DEC - - 2019

SOMEWHERE

ONLY

WE

KNOW

SOMEWHERE

ONLY

WE

KNOW

MAURENE GOO

FARRAR STRAUS GIROUX
NEW YORK

Farrar Straus Giroux Books for Young Readers
An imprint of Macmillan Children's Publishing Group, LLC
175 Fifth Avenue, New York, NY 10010

Printed in the United States of America
Designed by Elizabeth H. Clark
First edition, 2019
International edition, 2019
1 3 5 7 9 10 8 6 4 2

fiercereads.com

Library of Congress Cataloging-in-Publication Data

Names: Goo, Maurene, author.
Title: Somewhere only we know / Maurene Goo.
Description: First edition. | New York : Farrar, Straus and Giroux, 2019. |
Summary: Told from two viewpoints, teens Lucky, a very famous K-pop star,
and Jack, a part-time paparazzo who is trying to find himself, fall for
each other against the odds through the course of one stolen day.
Identifiers: LCCN 2018039566 | ISBN 9780374310578 (hardcover)
Subjects: | CYAC: Celebrities—Fiction. | Singers—Fiction. | Popular
music—Fiction. | Paparazzi—Fiction. | Korean Americans—Fiction. |
Love—Fiction.
Classification: LCC PZ7.G596 Som 2019 | DDC [Fic]—dc23
LC record available at https://lccn.loc.gov/2018039566

Our books may be purchased in bulk for promotional, educational, or business use. Please
contact your local bookseller or the Macmillan Corporate and Premium Sales Department at
(800) 221-7945 ext. 5442 or by email at MacmillanSpecialMarkets@macmillan.com.

In memory of my grandmother Swan Hee Goo,
who introduced me to all the great black-and-white romances.

And for Christopher, who introduced me to the real thing.

She went, ever singing,
In murmurs as soft as sleep;
The Earth seemed to love her,
And Heaven smiled above her,
As she lingered towards the deep.

—by ~~JOHN KEATS~~ **PERCY BYSSHE SHELLEY,**
"Arethusa"

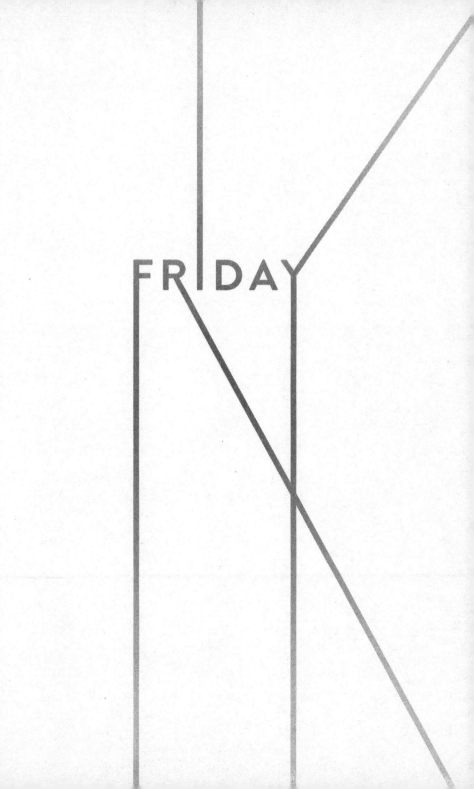

FRIDAY

CHAPTER ONE

LUCKY

WHEN YOU HAVE A FACE THAT'S RECOGNIZABLE BY AN entire continent, you have zero room to make mistakes.

Especially onstage.

I gazed into the screaming crowd, lights blinding me and the sound of my voice faint through the headset. The nonstop roar made it impossible for me to hear my own voice.

Once during a performance, when I threw my body into the outstretched arms of my backup dancer, the tiny microphone had shifted under my curtain of hair, and my voice cracked during the most dramatic moment of my hit single "Heartbeat."

It was the crack heard around Asia. Endless video loops of that moment were played on the Internet—some superimposed with cartoon rabbits and added screechy sound effects. My favorite one showed an animated pane of glass shattering at the exact moment of the voice crack. It was so masterfully done, I laughed every time I watched it.

My management label didn't find it funny, though. They saw it as a lapse, an imperfection on an otherwise perfect K-pop star.

That lapse was what I was thinking about as I stood on a stage in Hong Kong. The final stop on my Asian tour.

There was something about the vibration in the air, though—the currents of excitement filling in the spaces between me and the crowd. It was why I did this. Whatever I had been feeling days or seconds before I stepped onstage—like worrying about messing up again—all of that disappeared when the crowd's energy slipped under my skin and into my bloodstream.

Ferocious adoration by way of osmosis.

My silver stiletto boots were planted firmly in a wide stance, and my feet were killing me as per usual. I had this recurring nightmare of my boots chasing me around a parking lot. They were human-sized and ran after me in never-ending circles. My managers insisted on me wearing the same boots when I performed—my "signature look." Over-the-knee boots that stretched up the long expanse of my legs.

I was tall. Five foot ten—a veritable giant in Seoul. But there was no such thing as "too tall."

As I went through the familiar steps of the choreography for "Heartbeat," I managed to ignore the pain shooting up from the balls of my feet, the perpetual wedgie from my booty shorts, and the long strands of my pink wig sticking to the sweaty sides of my face.

Because I could do this choreography blindfolded, with two broken legs. I'd done this performance hundreds of times. At a certain point, my body moved on its own, as if on autopilot. Sometimes when

I finished performing "Heartbeat," my head hanging at an odd angle because of how the dance ended, I would blink and wonder where I had been for the last three minutes and twenty-four seconds.

When my body took over like that, I knew I got the job done. I was rewarded for the absolute precision with which I executed my performances.

And today was no different. I finished the song and looked out into the crowd, the screams of the fans piercing through me as I returned to my body with a *whoosh*.

I was finally done with this tour.

Backstage, I was immediately surrounded by people: my makeup artist, stylist, and head of security. I plopped down into a chair while my wig was adjusted and teased and my face dabbed with oil papers.

"Don't get rid of that dewy glow, though," I cracked to Lonni, my makeup artist.

Lonni pursed her lips. "You're seventeen, you don't need to be dewier. Also? Oil slick is not 'dewy.'"

Hmph. I let her continue mopping up my grease-face.

The back-up dancers stumbled backstage, a group of men and women in nondescript, sexy black outfits. I jumped up from my chair—making Lonni tsk in exasperation—and bent at the waist.

"Sugohaess-eoyo!" I said as I bowed. "Thank you so much." I always made sure to thank them in both Korean and English because the dancers came from all over.

They had suffered with me during every single practice and stop and never got any of the glory. My appreciation was genuine, but it was also expected. K-pop stars always had to be gracious.

They bowed and thanked me in return, sweaty and exhausted. "You killed it, Lucky," one of the dancers, Jin, said with a wink. "You were almost able to keep up with me."

I flushed. Jin was cute. He was also off-limits, as were most boys in my life. "I'll land that turn one of these days," I said with nervous laughter. They all shuffled off, going to their hotel together. I watched them with envy. Would they be hanging out in someone's room, eating cup ramen together?

No matter. My feet were going to crumble into dust. I plopped back into the chair.

A hand patted my back. "Hey. You too. Sugohaess-eo," my manager's assistant, Ji-Yeon, said. Ji-Yeon always told me I did a good job after performances, like a proud but stern older sister. She was a tiny rabbit of a young woman, her full-cheeked face obscured by edgy blunt-cut bangs and giant glasses. But she was a powerhouse who got things done.

She scrolled through her ever-present phone. "We're going to do a meet and greet for about an hour, so be sure to drink some water."

"What? A meet and greet?" I had stopped doing those a couple years ago. They were more for beginner pop groups. Once you reached a certain level, it got unwieldy.

"Yeah. Since it's your final show, we thought it would make a good photo op." She handed me a bottle of Evian.

"So, I'm going to be here for another hour?" I tried to keep the whininess out of my voice.

"It'll be fast. In and out. Do you not want to do it?" Ji-Yeon asked, peering over her glasses.

Don't be lazy. I shook my head. "No, it's fine."

"Okay, good. Now, let's get you out of this outfit and into something more comfortable for the fans," Ji-Yeon said with a slight twitch

6

of her nose, making her glasses shift up and down on her pale face. "Except the shoes, of course. Gotta keep those on."

Of course.

Minutes later, I was sitting behind a table signing albums, posters, whatever the fans had brought with them. And even though I had wanted to crawl into bed mere minutes before, the excitement of the fans zapped me with a familiar energy. Interaction with them was so rare lately.

"Can I get a selfie?" I looked at the girl with braces and a pixie cut and was about to say yes when my head bodyguard, Ren Chang, stepped in front of me and shook his head.

I threw the girl an apologetic look before the next fan approached me with a poster to sign.

In the early days, I had wanted to give a hug and speak to everyone who had waited in line to see me. But the bigger my fan base grew, the more nebulous and faceless they became. I battled the instinct to give canned and wooden responses. "Thank you for coming," I said with a smile at the older man as I signed his poster with a fat black Sharpie.

He nodded, not making eye contact with me. But his hand grazed mine when I returned the poster, and he got in close. I could smell the meal he'd had, feel the heat of his body. Without missing a beat, Ren pushed him back with a firm hand. Again, I smiled apologetically at the man, even though my entire being recoiled. Most of my male fans were perfectly fine—but there was an overeager, sweaty subset that approached me with an intensity that frightened me. In those moments, I still had to act gracious. Always grateful for what I had.

The line was cut off eventually and I stood up and waved and bowed to the crying and cheering fans. They roared when I threw out a peace sign and I was whisked away through the back door.

The second I stepped outside, the paparazzi and fans descended.
Camera flashes, voices yelling out my name, a crush of humanity.

Ren and a few other bodyguards closed in around me like a protective membrane. When people pushed against them, the force made the circle of security undulate as we moved through the narrow alley toward the van.

"*Lucky, I love you!*" a girl screamed. My instinct was to look toward the voice, to say, "Thank you!" But doing that would open the floodgates. I learned my lesson a long time ago.

Instead, I looked down, watching the steps of Ren in front of me. Keeping my eyes on his firm footsteps slowed my racing heart, gave me focus. I liked having something to focus on. Otherwise, I would spiral into sheer panic at the thought of being trampled, enclosed by a million people who all wanted a piece of me.

My guards slowed down, and I glanced up. The car was near, but people were blocking it. The police had arrived and the energy was feeding on itself—that stage of mania where absolutely no one had control. Where grown men with huge arms fought back teenage girls with dazed expressions, helplessly watching as the girls climbed over them as if they were trees, feral and hungry.

My heart raced, my palms grew sweaty, and a wave of nausea came over me.

"Stay close," Ren said in a low voice, stretching a thick arm across my torso.

"Like I have a choice?" I asked, my voice raspy from overuse. Feeling annoyed at Ren for no reason.

"Or you could get trampled," he replied mildly. Ren was my dad's age but had the fitness level of an Olympian. And the sense of humor of a Triscuit.

So I kept close—and within seconds, fresh air burst through the circle, breaking through the wall of bodies to reach me.

My heart resumed beating back to normal and I lifted my face up to the bright Hong Kong skyline. It flashed at me for a second before I was tucked safely into the van.

The first thing I did was take my freaking boots off.

CHAPTER TWO

JACK

I WATCHED THE PRESIDENT OF HONG KONG CONSTRUC-
tion Bank wax on about quarterlies or something equally boring until
my eyes started to water with general eyeball ache. Human eyeballs
were not meant to be fixed on one thing for this long. I glanced at the
time on my phone. Oh my God. It had been thirty minutes? *Thirty
minutes*! How long could a person talk about bank stuff for?

"Dad," I whispered, nudging him with my elbow.

Keeping his dark eyes fixed on the guy talking on the ballroom
stage, my dad didn't respond. His square jaw was set stubbornly, and
his meticulous hairline met the starched white collar of his shirt. Sitting
up straight in his hotel banquet hall chair, an uncomfortable one covered with a cream-colored satin fabric.

I poked him until he finally looked over at me with exasperation,
furrowing his brow. "What?" he whispered.

"At what point will this be . . . you know, fun?" I asked in a whisper.

"Kid, did you actually think a bank anniversary dinner would be fun?" he asked with a chuckle.

Good point. I looked around at the hotel ballroom full of banking people eating scallops in their formal wear. This was probably the most depressing Friday night of my life.

"Well, I thought the food would be good, at least," I muttered.

"Hey, it's free." He glanced over, squinting at me under sparse, straight eyebrows. "You have to stay."

I sighed and leaned back into my chair, smiling grimly at the other people at our table who had started to stare at us.

"You know, I had a very different gap year in mind. One that involved more backpacking, less ballrooms," I said.

"No kidding." His mouth twitched, holding back a smile.

When I announced that I had wanted to take a gap year in lieu of college, my parents had agreed to it—but only if I started interning at my dad's bank the fall after my high school graduation. It was October now, and the part-time work was already killing me with boredom.

The man onstage finally wrapped up his speech, and everyone clapped politely. Thank God. People rushed the dessert table, and I was about to get up and grab some cake when my dad stopped me.

"Jack, I want you to meet a few people," he said, waving a couple over. I groaned inwardly. He shot me a warning glance. "This internship isn't about going through the motions. You're supposed to be networking. Some of these people have great connections to the best colleges in the US."

Great. I put on my finest schmoozing smile. It was a good smile.

A tall Asian woman wearing dark red lipstick reached her hand out to me. "Jack! We're so glad you were able to make the event tonight. Shows initiative."

"Thank you, Caroline," I said. Her eyebrows rose with pleasant surprise. I was good at remembering names. "But let's be honest, I'm here for the cake."

She threw her head back and laughed, as did her companion—a burly Indian man in an expensive suit. Nikhil, if I recalled correctly. "Make sure you try the tiramisu," Nikhil said in a polished British accent. "So, how are you enjoying your gap year, Jack? I have fond memories of mine—backpacking through Europe and all that."

I shot my dad a very deliberate look. *See? Backpacking! It's a thing!*

But I said, "Oh, it's been great. I think there's so much you can learn outside of college, and I have the privilege of doing that." It was a subtle in-real-life subtweet, and I'm sure my dad picked up on it.

Nikhil snapped his fingers then. "Oh! I have a question about cameras, Jack!"

I startled. "You do?"

"Yeah, I've seen you in the office with that fancy camera of yours," he said. "You're a camera guy, right? I need a recommendation for one."

My dad shifted next to me, and tension crept up my back. "Oh, sure. What kind of camera are you looking for?"

Nikhil went on to describe what he wanted, and I tried to maintain a neutral expression. Yes, I knew a thing or two about cameras. I'd been hooked on photography for years, ever since I got my first fancy camera as a Christmas gift from my parents—a Canon Rebel that I took everywhere. As far as my parents were concerned, it was a hobby. They made that very clear when I went digging around into various art programs. They had reacted with extreme skepticism, pushing me toward business and engineering programs instead.

It had been what killed my enthusiasm for college. Why I had asked for the gap year. The idea of studying business or something instead of photography sent me into a literal panic.

The bigger thing I didn't tell my parents was this: I wasn't sure if I wanted to go to college. That college was something that felt far away now. So far away that I didn't know if it would ever be a part of my life. I saw where it got you. In a ballroom eating tiramisu while wearing an overpriced suit.

I glanced at my dad in that overpriced suit. This wasn't the life he wanted, either. My dad had studied creative writing in college. Even got an MFA. But life and circumstances had landed him here.

The conversation veered into financial stuff after I gave Nikhil some camera recommendations, so I made my way over to the dessert table. But everything looked unappetizing. My shirt collar was stifling, the buzz of the ballroom deafening. Existential dread filled me every moment I was here. Feeling time pass, feeling my actual cells grow older. I took a deep breath, my mind already whirring with how I could get out of this. Illness? My dad was a germophobe, so it might work.

I headed back to the table, sitting down next to my dad and coughing so hard he recoiled. "I don't feel good," I croaked out, laying it on thick.

"It's because you're perpetually cold," my dad scolded. "Do you even have heating in that hovel of yours?" My parents hated my apartment in Sheung Wan. As soon as I graduated, I had moved out with almost zero cash, and my current accommodations showed it. While my neighborhood was hip and fairly expensive, I had chosen one of the old walk-up apartments. They were tiny and usually above storefronts selling things like dried fish and medicinal herbs. But because the area was up-and-coming, it was still more than I could afford on my own, and I needed a roommate. In a one-bedroom. It was stressful, having to make rent and scrape by. My parents refused to help and I would rather die of starvation than ask them, anyhow. I wasn't sure how much longer I could keep it up, though, and I was trying everything I could to avoid the undergrad experience my parents were hoping for me.

"We do have heating," I lied easily. "Anyway, my throat is starting to hurt, too."

Dad leveled a penetrating stare at me. "Are you pretending to be sick to get out of this?"

I sniffled a very realistic sniffle. "Why would I do that? You know I've been pumped. My first bank banquet. Thing."

While skepticism lined his face, I could sense his phobia overriding his dad BS meter. "All right, this is wrapping up anyway. Go home and get some rest. Do you need Mom to send you some food?"

Most easily won victory ever. "Nah, that's okay. I can grab congee around the corner from my place."

He made some mumbly comment about Korean porridge being better than congee before I slipped out of the ballroom and into the lobby of the fancy hotel.

My family wasn't from Hong Kong. Both my parents immigrated to the US from Korea when they were kids, and I was born and raised in Los Angeles. And then a year ago, my dad got this enticing offer at the bank that he couldn't turn down. Hong Kong being the financial and banking capital of Asia.

It was always about the money. My dad had put aside his dreams of writing the Great American Novel when my mom's family put pressure on him to get a "real job." Which led him to a bank. And then he had kids. Which further entrenched him in the banking world. And that's how we landed here.

Two doormen opened the double doors for me and I ducked outside with a nod of thanks. I glanced up at the hotel from outside, a sleek, dizzying tower of glass surrounded by other tall skyscrapers. Many of them lit up with pink or green trim. A light fog had settled in from the water, giving everything a dreamy, futuristic feel. I rubbed my arms for warmth through my jacket. It was unseasonably cool. Summer heat usually lasted well into winter here.

Even though the homesickness almost killed me at first, I'd started to like it in Hong Kong. Sometimes you can go somewhere new and it feels weirdly familiar, as if you once saw and moved through it in a dream.

Not to romanticize it or anything.

I walked alongside the curved hotel driveway. Luxury cars lined the drive, and I narrowly missed getting hit by one of them—a black Escalade that screeched to a halt at the entrance. The valet guys sprinted to open the back-seat door, and a white guy in sunglasses with a shock of red hair got out.

I recognized that red hair. It was Teddy Slade, American action star. Holy crap, was he staying here? A preternatural sense of knowing someone was up to no good had me pause and follow him back into the lobby. He strode straight into an elevator being held open for him.

A woman in sunglasses and a dark coat stepped in right after.

The woman had the distinct profile of Hong Kong superstar Celeste Jiang. I couldn't believe it. I immediately texted Trevor Nakamura: I have eyes on Teddy Slade at the Skyloft Hotel. Celeste Jiang's with him.

15

Trevor was the editor-at-large for the biggest, sleaziest tabloid website in Hong Kong, Rumours.

And I worked for him.

He immediately texted back: **Everyone's been trying to catch this affair. Can you get a photo?**

For the past four months, I had been moonlighting for Trevor, getting him photos whenever I could. My parents, of course, had no idea I was doing this.

I texted back: **I can get it.** Then I watched the numbers on the elevator. They didn't stop until the penthouse floor.

Gotcha.

I received a warm welcome when I stepped up to the front desk. Fancy hotels treat everyone well because you never know who you are *really* talking to. I could have been Jackie Chan's son for all they knew.

"Good evening, sir, how may we help you?" A tidy young woman with a slight accent to her English greeted me. I assessed her—I knew at hotels like this they didn't let people go up into the hotel rooms if they weren't guests. There was a reason why celebrities stayed here. It was a small boutique hotel, and the staff probably recognized most of their guests. Everything was about discretion.

I shot her a quick grin and glanced down at her name tag. "Hi, Jessica. I'm meeting a friend who's staying here. Can I hang out to wait for him?" I let my gaze linger on hers for a beat too long.

She flushed and smiled back at me. "Oh, sure, the lobby by the elevators is probably best. That way your friend can spot you right away."

"Thanks, Jessica." I tapped her arm gently before walking into the lobby. Aware that she was still watching me, I sat down in one of the velvety blue-gray armchairs and pulled out my phone, as if texting my friend. I was actually researching the hotel—was there more than one room on the penthouse floor?

Yes. There were two. Easy.

I gave it a few seconds before I peeked over at Jessica again, who was busy helping another guest. I took a quick look around the lobby—dimly lit and filled with sleek furniture. And flowers. A lot of flower arrangements.

The elevator dinged, and I glanced up. A white couple speaking loudly in Australian accents stepped off the elevator, and an Asian woman wearing a patterned scarf stepped on. I got up and swiped one of the large flower arrangements set on a coffee table and slipped into the elevator after the woman, moving back into the corner.

The arrangement was more massive than it had looked sitting on the table, and it practically smushed the lady in the elevator. I couldn't even see her. I heard her huff as she moved around me and selected her floor. Peeking behind the foliage, I saw "17" light up after she tapped a card against the sensor.

Right. You needed a stupid key card to select a floor. "Bloody hell. Can't reach for my key card with this monstrosity I have to deliver," I said in a practiced British accent usually sported by boarding school–bred Hong Kong kids. "Would you mind hitting the penthouse floor for me?"

The woman let out a long-suffering sigh, and I heard the swipe of her card before she pressed the button.

"Endless thanks," I said from behind the giant flamingo lilies and pink-streaked leaves. She didn't respond.

Cool, lady. Who cares if you might have let Korean Ted Bundy into a hotel?

The woman got off on her floor, and I let out a tortured breath. "Good night!" I said as she walked out. She still didn't respond, and the doors closed behind her. "Good riddance."

The elevator shot straight up to the penthouse floor.

Time to get that photo.

CHAPTER THREE
LUCKY

"DO WE SERIOUSLY HAVE TO WATCH THIS NOW?" I stared at my manager.

Joseph Yim's gaze didn't waver from mine. "You're on *The Later Tonight Show* in three days. If there's any room for improvement, we have to know now, don't you think?"

His icy-blue button-up was crisp and tucked neatly into navy trousers. With his high cheekbones and steely eyes, Joseph was an imposing figure. He was only in his late twenties but was something of a wunderkind in the K-pop scene. So many number-one singles on the K-Pop Hot 100 came from his management label. People said that he had an uncanny knack for knowing who would be the next big thing. A jaeneung, a gift. And at the moment, his big hit maker was me.

If all went according to plan, in a few days I wouldn't only be the reigning queen of K-pop. I'd be an international pop star. *The Later*

Tonight Show was supposed to launch me into a bona fide household name in America.

America. The final frontier. Not many K-pop artists had conquered it successfully. K-pop was indisputably gaining popularity in the US, but there was yet to be a female K-pop star who was on American mainstream radio next to Beyoncé or Taylor Swift.

At this very moment, I was the star with the chops. My name didn't disappoint—Joseph considered me his lucky charm. Not a small army of vixens who could dance in sync to lush harmonies. Or beautiful moppy-haired boys who danced with the athleticism of gymnasts while rapping.

It was me. Lucky of the one name. Lucky of the angelic voice that made Joseph's eyes tear up when I auditioned. Lucky of the "naturally" small face and wide eyes that launched a thousand beauty products. Lucky of the blessed height that made her tower over her girl-group counterparts. Lucky of the precise and girlish dance moves that never deviated. Lucky with the flawless English.

I was lightning in a bottle, and the management label was pinning all their American mainstream hopes and dreams on me.

No pressure or anything.

A couple hours after the concert, Joseph and Ji-Yeon were still annoyingly in my hotel room, a laptop propped up on the marble coffee table between us. Joseph wanted to rewatch my performance from today, and both he and Ji-Yeon were staring at me expectantly.

I could go to bed. I'd gotten far enough in my career that I had way more freedom than in the past. But their expectant gazes further inflated the balloon of pressure inside of me.

"Sure, let's do it," I said with a tight smile.

With a quick tap on the space bar, Ji-Yeon started the video.

From my reclined position on the plush sofa, I watched myself hop, spin, and gyrate across the stage—my hands precise in their undulating motions around my face as I sang. My voice was tinny through the lousy laptop speakers.

We watched the entire thing from beginning to end. I could barely pay attention, blinking to stay awake. At one point, the image of myself on the screen turned into a dancing hamburger. Mm. A hamburger.

At least I'd performed perfectly. A tiny burst of confetti went off in my head. Joyless and feeble. The inability to get excited made me feel guilty, and I straightened up.

The video ended, and Joseph clapped his hands. "Good girl," he said with a low chuckle. "This is why you're going to make it. You're reliable."

Reliable! Truly, music to an artist's ears. I coughed into my fist to squelch the bubble of laughter rising in my throat.

Joseph's head snapped up. "I have an idea." Oh, God, not another one. "Let's watch your very first performance of 'Heartbeat' to compare with today's." He grinned at me. "Play them side by side. To see how far you've come."

"Well, this is *my* idea of a smashing Friday night!" I declared. Although Joseph and Ji-Yeon were fluent in English, they didn't quite grasp the finer points of sarcasm.

Ji-Yeon knelt down and pulled up a tablet to prop up next to the laptop, perusing through YouTube until she found it.

The video was from two years ago. My hair had been dyed a light brown and cut into a wavy bob. That bob would be copied by thousands of teenage girls shortly after this performance aired. The first three bass notes signaled the beginning of the song, and the camera panned down from the glossy waves of my hair, swaying hips, and farther down down

down my legs. I was wearing flat black ankle boots back then. I liked those.

As the performance went on, I found myself leaning more forward on the sofa until I was literally on the edge of my seat. I couldn't help but notice the wideness of my smile, the buoyancy in my steps. The sparkle in my eyes. When I glanced over at today's performance playing simultaneously, I saw the vacant look in my eyes. Two dark pools of nothingness. I stared hard at the Lucky from two years ago.

At thirteen years old, after I auditioned at the LA satellite studio of my current K-pop management label, I moved from Los Angeles to Seoul, alone and six thousand miles away from my family, and was put into a training camp immediately. My managers waited a couple years until the plastic surgery—giving me natural-looking ssangkkeopul, the double eyelids that had become so commonplace in South Korea that it was strange for any pop star not to have them. Then a discreet lil' nose sculpting. What people called the "K-pop combo."

It took about two years in a girl group, Hard Candy, before I shot to stardom. My managers plucked me out from the group to groom me into a solo artist. In the blink of an eye, I toppled every record, sold out every show, won every award you could win. And one of the keys to my success was that I had zero scandals. Not one photo of me drinking. Of a boyfriend. Of bad manners.

I was always humble, gracious, and contained.

Perfect.

And the media loved me for it. I was treated like some princess, protected fiercely by my public. The stories about me were always focused on my good deeds and success. In that order. Because my music wasn't particularly different—instead, it was the best version of what was always popular: catchy, upbeat dance tunes paired with sweet, soulful ballads.

"See that?" Joseph said, pointing at old Lucky. "You messed up that step there. You'd never do that now. You should be pleased with how much you've improved."

I didn't feel pleased. I felt unsettled. I remembered old Lucky. The joy I felt in my performances. How excited I was before every show, every photo shoot, every single release. Back then, I *had* felt like an actual artist from the sheer joy of loving what I did. For being able to do it at all.

I thought I still felt that joy when onstage. But watching old Lucky side-by-side with current Lucky made the contrast crystal clear. Goodness.

There was just no comparison to old Lucky.

CHAPTER FOUR

JACK

BALANCING THE SAINT BERNARD–SIZED FLOWER arrangement in one arm, I pulled out my phone as I walked down the hallway, the sound of my footsteps completely swallowed by the plush carpeting.

A quick search on Teddy Slade: The movie he was shooting here in Hong Kong was called *Endless Night*. I dodged a fancy credenza in the hallway as I scrolled through the list of cast and crew. I locked in on one name.

Okay, there were two rooms on this floor. I had a fifty-fifty chance. If it wasn't one room, I'd try the other. I stood outside the first door and took a deep breath. I set the flowers down and shrugged off my suit jacket, rolling it into a ball and tossing it down the hall. Then I tucked my phone deep into the foliage until it was shrouded by the colorful leaves and flowers.

My white button-down was wrinkled and sloppy, but I tucked it into my black pants and hoped that this mutant flower arrangement would hide me. My black sneakers couldn't be helped.

I hoisted the flowers back into my arms with a groan, then knocked on the door—three strong, assured raps. The blood rushed to my head, the familiar adrenaline kicking in.

Four months ago, I had snuck into a VIP party to impress the girl I had a crush on, Courtney. We were at a restaurant and spotted a few celebrities being ushered upstairs. "Oh my *God*, I would *die* to go up there," Courtney had said breathlessly, clutching my arm. Some caveman part of me puffed up, and I had taken the challenge.

Using some phony contact names that didn't exist, combined with dickish entitlement, I got us upstairs. And then managed to get Courtney close enough to her favorite actors to sneak a few photos.

A hand had grabbed me mid-photo. When I turned around, completely freaked out, a long-haired Asian guy was looking at me with a shrewd expression. "Hey kid, how did you get in here?"

I was ready to lie my ass off and run, but I hesitated when he grinned and said, "I know you snuck in."

Something about that smile made me relax. "Oh, yeah?"

He nodded. "What if I paid you for those photos?"

Since then, I picked up freelance work for Trevor now and again. And lately, the assignments were more frequent. I was gaining his trust. It wasn't my dream job or anything, but I knew that the more I did it, the better the money would get. And it used, in some marginal way, my actual photography skills. Had to compose those shots of celebrities getting into cars *just right* and all.

A few seconds after I knocked on the hotel-room door, I heard some shuffling on the other side. "What is it?" a gruff male voice called out from the other side.

"Flower delivery from Matthew Diaz." The executive producer of *Endless Night*, according to the Internet. I spoke in the heavy non-descript Asian accent used by racist stereotype movie characters since forever. The less we were able to communicate, the better.

There was a low-voiced exchange. My arms started to tire from holding this monstrosity in a basket. Come on, be trusting and slightly stupid, Teddy.

The door opened and there was Teddy Slade in all his affair-having glory. Red hair disheveled with a furry chest peeking out from a loosely tied robe. He was shorter than me, but sturdy, like a man who often had to be on-screen intimidating criminals.

"Flowers from Matt?" he asked, one hand on the doorknob, obscuring my view of the penthouse. I could hear some music. Music with saxophones. Really?

I was hoping for a quick shot of some kind of physical evidence— women's shoes that I could later trace to a photo from an event earlier today, anything. But first I had to get inside.

"Yes, sir. Please let me put on safe surface," I said, already inching my way through the door. My accent was offensive to my own ears but I knew Teddy wouldn't think twice about it. Most Westerners who visited Hong Kong spoke to me in slow, loud English, assuming I could barely understand. This assumption made people let their guard down, underestimating me.

"No, no, let me take them," Teddy said, reaching for the flowers.

I sidestepped him. "Sir, no. It's very heavy and delicate. Very rare flower from an ancient rain forest. It will injure if you try." Gotta love saying "ancient" reverently with a fake Asian accent.

So I pushed forward, almost knocking Teddy over with the floppy leaves. I didn't know where I was going, trying to find any spot for this thing. As expected, the penthouse was huge, with a giant wall of windows showing off the dazzling skyline. When I turned to place the flowers on a side table, I almost fell on my face when I noticed Celeste Jiang sitting on a nearby sofa. Clad in an oversized T-shirt, drinking a glass of water. Glamorous, poised, and deathly hot.

Holy crap. This was better than I could have imagined. I slipped my hand in the flowers, feeling around for the phone. I had about five seconds before this got weird.

Teddy walked up behind me, and when I glanced up, I saw my own reflection in a huge mirror. Also reflected was Teddy Slade standing beside the flowers and Celeste Jiang sitting on the sofa.

My phone tilted up and I snapped a burst of photos.

"Okay, you need to leave now," Teddy declared, all irate bluster. I glanced at Celeste before I left, noticing her bemused expression.

I pocketed my phone and Celeste caught me doing it. Her heavy-lidded eyes flicked down toward my hand, and one corner of her mouth lifted. "You know you could ruin a lot of lives with that photo?" Her expression was neutral, the words said in a low and unhurried voice.

For a moment, I froze. I'd been yelled at, chased down streets, but this was the first time someone looked me in the eye and said something so . . . straightforward. Was she asking me not to publish the photo?

But then Teddy was standing over me, and I bolted out of there. "Have a nice night, Mr. and Mrs.!"

The door shut behind me forcefully, and my heart was pounding in my ears as I grabbed my blazer off the floor and flew toward the elevators.

You guys ruined your own lives, Celeste.

CHAPTER FIVE

LUCKY

"STRAIGHT TO BED TONIGHT. YOU ONLY HAVE A DAY OF practice before our flight to LA," Ji-Yeon fussed as she tidied up the hotel room. Joseph had left for the night, and I was changing into pajamas.

"Yeah, yeah," I said, pulling on my sweatpants.

Ji-Yeon tsked. "Don't complain."

"Okay, but can I *eat something* at least?" My stomach grumbled at the words. I'd subsisted on coconut water and granola bars today because of the hectic tour schedule.

Ji-Yeon leaned against a wall and squinted, thinking about it for a second. Thinking about whether or not I should *eat*! Finally, she nodded. "Okay, I think I remember seeing some juices and salads on the menu."

I couldn't reply because a cartoon hamburger was twerking in front of Ji-Yeon's face. I would kill for In-N-Out right now. Sometimes the homesickness for LA hit me so hard. I pushed it down deep into the recesses of my rib cage like I always did. If I let it overpower me I would never be able to keep doing this. Homesickness, like so many other things, was a luxury I didn't have at the moment. It would have to be dealt with later. Always later.

Ji-Yeon ordered the food, then popped out into the hall to alert Ren to the coming room service. Ren usually stayed at my door all night. There were more security guards in the lobby and in the car, too, just in case.

It would seem over the top, except there was that time one of my sasaeng fans (superfans who were essentially stalkers) was waiting for me in the back of my car.

The Hong Kong skyline was colorful and dramatic and filled my hotel room, the wall of windows making me feel like I was floating in the sky. The buildings were massive and so close together that they looked like overlapping, neon-lit pieces of paper within reach. But when I moved closer to the windows to gaze at it, Ji-Yeon shut the curtains briskly. With finality. And even though I was so tired I could sleep for a hundred years, the old nighttime anxiety set in.

As a kid, I hated dusk and the impending rituals of bedtime— brushing my teeth, putting on pajamas, shutting off lights. A sense of dread always followed me as the day grew closer to ending.

"Here you go." Ji-Yeon placed a small dish next to my bedside table. Two sleeping pills and one Ativan. The sleeping pills were standard, everyone took them. But the Ativan—that was top secret. Mental illness was still taboo in South Korea, and if anyone found out I was taking medication for anxiety, well . . .

K-POP PRINCESS POPPING PILLS

The Korean press would eat me alive. The rest of Asia would follow. And then my career would collapse into itself, like a star that finally gave in to gravity.

I scooped them up in my palm, my long peach nails scraping the plate, and tossed them back with some water.

After setting up my dinner of salad greens with a light olive oil dressing and a side of almonds, Ji-Yeon went into her own room off my suite. Although I coveted my privacy, I also had a terrible time falling asleep alone. Having Ji-Yeon close was comforting, and it was one of the few diva cards I pulled.

But, tonight, as I fretted about my impending American debut, I needed a little more comfort than usual.

I pushed my salad aside and FaceTimed my mom. It was early in the morning for my family, but they could deal. My parents always made time for my calls since they were so few and far between lately on my tour.

On the third ring, my mom answered—the screen dark and fuzzy for a moment before it adjusted on her face, eyes set far apart from her button nose, strands of wavy hair framing her smooth face.

She squinted into the screen. "Is something wrong?" My mom's typical greeting.

"Hi, Umma. No, nothing's wrong. I'm just calling," I said, my voice choking up. It had been three weeks since we talked, and I hadn't felt the distance until *right* this moment. Seeing and hearing my mom's voice instantly stripped me bare of my pop star confidence. I was normal me again.

My dad's face popped into the screen then, shoving hers out of the way. His salt-and-pepper hair was disheveled, and he pulled his black-framed glasses on. "Oh! Why are you still awake?!" My dad always looked like a flustered professor at a wizarding school.

"It's only like, ten o'clock here," I said with a laugh, watching my parents jostle for prime screen space. "Did I wake you?"

My mom waved her hand dismissively. "Not me. I wake up earlier than your dad now."

"Yah, in what world?" my dad said, mixing Korean and English as he always did. "Only this week because—"

"He's watching that *Game of Thrones*," my mom interrupted. "I don't know how he can watch that before bed." She shuddered. "Horrible."

"You're watching that?" I asked with my eyebrows raised. "Appa, that is like, so violent. Also, can you even follow the storyline?"

My mom burst out laughing and my dad pushed up his glasses in agitation. "Wow, wow. Okay, you think your appa is a total babo." The Korean word for "fool" never failed to make me giggle.

"No, I don't!" I protested. "It has so many characters and like, complicated fantasy world-building—" I stopped talking when a puff of cream with black eyes suddenly obscured the screen. Fern, their Pomeranian. She yelped loudly, and then it was chaos for a few seconds as my mom tried to hold her up to the phone while in selfie mode. Her nose pushed into the camera and I started laughing when I heard a voice screech in the background.

"Oh my *God*! Why are you guys being so loud this early?"

Ah, the unmistakable sounds of an irate fifteen-year-old.

"Your sister's on the phone! Say hi!" my dad said, moving the phone around until I was staring at my sister's face. It was like mine, but not— fuller cheeks, wider mouth, bigger eyes.

31

"Hey, Vivian," I said.

"Hi," she muttered. "I hate FaceTime."

"What are you up to today?" I asked, fully knowing what her answer would be.

"Nothing." She avoided looking at me, but I saw her shoot me a furtive glance. "Did you microblade?"

I touched my naturally full eyebrow. "No."

"Hm. Looks weird."

Nothing like a younger sister to bring you down a peg.

My parents interjected, talking about their plans for the weekend. The regularness of it was so nice—a conversation separate from my job, my schedule, my fans.

When I yawned, my mom frowned. "Hey, you should go to sleep now. You had a long tour and now you have to prepare for *The Later Tonight Show*, right?"

I nodded. "Yeah. Monday. You're going to come watch, right?" They would be waiting for me in the greenroom right after the taping.

"Of course!" my dad said. "We'll make sure you eat well so you have lots of energy."

The worried expressions that crossed their faces made me teary again. I pasted on a bright smile. "Oh, I've been eating *so well* on this tour. A lot of dumplings and noodles and stuff."

They nodded, pleased to hear it. It was a lie, of course. One of many to keep my parents from freaking out. If they knew how little I ate and slept—well, I wouldn't be able to do this. I knew the sacrifices my family was making to get me here. The least I could do was keep them from worrying about me.

We hung up and the homesickness still weighed me down. Or was that the sleeping pills? My limbs felt heavy, but my mind was racing.

I crawled into bed without washing my face or brushing my teeth, like a monster, the fluffy white comforter swallowing me up. The luxurious sheets slid against me, cool on my cozy pajamas. I was dressed warmly for bed, a habit I picked up while living in Korea.

The first night I spent at the training room dorms, I had gone to bed in a tank top and underwear and the other girls had ridiculed me within an inch of my life. Like, calm down, it's just undies. Or as I had called them, ppanseuh, the word my parents had used for underwear. Another faux pas that made my Americanness more clear. Apparently that was an old-fashioned Japanese word that only grannies used. The cool kids said "paenti." Like panty. Straight-up panty, a word that gave me the creeps. And no one slept in *just* their paenties.

You know, my boots were annoying the heck out of me lately. It's like, don't let Lucky wear flat shoes, God forbid she's only five-ten! FIVE! TEN! THAT! IS! TALL!

When I thought in all caps, the pills were definitely kicking in. I tossed around in bed, punching my pillow to fluff it up some more. But whether it was from hunger or annoyance or what, I couldn't fall asleep for the life of me. I had an early wake-up call for practice. I couldn't flub on *The Later Tonight Show*, no sirree.

Mm. Hamburgers.

That was the problem. I was still freaking hungry. I kicked off my blankets and cracked open my suitcase. I kept my thermal shirt on but wriggled out of my sweatpants and into a pair of ripped black jeans. I pulled on my favorite baseball cap—a plain olive-green one that drew absolutely no attention to itself. My pink wig was being carefully guarded by Ji-Yeon and off my head, thank God. Then I threw on a camel-colored trench and looked for my sneakers but couldn't find them anywhere.

"Note to self," I mumbled. "Someone is stealing my shoes." I glanced down at the white hotel slippers by the bed. Those would do.

I was about to open the door and breeze outta there when I realized who was outside. *REN!* I shook my fist at the door and bent my knees in dismay.

Then I straightened up, my hair whipping back from the swift movement. No, I could do this. I was smart. Everyone said so, even if it was because my management label claimed I got into Harvard.

HA HA HA.

Yeah, cool, I was applying to Harvard while subsisting on sweet potatoes and learning how to pirouette counterclockwise.

Okay. Think, Lucky. Think.

After a second, I rapped on the door. "Ren?" I called out in a thin, pathetic voice.

"Yes? Everything okay?" Ren's voice rumbled through the door.

"Nothing huge, but, uh . . . Ji-Yeon's sleeping and um, well. I need medicine. For my period cramps."

I could feel the revulsion through the heavy door. "Sorry," I added sweetly.

"What kind do you need?" he asked, all huff and puff and gruff.

"Midol. Or the Chinese equivalent. Tell them the problem, they should know at the front desk."

I heard him grumbling and waited until the heavy footsteps receded. A few seconds after that, I cracked the door open to peer down the hallway. I was on the penthouse floor for privacy and there wasn't a soul in sight.

Closing the door gently behind me, I sped down the corridor, switching from a run to a creeping gait, to a run again. What was the best way to sneak?

The elevators were at the end of the hall, and there was one open and waiting for me. I ran inside and hit the button that said "1," feeling myself relax, when a hand gripped between the doors and pushed them open. Shoot. I stepped back into the corner and hid my face.

"Thanks," a guy's voice said. I glanced up. It was some young Asian guy clutching a jacket. I shoved myself farther into the corner, as far away from him as possible. But he wasn't paying attention to me.

The dude was grinning and pulling on a wrinkled blazer. Then he untucked his shirt and fluffed up his hair.

I couldn't help but look at him. What a weirdo. Cute weirdo. Incredible hair. Tall. Broad shoulders coupled with long limbs. But totally giving off the strangest vibes. A kind of manic euphoria. I inched closer to the wall when he started chuckling as he looked through his phone. Okay, sir.

I tried to calm my racing heart, praying for no more passengers. Luckily, there weren't any, and I barely breathed until the elevator stopped on the first floor.

When I stepped out, I was in a carpeted hallway, not the lobby. I glanced back at the elevator in confusion.

"If you're looking for the ground floor, that's level 'G,'" the guy said, barely looking up from his phone.

With as much pride as I could muster, I said, "No, this is it," and strutted away. Despite not knowing where the heck I was. In hotel-room slippers.

Hotels. I knew hotels. I would go in the lobby and ask, low-key style, where the best burger was. So I took the stairs one flight down.

Piece o' cake! I got this! I stepped in rhythm to my cheerleading. *This is nothing. Remember that week when you slept for eight hours total and*

had to be hospitalized for dehydration during the MTV Asia Awards? This
sneaking around is freaking nothing!

The impeccably designed lobby was no-frills. My managers always booked me in discreet boutique hotels, hoping they would be better hideouts than big showy ones.

Two of my security guards were chatting idly by the valet stand and I hid behind a giant potted palm next to the front desk.

"Hi, there," I greeted the front desk staff with what I hoped was a chill, very normal voice. "Would you mind pointing me to the nearest delicious hamburger?"

One of the young men behind the counter smiled serenely. "Of course, miss, there's an American-style restaurant in the mall that is connected to the hotel." His head was turned in the direction of the door but then he slowly looked back at me, recognition dawning on his face.

Blast. Even without the pink hair, I might be recognizable. I lowered my cap. "Thank you very much!" I called out over my shoulder as I slipped through the glass double doors into the mall.

Hong Kong malls were no joke. This one was a giant, endless maze encased in glass and light gray granite, with infinity floors and sculptural light fixtures shining everywhere.

I stood frozen in place as I found myself surrounded by people. Mostly young people. What was everyone doing out this late at a mall? Looking around, I saw a few bars and posh lounges open. A city that never slept.

And I didn't know if it was the anxiety meds or what, but the usual panic that came over me in large crowds didn't surface.

Maybe it was also because visions of hamburgers still danced in my head. So I kept walking, keeping my head down and the collar on my trench popped up. Was this more or less conspicuous? I felt like the freaking Pink Panther.

I reached a mall directory and stared at it. What in Sam Hill was this? Everything was digital. I touched the screen a few times, but the thinking required to figure this out was going to melt my face off.

All right, Lucky. Follow your nose. Yeah, great plan. I had a very sensitive nose.

The mall was endless. I walked by luxury store after luxury store. And fancy restaurants, but nothing that looked like it would promise a good, greasy burger. A few minutes later I ended up near some escalators leading out of the subway station. Navigating a Hong Kong mall while fighting against sleep and anxiety medication was a grand idea. My head felt a bit woozy, and things started to blur together into soft lights.

Trying to orient myself in this state, I missed the giant group of people coming out of the station and was swept up into the crowd.

Worried about being recognized, I kept in step with everyone until I felt a rush of cool air.

When the crowd dispersed, I found myself standing outside on the streets of Hong Kong. Alone.

CHAPTER SIX

JACK

YOU KNOW THAT SCENE IN HARRY POTTER WHERE THEY
ride that bonkers double-decker bus through London?

Hong Kong buses weren't that different.

Sitting up on the second level of the double-decker (one of many
cultural remnants of Hong Kong's British colonial history), I could see
the winding streets of Central—full of people, since it was a Friday
night.

Hong Kong, the entire territory, is fairly large—spread out between
Hong Kong Island, Kowloon, the New Territories, and a bunch of
smaller islands. Kowloon is across Victoria Harbour from the island,
connected to mainland China. But I lived on Hong Kong Island,
and the bus was currently taking us through Central, the economic
and financial center of the city, on the northern part of the island
near the water. It was full of skyscrapers and high-rise apartment

towers, close to the big tourist spots that everyone associated with the city.

In Asia, there was this electricity of the *future* everywhere. And something about that made me feel alive. And in a huge city like this, there was infinite space for improvisation. For reinvention. You could do whatever you wanted. It was the opposite of growing up in a Southern California suburb—where there seemed to be one path that everyone was following. Where nighttime activities were limited to strip malls and movie theaters. Where, even with the vastness of the landscape around you, you felt trapped.

I loved the bus for a lot of reasons, and right now it was a good place to get work done. Still high off my coup, I was uploading my photos to Trevor. They came out great. Even in the dim lighting, framed by leaves, you could see Teddy and Celeste in a hotel room together. With some random silhouetted dude bent over a giant flower arrangement. I had played around with the photos to sharpen their faces and put myself more in shadow. These were gonna be my biggest payday.

Celeste's words echoed in my head as I sorted through the photos. *You could ruin a lot of lives.* A few months ago, that comment would have bothered me. Buried itself under my skin and made me feel bad about myself. But dozens of encounters with celebrities later—watching them have affairs, treat service staff like trash, throw fits, scream at their children—I'd grown numb to it all. This was a job now. That's it. Nothing personal, but it was the price of fame, Celeste.

I immediately got a text back from Trevor: **Good work. One more big scoop and you're looking at a full-time position.**

Full-time? I sat straight up in the colorfully upholstered seat. I knew that Trevor was liking my work lately, but this was a new thing. A new opportunity. It would give me something to do in place of college. And even if my parents found out—well, I could support myself now. I wouldn't have to live with their disappointment in my life decisions. Their hopes of me studying business or engineering or whatever in college. Just because my parents chose stability over excitement didn't mean I had to.

The bus came to a sudden stop and when I glanced up out the window, I realized I had made a complete loop—I was back near the hotel. I checked my phone. It wasn't even eleven yet. I still had time to meet up with a friend or two for a drink. The legal drinking age in Hong Kong is eighteen, which blew my mind when I moved here.

I texted my roommate, Charlie Yu.

Do you have time to grab a drink?

A minute later he responded.

YAYERS. In an hour when I can take a "lunch break" 😊

When his uncle retired, Charlie inherited his taxi business and his classic red Toyota. Taxis were a Hong Kong institution and Charlie worked nights. He often took extended breaks to grab a beer with me.

Cool—I got a HUGE scoop for Trevor. DRINKS ON ME.

Charlie replied: **GET THAT MONEY.**

I shook my head and smiled. Charlie and I were unabashedly hustling for cash all the time. Our complaints about our jobs and lack of money filled our apartment as we played video games and ate ramen. It was our main source of bonding.

I texted back: **Always.** 💲 **I'll pick a spot and text you.**

Make sure you pick a place with actual chicks. Not like that last dive bar full of weird old bros who all looked and smelled like retired fishermen

That dive bar was cool, thank you very much. But Charlie was all about the girls. It would be sleazy, except he managed to have this eager charm when flirting. Plus he looked like the bad boy who'd pick you up on his scooter to whisk you away from your strict parents.

I was texting back when someone knocked into me. It was a girl, staggering her way down the aisle. Okay, Drunko. I went back to texting when I heard a loud moan behind me and then, "Baegopa jughaeso!" I looked up from my phone in recognition. It was Korean for, "I'm so hungry I could die!"

When I glanced behind me, I saw the drunk girl in a seat with her head resting against the window, her eyes fluttering shut.

Why did she look so familiar?

I took in the green cap and long hair, her face in shadow. Oh, she was the girl who was on the elevator at the hotel. When I looked down at her feet, the hotel slippers confirmed it.

The girl on the elevator who seriously didn't want me to talk to her as she practically absorbed herself into the walls.

So, despite my curiosity, I turned away. Didn't wanna be a creep when this penthouse snob had clearly wanted to be left alone.

But she kept mumbling things. In both English and Korean. Was she American?

Other people on the bus started looking at her, but no one did anything.

I looked straight ahead. Don't get involved in this, Jack. She doesn't need your help.

One by one people left the bus and the girl stayed. When I finally turned around to look at her again, she was passed the eff out, her mouth slightly agape.

Because I couldn't get a good look at her face, it wasn't clear how old she was, but she looked around my age or younger.

And she was Korean American. Maybe. It was irrational, but I felt some kind of obligation to take care of my own people in Hong Kong. This wasn't at all what I had in mind for celebrating tonight. I could almost hear Charlie, a miniature devil on my shoulder, egging me on. *She's cuuuuuute*, he said in a squeaky voice.

I got up and walked over to her, the jerky movements of the bus making me sway. "Um . . . hey."

She didn't move a muscle. The brim of her cap hid her face.

"Excuse me." I paused. "Miss." Well, that was the first time I'd ever called anyone "Miss."

Again, no movement or acknowledgment of my presence. I leaned in toward the girl and poked her gently in the shoulder. Nothing. I nudged her slightly harder. Her head shifted on the window.

"Ya," I said loudly, hoping the informal Korean would jolt her. It was kind of rude, but desperate measures. I saw her lips twitch, registering something. Then she murmured, "Baegopa." She was still talking about being hungry.

My Korean sucked so I spoke English. "If you get up, you can eat." My gaze stayed on her mouth, which was undeniably pretty. Her lips were stained pink, as if they had had lipstick on them earlier. The top lip more pillowy than the bottom.

Whoa, stop looking at a drunk girl's lips.

I slipped into the seat next to her, hoping to find her phone on her and maybe call someone to get her. As I eyed her coat pockets, she fell into me.

The falling was slow. Luxuriant. Her jacket slid against my blazer as her shoulder hit my arm. Her head landed on my shoulder gently and a small sigh escaped her. Her long hair fanned over my arm. Silky black strands touched my bare knuckles.

Wow.

Snap out of it, Jack. I gently moved her head off my shoulder and was about to push her to her side of the seat when she woke up.

"Hi." Her sleepy eyes looked at mine. Straight into mine.

It was the first time I had a good look at her face and I had to clear my throat from the unexpected electricity of it. "Hi. Hi, there. You fell asleep and I was trying to wake you up."

She blinked and looked around. "Where am I?"

"The bus. In . . . uh, Hong Kong?" I had no idea how out of it she was.

Her eyes registered the seats, the windows, the city, and then me. "Oh. *Oh.* Wuh-oh." She started laughing. "Goodness, I'm in trouble." The expression was so old-fashioned and odd that it made me pause. *Was she American?*

"Do you need help getting back somewhere?" I asked, being careful not to cross from friendly to overly enthusiastic.

She shook her head. "No, I'm okay. Like, okeydokey!" She held up her fingers in the "OK" symbol over her eye. Something about the movement was familiar. Then she laughed hysterically and I felt a gnawing sense of obligation, again.

"Are you sure?"

"Sure I'm sure," she said with a hiccup. Oh boy. A hiccup. Like a freaking drunk cartoon mouse. The bus stopped and she got up so suddenly that I fell over into the aisle, on my butt. "Here's my stop!" she exclaimed, holding her index finger up in the air.

She staggered along the aisle in those ridiculous slippers and I scrambled up after her.

I tugged on her arm before she stepped down into the narrow stairs. "I'm going to help you. These stairs are steep."

43

She shrugged. "No problem." She sounded like a cowboy. Vowels dragged out, overly pronounced. I couldn't help smiling. Was she making fun of me?

We made it down the stairs, barely, and the driver didn't even glance at us as we fell out into the street. I looked around. We landed in the middle of all the bars, where I had been planning on meeting Charlie.

The girl's eyes grew huge as she took everything in. We were surrounded by people and brightly lit signs. Off every side street were steep hills filled with bars and cafés. "I think I can find a hamburger here," she declared.

"A hamburger?" I asked, looking at her intently. She was alert now—sleepiness completely wiped from her bright expression.

"Euh," she said in Korean, nodding her head. "I'm hungry."

"I gathered," I said with a grin. "Well, I'm not sure where you can find one around here."

"Where are *you* going?" All of her focus was suddenly on me. I started to feel hot under her gaze. It was like having a beam of sunlight on you—pleasing but a little too intense.

I paused and angled my head to get a good look at her. One second she seemed drunk out of her mind, and then another she seemed weirdly sober.

"Why? You wanna come?" The flirtation was instinctual and I immediately regretted it.

She tilted her head to match mine. Precisely, like a dance move. Her delicate finger pointed at me. "Yes. Take me with you."

CHAPTER SEVEN

LUCKY

THE CUTE GUY LOOKED SURPRISED.

It was satisfying to catch this rando off guard. To have a moment of boldness. Now that I was outside, on the busy night streets of Hong Kong, surrounded by young people in pursuit of fun . . . well, I wanted some fun, too.

I couldn't even remember the last time I had been anywhere without Ren, without supervision. Not only had I never snuck out, I never even had the desire to do it.

But I *did* do it. This night was turning out to be something beyond wanting a hamburger now. There was a chance that it would be impossible for me to go unnoticed after my performance on *The Later Tonight Show*. For the tiny bit of anonymity I had to get even smaller.

I looked up at the high-rise apartments and bright lights and felt a cool breeze sweep over my cheeks. I closed my eyes for a second. Yeah,

I wanted a tiny piece of the freedom everyone else had. I wouldn't be greedy. A thimble-sized serving of it would do.

The guy didn't seem to know who I was, which was *purrrrfect*. I'd be able to hang out with *a boy* like a normal teenage girl. The idea energized me, even through the drowsy effect of the meds.

And there was something about this guy. Beyond his handsomeness level, which was off the charts. Even though I had been out of it on the bus, I remembered the inexplicable comfort I felt when I opened my eyes to see his worried face watching mine. The proximity of strangers usually made me recoil—put up a barrier. But the warmth in his eyes had put me at ease. There was concern, not curiosity, behind them.

He didn't have to help me on that bus. Hold my arm so I wouldn't eat it coming down those stairs. And he didn't have to smile at everything I said, either, as if he found me endlessly entertaining.

Granted, he probably thought I was drunk.

"How old are you?"

The guy's question came outta nowhere. I looked at him. "I'm twenty-one."

He laughed, sharp and quick. "Okay, and I'm . . . Steve Jobs's ghost."

Sarcasm. I smiled, pleased, resisting bopping him on his very-well-shaped nose. "Nice to meet you, Steve Jobs's ghost. You're a lot more Korean in real life."

Steve Jobs's ghost ran a hand through his thick hair, fingers long and unexpectedly elegant. My eyes followed those fingers like a creep.

"Hey, how could you tell?" he asked.

"You spoke Korean earlier." I remembered the rough "Ya" as he poked me. I thought I had been dreaming when I had heard it. "Also . . . your face." I waved my hands in front of it to clarify.

The face made a face, but it was good-natured. "Well, your age doesn't matter, I guess. Nobody cards here."

Even in my woozy state, I could tell the guy was feeling conflicted about taking me along.

In what universe was a guy conflicted about hanging out with *Lucky*?

Everything about tonight was so different. So fresh. I felt buoyed by it.

Steve Jobs's ghost took a deep breath. "All right, follow me. Are you sure you want to drink, though? You're already wasted." He started walking and I sped up to follow him, right at his heels. The surface of the stone-paved streets hurt my feet through the thin soles of my slippers.

"I'm not wasted! How *dare* you," I protested as I took in my surroundings. We were walking up a steep hill and the bars and restaurants had their windows and doors thrown open. People were sitting on low plastic stools slurping noodles, standing at bars swigging beers, huddled in the street smoking. There was so much to look at, hear, and smell. It was sensory overload but it wasn't necessarily unpleasant.

I lagged behind in all my gawking and the guy waited for me on a steep set of stairs, his hands resting on his hips. "Okay, you're not drunk. Wearing hotel slippers. In public."

"Don't *judge* me," I sniffed. As I followed, I spotted a couple making out in a dark corner. Well! I averted my eyes. "What's your real name, anyway?" As the words came out, I nearly tripped on my oversized slipper and Steve Jobs's ghost reached out just in time before I fell on my face.

He was still grasping my arms when I looked up at him. There was that concern again in his eyes. It was undeniably attractive. "Jack," he answered.

It wasn't so bad being caught by a cute guy. I felt like it should have been in slow motion. I leaned into his hands, relishing the feeling for a second. "Your name is Jack?" My face was incredibly close to his.

His dark eyes grew wide. Then he blinked. "Yeah."

"That is like, a fake name," I said with a giggle. "Like some jaunty reporter in a Katharine Hepburn movie."

Jack steadied me back into a standing position. "Huh. Are you American?"

"Why, yes I am!" I was totally tickled by him noticing. Sometimes my English felt rusty and this interaction with Jack was probably the most I'd spoken it in months. I used a mix of Korean and English with my managers. And then Korean with almost everyone else. "Are *you* American?"

Jack started walking up the steep hill again. I almost didn't hear him when he answered. "Yeah, I'm from California."

No way. I stopped in my tracks and gasped so loudly that a few people walking by stared at me. "*I am also from California!*" More people stopped and looked, some snickering. Even in my fuzzy brain state, it occurred to me that people staring wasn't good. Years of celebrity were imprinted into me so deeply. I scampered over to Jack, lowering my hat and keeping my face close to his shoulder.

"What's your name?" he asked.

My name? It almost slipped out, but I stopped myself. The image of a Pomeranian's nose on my phone screen flashed through my mind.

"Fern," I blurted out.

"Fern?" Jack's expression was dubious.

"Yeah, Fern. That's my name, Jack." I looked up at him. "Hey. Jack. You're tall, too."

Amusement crossed his face as he glanced down at me. "I guess so. We're both a couple of tall Californians."

"Must be that California milk. Happy cows are from California," I intoned in the voice of a commercial announcer.

"What's your story?" he asked with a choked laugh. "Why are you in Hong Kong?"

I didn't answer. We were stepping onto an escalator lined with colorful lights and I was overcome with a surge of recognition.

"Wait! I know this place!" I held on to the handrail and craned my neck to see in front of us. The escalators were going up, covered by a curved glass roof, going right through the middle of the hilly neighborhood, and it stretched out for what seemed like forever. The twinkle lights were different on each level. Purple. Green. Red.

I grabbed Jack's sleeve. "Oh! *Chungking Express!*"

His brow furrowed in confusion. "What?"

"Are you kidding me?" I cried. "You don't know *Chungking Express*? My favorite Wong Kar-wai movie!"

"Ohhh," Jack said in recognition. "Yeah, I've never seen any of his movies."

I pretended to stagger over. "You're visiting Hong Kong and have never watched his movies?"

"I'm not visiting. I live here."

"*Even* worse, dude," I said, slapping my forehead. "You need to educate yourself. He *is* Hong Kong."

We stepped off on the purple floor and got on the escalators with the green lights. Jack touched my back lightly until I was safely holding the rail. "Are you mansplaining Hong Kong film to me right now, Fern?"

The lights, the views of the city, the familiarity of this place were filling me with warm fuzzy feelings and I returned the jab. "Well, no, I'm physically incapable of doing that as I am not a man."

His tentative smile turned into a grin. The brightest smile I had ever seen. I almost turned away from it, nervous suddenly.

"You're right," he said. Something flickered in his eyes then. An alertness that wasn't there before.

"Also, his movies are magical," I added. He didn't answer, still looking at me with that curious new expression.

We were quiet for the rest of the ride, and when we got off, I locked that memory away, promising myself to never forget it. To savor it.

Jack led me through some more alleys and streets, and I felt like my fake namesake, a little doggie being taken for a walk in a new place. I wanted to sniff every corner, investigate every business, but Jack kept us moving.

Then I heard the music. Strains of trumpets and piano and bass. Jazz. I stopped in my tracks. "Ooh, I wanna go *there*."

Jack turned around, his hands in his pockets. "Hey. Hey, Fern!"

But I was already walking toward it, my body drawn to the music.

CHAPTER EIGHT

JACK

HOW DID I BECOME A BABYSITTER FOR A DRUNK GIRL IN hotel slippers? Named *Fern*?

She had walked into a bar popular with Western expats. It was dimly lit, filled with oversized industrial equipment as decor. Every table had a bowl full of bronze palm-sized animal figurines. You were allowed to touch them but not take one. Bad luck, karma, whatever. There were also real, dead butterflies hanging from the ceilings by strings. It was the most whimsical place Fern could have stepped into tonight.

I followed in after her, the top of my head grazing the curtained entrance. My eyes adjusted to the dark as the music from the live jazz band filled the bar, rich and inescapable.

Fern was standing in the middle of the room, enthralled by

everything around her—hands clasped to her chest, her body bopping slightly to the music.

Yeah, I was a babysitter tonight, but I was kidding myself if I said I felt burdened by it. This girl was totally wacky and quite possibly in an altered state, but still . . .

She had these moments of sharpness that zeroed in on me in this way that was startling. Like her lightning-quick mansplaining retort. Challenging me. Keeping me on my toes.

As I watched her engrossed by the music, I felt myself being pulled under a familiar rush. I crushed so easily. Charlie always sang the lyrics to this old rap song around me, "I'm not a player, I just crush a lot."

It was true. I crushed fast and hard. But then it faded away quickly and it was gone before it had even started. I'd never had a real girlfriend before because of how short-lived my crushes were. But what was I supposed to do? Stay in relationships out of some sense of duty? Would that even be fair to the girls? The whole point of love was that you truly felt it, that it was so strong that you had to be with that person, as if drawn by some otherworldly force.

At the moment, there was a strange pull to this girl. A girl who was probably drunk, and this whole interaction was starting to feel questionable.

I nudged her with my shoulder. "Yo, Fern. There are cooler places to go that aren't full of douchebags."

Her eyes never left the musicians playing on the small stage tucked into the corner of the bar. "No, let's stay here for a little while!" she shouted to be heard over the music. The bass player seemed to hear her and glanced up, shooting her a wink. She clasped her hands tighter, balancing on the tips of her toes in delight.

Oh, brother.

In her excitement, Fern had this air about her that I couldn't quite place . . .

Oh my God. What if she was *dying*? I glanced down at her slippers. Were they the hotel slippers or were they like, hospital slippers? Wait. No, I saw her at the hotel. That fancy hotel. She must be rich, or something.

Rich people die, too.

My eyes skimmed over her—starting from her baseball cap down to her slippers. She looked okay?

What was her deal? I got this nagging feeling she was hiding something.

The music stopped and Fern clapped enthusiastically, jumping up and down. Like a little kid. Her excitement was infectious and I found myself grinning when she looked at me. "Ooh, you're into it now," she said, teasing me.

I wanted to tease her back but the bass player walked up to us before I could. The band had come offstage, taking a break. Up close, the bass player looked like he was half-Asian, half-white. And full hunk.

"Hi, there. Want to join us for a drink?" he asked, his voice rich with a Southern American accent, all smooth and liquid. Not even looking at me.

Give me a break. I looked at Fern, waiting for her to reject this creep. Her pause lasted forever.

CHAPTER NINE
LUCKY

JACK AND THE HANDSOME BASS PLAYER WITH THE long eyelashes and toothpaste-commercial smile were staring at me expectantly.

The music had stirred something in me. Even though I had just finished a fifteen-city tour, I still got excited seeing music performed live. The way musicians came together and fed off of each other's energy. Taking subtle cues from one another, a language without words.

It reminded me of how I felt when I was an obsessed fan myself. The pure euphoria of going to a concert.

I want to make people feel how this music makes me feel.

That's what I thought as a twelve-year-old.

I was starting to get sleepy again, more fuzzy-headed than before. I looked at the two guys waiting for me to say or do something.

The night was young.
And I was hungry.

CHAPTER TEN
JACK

FERN'S EYES MADE A PATH FROM THE GUY'S CHISELED face, over the rolled-up sleeves of his black button-up, down to his scuffed black Oxfords. The dude was good-looking, fine. If she wanted to stay here and hang with him, I'd be okay with that.

I think. Damn it. She still seemed wasted and I wasn't sure if this guy was a dirtbag or what.

I was wondering what to make of this annoying chivalrous instinct, not sure if Fern even wanted it, when she glanced over at me questioningly. Something about that subtle thing, that tiny check-in, got to me.

"Sure, but can my friend Jack join?" she asked the bass player.

The guy barely looked at me. "I guess." Cool, thanks, bro. Real excited.

He led us over to a group of people sitting on low stools scattered around a coffee table covered with drinks. "Y'all, make some room for . . ." He looked at Fern.

"Fern. And Jack!" Fern said, patting my shoulder. Hard.

The group of people—a mixed bag of ethnicities, ages, and genders—nodded their heads in greeting. It was the chilly greeting of Hong Kong hipsters.

Fern plopped onto a stool and pulled me down next to her. The bass player sat on the other side of her and motioned for a server to come over.

"I'll have a gin and tonic," he said, his voice all velvety and authoritative. He glanced over at Fern with a lazy smile. "What do you want, darlin'?"

Laying it on thick, there, Rhett Butler.

"A hamburger," she said primly, folding her hands in her lap.

He chuckled. "What about a drink?"

Oh, please. I tapped my foot, not wanting to make any decisions for her, but another drink seemed like a supremely bad idea. I was itchy to get out of this bar, away from this pretentious snake pit.

Fern was still poring over a menu and staring at all the food photographs. "There are no hamburgers here."

The server gave a flat smile under his handlebar mustache. "We don't have hamburgers. Only snacks and desserts."

Fern's eyebrows rose. "Dessert. Hm, that's novel." I looked down to avoid cracking up. Her old-fashioned words and phrases always popped up at the weirdest moments.

After a quick flip through the menu, she looked up at the server. "I'll have the ice cream sundae, please."

Sleazy McJazzy rolled his eyes and lifted his chin in confirmation with the server.

Musicians were the freaking *worst*.

He started to chat with Fern and I glanced down at my phone. Charlie was texting about meeting up.

Uh . . . about that. I kind of met this girl and she's eating ice cream right now.

Charlie's text came swifter than anything: **WHAT**

Then: **Why is she eating ice cream? Wait never mind. FORGET I EXIST AND ENJOY THE NIGHT BRO**

No one got more excited for this stuff than Charlie. He liked to play the womanizer part, but I was pretty sure he was a romantic at heart. I slipped my phone back into my pocket and glanced over at Fern and the guy again. He was speaking low into Fern's ear.

It wasn't that loud in here, buddy.

The sundae arrived and Fern dug into it like someone who hadn't eaten in days. Weeks.

"Whoa," I said. "You're gonna get brain freeze."

She paused in her inhalation to look at me before her face scrunched up. "Ow!" She clutched her forehead, knocking the cap off her face. It wasn't nice to laugh at her suffering, but I couldn't help it. She started laughing, too, whipped cream smudged on her chin.

McJazzy didn't seem to like this laughter business and leaned into Fern, his cheek practically touching hers. "That looks good. Can I try some?"

God bless Fern, she handed him her spoon. "Why not?"

He looked down at the spoon for a second. "How about you feed me?"

Gross. I tensed, my patience growing thin with this guy.

Fern let out a big burp in response and he recoiled away from her.

58

I burst out laughing again and got up. "On that note, I think we need to head out!"

She got up to follow me. "Okay. Bye!" She waved at everyone. McJazzy got up and grabbed her arm. Oh, God. Was I going to have to fight this grown-ass man?

"Why are you letting this kid drag you around?" McJazzy asked, sneering at me. "Is he your brother or something?"

Fern looked down at his hand and extricated herself. Hard. Slapping him away. "*No*, he's not my brother. And you need *ta' chill*!" she bellowed. "You're like, *old*."

Okay, now this was going from funny to a potential scene.

"Fern," I said, reaching for her, but I drew my hand back, thinking better of it.

She spun around and poked me in the chest. Hard. "Hey, Jack? You're cute but need to like, *relax*!"

I was cute?

Then she kicked McJazzy in the shin, lightly. "And you need to stop creeping on me!"

Holy crap. The expression on McJazzy's face was priceless. But the amusement was short-lived because when I looked back at Fern, she was standing on her tippy toes, reaching for one of the butterflies on the ceiling.

Noooooo.

She snapped one off its string and it was like someone switched off the life in the entire bar. It went silent.

Oh, crap.

Fern didn't notice. Instead, she held the butterfly between her fingers, examining it with open pleasure.

I rushed over to her, hoping that no one working here had noticed. There was a hard-and-fast rule at this bar: If you touched one of the butterflies, you were kicked out. I knew because I had done it before in the past.

The burly bouncer reached her before I did. "Miss, you need to leave."

She held the butterfly up to his nose. "Were these killed on *purpose*? To display *here* for our viewing pleasure? Like barbarians?!" Her tone managed to be both accusatory and curious.

The bouncer swatted her hand away. "How old are you?"

"What does it matter? I want to talk to the manager!" She started to reach for another butterfly.

I grabbed her hand. "Fern! Let's get out of here!"

The bouncer looked at me. "Are you going to take responsibility for bringing a minor in here?"

The whole bar was watching us now. Great. I switched to my "Aw shucks, who, me?" expression and lifted my hands. "Sir, please excuse my sister—" I heard McJazzy yell out, "I *knew* it!" I gritted my teeth but kept smiling. "She's not well. Look at her shoes."

The bouncer glanced down, but his expression remained unamused. While his attention was at her feet, Fern snatched another butterfly off the ceiling. People gasped and the bouncer's head shot up. "That's *it*. I'm calling the police."

Suddenly, Fern lurched forward, pushing the bouncer. "Aren't you *overreacting*?" Her words were slurred and her eyes were starting to close.

So I did the only thing I could do. I yanked her into me, brought my lips to her ear, and whispered, "*Run.*"

CHAPTER ELEVEN
LUCKY

THE CUTE GUY NAMED JACK WAS HOLDING MY HAND and we were running down the street.

It took all my concentration not to trip in my slippers. As we booked it down the steep and busy street, I glanced over at him. His eyes were narrowed as he looked ahead, my hand firmly in his grasp.

Who was this guy? Why was I trusting him? *Did* I trust him?

Suddenly, none of this seemed like a good idea. All my grand notions of this being a wonderful, whimsical night to remember forever when I was an old crone turned to ashes as I struggled to keep up with him, feet hurting.

The second I stepped outside onto the street, I should have turned back around. Into the mall. Eaten my forbidden hamburger and called that my rebellious deed of the trip.

Instead, I had walked down into the street and into a bus! It was so risky, so stupid, so—

I burst out laughing, knowing it was sudden and bizarre, as we turned a corner.

Yes, all of this was a bad idea. And yet, it was kind of sexy times.

Jack glanced over at me, startled by the sound.

When our eyes met, I stopped laughing.

He was too cute and I was too fuzzy-headed.

Finally, after turning the corner into an alley, we stopped. Jack pressed both of us back against the brick wall of a bank, all stealthy and practiced somehow.

Yes, great idea going into an alley with a complete stranger, Lucky.

We took a second to catch our breaths, and then Jack peeked around the corner, reaching across me, his body shielding mine briefly. Hm. I breathed in deeply—I knew it was creepy, but he smelled good. Soapy and a little sweaty.

"Okay, I think we're good," he said, not noticing me sniffing.

I grinned. "I'm good. You're good. What are we good about?"

Jack's mouth formed an unamused straight line. "You were about to get kicked out of a bar, and possibly landed in jail for like, assault. In a foreign country." He practically smoldered. In fact, this guy's whole look was kind of smoldering. Like Heathcliff meets K-drama meets Cali.

"How do you know I'm foreign?" I literally hiccuped the last word out.

He shook his head, raking that lovely hand through that lovely hair again. "What? We talked about it. You're from the US."

"Ha! That's what you think. I live in Korea."

Jack's eyes roved over my face quickly, but not without interest. He had a way of looking at me so thoroughly. Giving me his undivided attention. It suffused me with a strange, but not entirely unpleasant, warmth.

"I guess I can see that. You've got Korea vibes," he said.

"You also look Korean but you don't see me talking about it!" I hollered. God, yelling felt good. I didn't get to do it enough.

"What?" he yelped, his eyes big and incredulous. "Okay, forget it. You're not . . . making sense like, at all. Let me get you back where you need to be."

A panicky chill swept through my body. By some miracle, I had escaped from Ren Chang, the best bodyguard in Asia, and I didn't want to go back now. The freedom had been too short, not enough, too—fuzzy. "No!"

Jack took a ragged breath. "Come on, you're drunk or something. It's not safe."

"How dare you!" I jabbed a finger into his chest. "I do not drink!" I had a feeling I liked saying "how dare you."

"Okay. You don't drink." His expression was maddeningly patient. As if he was dealing with a petulant child. "No worries, let's get a car," Jack said while pulling out his phone.

Again, the panic continued to swell. "I can't go back, please!"

The words were "Alarming Things Women Say for Four Hundred, Alex," and they worked. Jack's head snapped up and he looked at me with concern. "Why? What's wrong?"

And although I knew those words came from worry I hadn't quite earned, my eyes welled up with tears. Outta *nowhere*. When was the last time anyone besides my parents asked me, "What's wrong?" It was the question asked when my face looked drawn or sad. Or when I was crying. It was the question asked by people who truly knew you and cared.

It was easy to sound happy and relaxed on a FaceTime call, or in texts.

But soon, I could see my family in real life. The money would be so much better, and I'd actually be able to fly my entire family out to see me. Despite having two hit albums, my contract still gave much of the earnings to my management label.

It was how it was done and had always been done. I was supposed to be grateful for the fame, for making it to the top in a competitive field. Being an idol? Up until very recently, it had been enough.

At some point, something changed. Watching that video in my hotel room? I knew something was missing now. I just wasn't sure what it was. And right now, this night with this guy was helping me avoid it. To forget that my accomplished dreams were no longer fulfilling.

My cheeks were wet, my eyelash extensions clinging to them. Jack slipped the phone back into his jeans pocket. "Hey . . . hey. Don't cry." He kept his distance, but I felt his warmth anyway.

The big feel I got from this guy since we met was . . . *caring*. He cared and he had no reason to. That's why I had followed him down a dark alley.

Suddenly, I was so, so tired. And embarrassed. I wasn't acting like myself and I was a mess, and this guy was now spending too much time with me, and it was all going to get leaked out in the press.

I tried to dry my eyes with the long thermal sleeves peeking out from my coat and swiped up some stringy snot along the way. Oh, God.

My eyes flew up to Jack's face. Jack, who would be taller than me in heels. He tried to avert his eyes but it was too late.

"You saw my komul right now!" I wailed. Certain words, like snot, would always be Korean first no matter what.

Jack coughed while trying to hold back his laughter. "No, I didn't!"

"Yes, you did!" I turned away from him, my face planted into the wall. The rough brick scratched my cheek, but I didn't care.

"I swear!" he said from behind me.

But with my forehead pressed into the cool building, the surroundings dark, I felt my eyelids droop. And I gave in to the exhaustion.

CHAPTER TWELVE

JACK

YOU KNOW WHAT'S DIFFICULT? CARRYING A HUMAN being on your back. Especially a human being who is dead asleep.

I shifted my weight from one foot to the other, and Fern let out a complainy sniffle. So sorry, literal monster on my back!

If I were famous, some paparazzo like me would snap a photo of this moment.

How did my night turn into this? From being worried about a cute girl falling asleep on a bus to piggybacking her home? Not her home. Mine.

She had absolutely no identification on her. I had a feeling she was staying at the same hotel as Teddy Slade, where I first saw her in the elevator. But bringing a drunk girl into that lobby without knowing anything about her was probably *not* a good idea. And no way was I stepping back into that place after the stunt I pulled today. Celeste Jiang had known what I'd done and I didn't want to risk it.

I had dug through Fern's pockets earlier, hoping to find a phone, to call someone to pick her up. But nothing.

It was like she fell out of the sky.

By the time I got to my apartment building, I felt like I was going to die. Like, blood pouring out of my eyes type of death. I heaved her off my back as gently as possible. She slumped down onto the granite-tiled floor in the entryway. The medicinal herbs shop on the ground floor of my apartment building was closed for the night, the metal grate in place, but its scent was still strong around us. I fumbled to enter the code to let me into the building. When the door unlocked with a loud *clang*, I propped it open with one foot and reached for Fern, draping her arm across my neck and heaving her up by the waist with my other arm.

Why did I live in a walk-up? All of my life decisions that led me to this moment played in my head like a punishing movie montage, and I cursed every single one of them.

When I finally reached the fourth floor, I was panting and my entire upper body was cramped with pain. Leaning both our bodies against the wall, I tried to dig my key out from my pocket but Fern immediately slid down onto the floor.

I let her sit there for a second while I unlocked the door. I grabbed a shoe from the entry, one of Charlie's rubber house slippers, and wedged it into the door.

Fern was a limp noodle of a human being now, completely slouched over, her slippered feet pointing in opposite directions like the Wicked Witch of the East.

After a few attempts to move her, I was sweating. Christ, why was this girl so freaking difficult to move! I was finally able to grab her under her armpits and drag her into the living room. Straight-up hiding-a-dead-body style.

I heaved her against the sofa, where she continued to slump.

"Oh my God," I said to the ceiling, dragging my hands down my face. There was so much that could go wrong.

One, if Fern woke up and didn't know where she was, and saw me, she would freaking flip and I would look like some creeper who probably roofied her at the bar. Two, if my landlady caught wind of this somehow, I would literally be beaten to death with a shoe.

I took a deep breath. *Okay, it's cool. Keep your head on straight, Jack. You excel in crises, right? This is your jam. You can get out of anything.*

I rolled up my shirtsleeves and threw the extra dead bolt on my door. In case my landlady decided to pay a surprise midnight visit. Which wouldn't be the first time. She was an insomniac and got bored easily. I glanced at Fern to see if the sound stirred her awake.

With her head dropped forward and her limbs splayed like a rag doll, there was no chance of anything short of an EDM concert waking her up.

I grabbed a pillow and a blanket from the bedroom and tossed them on the sofa.

As I stood there staring at her and the fake leather sofa cracking and peeling with age, I felt guilty. Maybe she should get the bed. That seemed like the right thing to do?

If Charlie only knew. We actually shared the bed—switching off every other week, one taking it while the other slept on the sofa. We each had our own set of sheets and changed them every week. It was straight-up Wild West, but it worked.

What would he say if he knew this strange girl was sleeping in our bed?

Fern was fully slumped over now, her head almost touching her knees.

Time to move her.

I closed my eyes, willing my overtired muscles to be cool with it.

Oof. Fern's foot hit my calf as I hauled her into the bed. After looking at her for a second, those silly slippers stuck out at me and I sighed deeply. I lifted one of her feet by the back of her ankle and quickly tugged off the slipper. Trying not to linger too much on touching her skin, I made quick work of the other slipper as well, my fingertips barely touching her.

Fern let out an odd sound and I froze. But the next thing to come out of her mouth was a snore.

I gritted my teeth. I was going to have a heart attack because of this person.

Suddenly, she threw her arm across her face, knocking her cap off.

I finally had an unobstructed view of her.

She had a lot of makeup on, almost like she had been made up for some occasion. Which was at odds with the fact that she had been barefoot in hotel slippers. But the rest of her—long-sleeved shirt and jeans—looked normal.

What was she doing here?

Whatever the case, I was staring, so I eventually drew the blanket over her and turned off the bedside lamp.

I looked at my phone in the dark to check the time, the screen washing everything in a cold blue light. Every part of this made me feel like a serial killer. It was late, past midnight. Charlie usually got off work around seven in the morning, so we were safe from him busting in here.

I hoped, anyway.

After washing up, I climbed into my makeshift bed on the sofa, hearing Fern snoring lightly in the next room. A billion thoughts raced through my mind, making it pretty much a guaranteed nope for sleeping.

What if she woke up before me and freaked out?

What if she freaked out and screamed, making my neighbors, or worse, my landlady, run in here?

What if she freaked out, screamed, and someone called the cops?

Every scenario ended with me in Hong Kong jail and being some weird Reddit urban legend.

Because I couldn't sleep, I swiped through my phone—going through social media accounts on autopilot.

As I scrolled through Twitter, an image popped up that made me pause.

It was an account for a comedian I followed—and it was about his upcoming performance on *The Later Tonight Show*. The image attached to the tweet showed the comedian's face alongside another.

A Korean pop star.

Her name was Lucky and she was going to perform in a couple nights. Fresh off her Asian tour.

Oh.

My.

God?

Long, pink hair floating around a radiant face smoldering into the camera. Full cheeks, wide eyes, a smirky smile.

Holy crap. It was Fern.

I actually recognized her vaguely from some stuff in Rumours mentioning her tour. But without the pink hair, she wasn't as recognizable to someone who didn't follow K-pop that closely.

Okay.

Okay. So I have a K-pop star sleeping in my bed right now.

No, not *my* bed. The bed I share with my roommate! Right. That made it better.

I scrambled over to the bedroom and crouched at the edge of the bed. Trying not to make a peep, I tilted my head to get a better look at her face, shining my phone's screen on it.

I gasped. There was no denying it. It was her.

All right, Jack. Chill. Remain calm. No big deal that you might have inadvertently KIDNAPPED A K-POP STAR.

I quickly Googled "Lucky K-pop" and found endless links and images. Her music videos, live performances, fan pages. And paparazzi photos of her covering her face as she exited a plane at the Hong Kong airport. Then photos of her in concert just *today*, of her dancing and singing in an outrageous booty-short bodysuit thingy with super-high-heeled silver boots.

Stunned, I fell against the bed, my back making the mattress shake. I froze, but she didn't move a muscle. I needed to reconcile these photos with the drunk girl in my bed, whose snot had rubbed against my shoulder as I carried her. Why was she out by herself? Was someone looking for her?

I went deeper into my Google search and found out she was

supposed to perform on *The Later Tonight Show* on Monday. Scrolling through a K-pop news site, I saw an article that said this performance was going to be her American debut and that there were huge expectations for it, hoping it would launch her as a star there.

Knowing what little I did about K-pop, I knew it was hard to break out in Western countries. Would she become famous in the US? Was I alone in my apartment with a potential mega superstar right now?

Mega superstar.

LUCKY NIGHT OUT

The potential headline splashed through my head in flashing lights. Lucky . . . she wasn't some cute drunk girl who needed help. She was a celebrity. One on the brink of becoming *huge*.

And extremely sought after.

If someone had snapped any photos of her tonight in that bar, they would have made the Asian tabloids for sure. It would have been a huge scandal. K-pop stars were tightly reined in, their images had to be squeaky clean. Drunk Lucky in a Hong Kong bar? With a *guy*?

Me. I was that guy.

This was the story. My brain glommed on to this immediately—cogs and gears turning. What if Lucky spent an entire day with some random guy in Hong Kong? What if it was all documented? That story would sell for *a lot* once she hit it big in the US. And if she didn't, it would sell to the Korean media, regardless.

It was a decidedly uncool thing to do to someone. If they were my friend. But I didn't know her, and beyond that, she was a huge celebrity. And if she was going to be famous in the US, being seen with a boy wouldn't ruin her reputation—it wasn't like that there.

I made the decision then—to manage an all-nighter, ensuring that I'd be awake before her. I crept back over to the sofa, my thoughts going a million miles per hour. If I pulled this off, I'd get that job, and so many of my worries would melt off—making rent, my parents' college expectations.

They would peel off of me, layer by layer.

SATURDAY

CHAPTER THIRTEEN
LUCKY

THE FIRST WEIRD THING I NOTICED WAS THE LIGHT.

What happened to my black-out curtains? I never woke up to sunlight.

Second was the faint snoring. Was that Ji-Yeon? Did she spend the night in my hotel room? She'd done that in the past when I had particularly anxious nights.

I shifted under the covers, then froze. I was still wearing my jeans and my neck was all crunchy-feeling. Why was I—

The hotel hallway.

The dude in the elevator.

The mall.

The bus.

The boy.

The bar.

The boy.

I shot up—brain fully awake and registering everything around me: The small bedroom crammed with a hodgepodge of black wood furniture. A poster of some old action movie. Threadbare floral curtains fluttering around a large window. The cracked-open door and the sound of light snoring drifting into the room.

OH MY GOD.

My hands flew to my mouth, muffling my involuntary scream. What in Sam Hill did I *do* last night?

I spied my coat neatly folded next to my hotel-room slippers at the foot of the bed, placed side by side. Which led me back to the view of the other room . . . two feet poking out from a pile of blankets on a truly hideous sofa.

Was that *him*?

I remembered the guy like a fuzzy dream. Tall. He towered over me. Lean but sturdy. I remembered him *feeling* sturdy. Oh, good gravy. My face burned at some memory I couldn't quite grasp. I tried to piece together an image of him. Thick, longish hair pushed back from his face, tucked behind his ears. His face, though . . . my memories couldn't focus on any definitive features on his face.

I was so out of it last night and somehow ended up in a guy's apartment. He brought me back to his place. He was a stranger. All my girl alarm bells were going off at the moment. I needed to get the heck out of here.

He was still asleep. Only needed to slip out of here unnoticed. I found my hat on the nightstand, pulled it low over my eyes, and practically slithered out of the bed, careful not to make any sudden sounds.

I dropped to the floor and crawled toward my jacket and slippers. Why was I crawling? In case the paparazzi were poised outside the window? A shudder went through me at the thought. Yeah, I had to get out of here like, *now.*

But the second my fingers brushed the slippers, the sofa pile moved.

I let out a low hiss and pulled back. *Blast.* Then I heard muffled cursing from the pile of blankets before a series of frantic movements began underneath them. I leaned back against the bed and froze, watching the blankets. Afraid of what would emerge.

First, a hand fumbled around the coffee table until it found a phone. The phone disappeared under the blankets for a second before all the blankets were thrown aside to reveal a real live boy sitting up in the middle of the pile.

Ah, there was his face.

Dark, heavy-lidded eyes, bleary from having just woken up. Finely sculpted bones—he had cheekbones I would murder for and a jaw that could cut glass. But it was his mouth that startled me. An outrageously pouty mouth. He looked like a bratty playboy from a K-drama.

I must have made some kind of sound, because suddenly he was looking at me.

Those sleepy eyes widened and his *how-dare* mouth dropped open. We stared at each other in silence for about .5 seconds.

I scrambled up and shot out of the bedroom, toward the front door of the apartment.

"Wait!" he called out from behind me, but I fumbled with the dead bolt until I was out the door. Halfway down the hall, I noticed the flickering lights and the smell of cigarette smoke.

Then I stepped in something wet and registered my *bare feet.*

Waves of revulsion rolled over me as I tried not to think about what I might have stepped in. Ew, ew, *ew.*

I took a deep breath, pushed my hair off my face, and closed my eyes. Mind over matter. Trying to summon my meditation app's breathing exercises. It was all about focusing on your breath so that the absolute horror of your surroundings and current life could melt away or something. It did help, though. It got me through excruciating dance numbers with a sprained ankle. Got me through the scent of grilled meats at late-night barbecue spots when I was subsisting on sweet potatoes.

My mind finally stilled as it was on the edge of freak-out mode. Tightly wound self-control kept me anchored, kept me still. When I opened my eyes, I was as cool as a cucumber. I had no idea where I was in the city, and not wearing shoes would attract unwanted attention. Not to mention, it was totally gross.

So I grudgingly made my way back to the apartment. Except I didn't know which one I came from. I walked door to door, hoping one of them would trigger some sort of familiarity by appearance alone.

Moments from last night kept flashing through my mind, including the boy's face. And then suddenly, I wasn't merely imagining his face. I was seeing it.

Right in front of me.

He was standing in the hallway, holding up my slippers. "You forgot something."

Even though his hair was all mussed, his eyes still bleary, and clothes rumpled, there was a confident gleam in his eyes. His lips curled up into a knowing smile.

I snatched the slippers from him. "Where am I?"

"You're at a luxury apartment complex in Hong Kong," he said. Every part of him exuded extreme enjoyment at this predicament. It turned that lovely mouth into a punchable one.

"Listen. I don't know you." I poked his chest with my slipper.

"You're just some random creep who brought me back to his place, so I don't think this is the time for you to be acting *sassy*, do you?"

For a moment, his confidence seemed to flag, but then he bounced back with triple the zest. "You know me. Jack. Jack Lim."

Jack. I remembered now. I recalled a flash of his smile on a steep street saying the same thing. And I remembered a few other things: A sturdy hand on my back as I stumbled down steep stairs on the bus. A slightly disapproving-auntie vibe as he sat next to me at a bar. That perv musician asking me to feed him ice cream. The butterflies, and Jack rushing me out of the bar. I also remembered that he didn't know who I was.

A tiny flare of trust started to spread through my chest.

My eyes whipped up to his face, looking for a hint of last night's chivalry in that self-assured expression.

He raised an eyebrow. "Hi?"

I frowned. "Are you American?"

An exaggerated wince. "Don't hold it against me."

Who *was* this guy? I had never met anybody so *on* in my life. And I worked in the freaking music industry!

"We already established this, Fancy Shoes. We're both from California." His gaze held mine warmly, and I flushed.

My instinct was to hide my face, but I remembered that he didn't know who I was.

"Well, I wouldn't call myself a Californian, anymore," I said hesitantly. "I haven't lived there in years." The information slipped out too easily. Years of training usually had me more careful with what I revealed—not that me being American was some big secret or anything.

I knew I should be wary of this grinning confidence of his. It wasn't that I trusted him exactly. It was that I didn't want to *care* about trusting him. I was tired of living in a constant state of vigilance.

So I stood there instead of running away.

"You still have a Valley girl accent," Jack said. I was about to protest, but the way his eyes stayed firmly on my face was distracting, and I felt the first annoying tingles of crushness.

How many times had I been half-naked on a stage, on a TV screen? After getting used to the feeling of being ogled, I'd grown numb to it. Men looked at me all the time—with equal parts reverence and lust. I'd learned to stop noticing. But for some reason, this guy's eyes on my face, the genuine interest in his expression, made every inch of me hyperaware of him. I remembered, vaguely, his focus on me last night. Always concerned and interested.

I couldn't stop noticing his attention because it was physically impossible.

While I stared back at him, Jack continued to speak, half-perplexed, half-amused. "So. Fern. What are your plans today? I think you owe me breakfast after last night."

My mouth dropped open. *Fern?* Oh, God. Right. "Wha . . . why, what happened?" I frantically tried to remember if any funny business had happened between us.

"Nothing!" he exclaimed too quickly, his slick exterior slipping away for half a second. And was it my imagination, or did his cheeks turn red?

I was relieved, but I couldn't quite figure out if it was from *not* having been despoiled, or if it was from knowing that if I *had* been despoiled, I would have wanted to remember it.

Either way, his blushing was cute.

82

He gathered his wits almost immediately. "I mean, I rescued you from getting arrested. That's all."

"You *rescued* me?" I scoffed.

He nodded. "Well, yeah. You were about to throw down with a huge bouncer."

I couldn't help but laugh. "I would never."

"How drunk were you? Why were you out alone anyway?" he asked.

My huffiness returned. "That judginess in your voice right now? The least attractive thing, ever."

"I'm more concerned about your well-being than how attractive I am to you."

"Okay," I said with a snort.

Jack grinned again. "Okay."

It took a lot of willpower not to smile back at this guy. "Anyway, I wasn't *drunk*."

He guffawed. "*Okay*."

I realized that I had no other explanation I could give him. *I wasn't drunk. Only completely out of it from sleeping pills mixed with anxiety meds, which I need to take to fall asleep every night of my life.*

Yeah.

"Whatever. I need to get back to my hotel, so . . . thanks for whatever it is I should thank you for," I said, pulling on my slippers, hopping from one foot to the other. Jack reached out to steady me with one hand, quick and unthinking. His hand was firm on my elbow. I glared at him and yanked it away, almost toppling over in the process.

When my slippers were finally on, even though I knew I looked silly, I felt somewhat in control. Untouchable. Like how I usually felt.

It was time for my cool exit.

I turned and started to walk away, my steps brisk and deliberate. This kid Jack would remember the day he had *THE* Lucky sleep over at his place and—

"*Fern*!" he bellowed down the hall. "How are you getting back? You don't have a wallet or your phone."

I faltered but kept walking, feeling around in my pockets. *No!* I had a vision of my phone on my hotel nightstand. Right where I had left it before going to bed. And I never carried a wallet anymore, it wasn't necessary.

"I've got my legs," I shouted without looking back, reaching the elevator.

"Yeah, you do."

I almost tripped. The nerve!

"Problem, though. We're about ten miles out of the city."

I whipped my head around. "WHAT!"

Jack grinned. "Let's get breakfast."

CHAPTER FOURTEEN

JACK

OKAY, SO I WAS LYING. WE WERE SMACK-DAB IN THE middle of the city. But "Fern" didn't have to know that. I needed to buy time with her and I was using everything in my arsenal to do it. Persuasive charmer mode initiated.

As we walked down the stairs, I glanced over at her again. She had insisted on going back into my apartment to wash off her makeup. "*Good GRAVY!*" she had yelled when she saw her reflection. With her face freshly scrubbed, Lucky looked considerably younger. For a few seconds, I was able to forget that she was the biggest pop star in Asia.

She caught me looking at her as we went downstairs, and instinctively reached for her cap, slim fingers grazing the stiff brim. Her long hair fell around her face and she seemed to shrink into herself. I blinked. Suddenly, the larger-than-life feel of her diminished.

"Are you in town with your family or something?" I asked. This charade rested on my acting chops—and right now I had to act curious about her in the way that anyone would be about a stranger.

She hesitated before answering, "Uh, no. I'm here with my church choir."

Good one. "For fun?"

"Work. We're doing a few performances. Our choir is pretty famous. In the . . . church choir world." Her voice trailed off, and I held back laughter.

"So, aren't they going to wonder where you were all night?"

She chewed on her lower lip. "Yeah . . . which is why I need to go back early enough before they notice. Which is why I *don't* want to go to breakfast with you."

"You owe me, though."

The most vicious scowl crossed her face. "We've already established I don't have any money on me!"

Right. "You owe me your lovely company, then."

She stopped on the stairs and leaned in close. Menacingly. "I don't owe you my company, *ever*."

Her reaction startled me. "Sorry. I was kidding." It was a flash of the powerful superstar she was. My determination to make this story happen grew stronger with each step we took.

"Have better jokes," she muttered as she continued down the stairs. Ouch. Maybe time to reel back some of this arrogant charmer bit.

"I want to keep hanging out, that's all," I said. It was the truth.

I was hoping the words would disarm her, enough to convince her to stay with me. I had no idea how much time I would have with her, but I knew that she had ditched her hotel last night for a reason. I only had to add to that reason, make it more enticing as the day went on.

It worked. She looked at me with pink cheeks. "Okay, fine. Why didn't you say so?"

I smiled the rest of the walk down the stairs, and when we reached the ground floor, I opened the door into the small lobby. Harsh daylight washed over us, and Lucky's head immediately tilted down, her hand reaching up to block her face.

How many times had I seen this pose? All the celebrities photographed in airports, grocery store parking lots, their own backyards? It always reeked of wary entitlement to me, like, "My livelihood depends on your attention but I also demand a level of privacy that is unrealistic."

But being here, on this side, all I felt was Lucky's wariness. Laced with fear. It made me wonder again about why she had left her hotel room last night.

I did a quick sweep of the lobby to make sure it was empty. "Wow, pretty dead around these parts," I said loudly, stepping onto the tiled floors, my body casting a shadow over her.

She relaxed visibly, her shoulders dropping a millimeter and her face peeking out from behind her jacket sleeve. When she confirmed that it was indeed empty, she dropped her arm but still kept her head tilted down.

Realistically, I knew she could be recognized in Hong Kong. She was famous all over Asia. But it was a huge, bustling city, and she wasn't in pop-star mode—in fact, she was almost unrecognizable without the makeup and pink hair. Too bad it was hard to hide the fact that she was a stone-cold fox.

"Jack!"

My body tensed at recognizing that voice. I saw Lucky freeze up next to me, and I reassured her with a small smile. "My landlady."

Mrs. Liu walked toward us from the front entrance, a bamboo broom clutched in her tiny, gnarled fist. She was the size of a fifth grader, her rounded back hunched, her puff of white hair shellacked into place. Shrewd eyes set into a remarkably unlined face sized us up, coming to rapid conclusions. "Who's your friend?"

"This is Fern," I said, subtly pushing her behind me, trying to place her in shadow. I didn't think Mrs. Liu would recognize her, but she often surprised me. She was Harry Styles's biggest fan, for one thing. "We're leaving now, so byeeee."

"Stop!" she called out before we could duck out the door. "No sleepover guests, remember?"

Oh my God. I glanced at Lucky, who was turning a deep shade of red.

"Mrs. *Liu!*"

She glared, pointing the small broom at us. "Don't shout at *me!*"

"She didn't sleep over, she met me here," I said, the ire sounding flimsy even to my own ears. Mrs. Liu had a way of cutting through my crap.

Lucky shifted uneasily next to me. Mrs. Liu zeroed in on her. "You. Don't sleep over with bad boys like Jack."

I sputtered. "Wha-what?! Bad boys . . ."

A snort of laughter came out of Lucky, and Mrs. Liu kept going, "Jack, you know that washer you brought up to apartment 301?"

"My *back* remembers," I muttered, rubbing said back. "Next time, get the delivery guys to do it!"

She shook the broom at me. "And pay extra? What's the point of you living here if you don't help an old lady once in a while?"

"Um, my *rent*?" I said. Then I winked at her. "And I make the women happy."

Mrs. Liu cackled. "More like, make us laugh. Anyway, the washer isn't working. Can you look at it?"

I shook my head. Because I reminded her of her handy son living in Germany, Mrs. Liu always expected me to have the same skills as him. "I'm not going to be able to fix it!"

"At least try, you lazy!"

"Lazy?" I yelped.

Lucky was watching our back-and-forth with open delight. Mrs. Liu coughed then, while trying to get another jab back at me.

I frowned. "Did you sleep with your hair wet again? That's how you got sick last time. I told you not to do it anymore!"

Mrs. Liu waved her hand. "I'm not sick. It's so dusty in here. I have to clean, out of my way!" She pushed by us. "Bye, now."

"Well, if you get sick, don't blame me!" I called out before storming outside, cursing the day I decided to live in this apartment building.

CHAPTER FIFTEEN
LUCKY

SEEING JACK FLUSTERED BY A LITTLE OLD LADY WITH A broom was already a highlight of my day. Their relationship, as shouty as it was, seemed pretty darn cute.

I observed him as he opened the door for me. The cool-guy act was merely that—an act. Because in his spare time, he was helping old ladies move heavy appliances. Caring about their damp hair.

I was about to follow his huffy figure out the door when I felt a firm hand grip my arm.

I turned to see Mrs. Liu looking up at me, her expression deadly serious, her eyes sharp and sweeping over my face. They lit up as soon as they confirmed what she was looking for.

My blood turned to ice. She recognized me.

The words that came out of her mouth, however, shocked the daylights out of me.

"Don't hurt him, Lucky." Her eyes softened, her grip still strong. "Jack's a good boy, even if he doesn't show off about it."

And then she walked away, whistling and sweeping along the way.

Her words vibrated deep in me, and I had to steady myself after she disappeared around the corner.

"Fern!"

I glanced over at Jack and followed him, this guy I didn't know but was growing curious about.

Curiouser and curiouser.

CHAPTER SIXTEEN
JACK

WHEN WE STEPPED OUTSIDE, LUCKY STAYED CLOSE. IT surprised me how quickly she trusted me.

A tiny, tiny ember of guilt lodged itself into my chest.

Listen, you speck of guilt. I know you think I am not doing the "right" thing. But this is the price of fame. Your every move is recorded. And plus, Lucky's going to get a fun day out of this. I can be charming, all right?

Hong Kong in the early morning felt like a secret. It was so early that we were outside before the rush of traffic, and the shops were starting to open. The streets were quiet, hushed, and cast in a soft yellow morning light.

"You good?" I asked Lucky, feeling her anxiousness in every step we took, every glance down the street. I wondered what kind of trouble she was in. Her unease made it clear to me that she had definitely snuck out last night. There was no way it was cool for her to have slept over in some random guy's apartment. And she'd been in no state to call and update anyone. Someone had to be looking for her.

She nodded. "Yeah. I'm good."

And she was probably hungry. "Okay, so what are you in the mood for? There's this great bakery that makes sourdough bread that I dream about—"

"I want fish congee," she interrupted, her face tilted up for once, her dark brown eyes zeroed in on mine.

When I recovered from that direct stare, I raised my eyebrows. "Fish for breakfast?"

She snorted. "Wow, you're *very* American."

Some latent Korean pride in me sparked to life, making me sputter, "Okay, Miss Korea."

"Good one." The sarcasm surprised me, her vulnerability dashed for a second. "Don't you ever have rice for breakfast?" she asked.

A cab rushed by, the air whooshing between us. "No, actually, I don't. Are you going to take away my Korean card now?"

"I should," she said, but she was grinning, her movements more natural and at ease. "Anyway, it's a typical breakfast food here. You should know that."

I looked over at her, surprised. "Have you spent a lot of time in Hong Kong?"

Her mouth opened to answer, but something in her brain seemed to hitch and she took a beat longer than necessary. "Um, not really. But I've been here before." I could imagine she'd been here a dozen times on tour, but never had a chance to actually *be* here.

While I knew I was doing this for a story, I also felt real excitement to share that with her. "Well, lucky you." The word slipped out before I could think, but her face stayed impassive. "We happen to be near some of the best congee in the city. I'll take you to my roommate's favorite."

There was a skip to her step as we headed to the café and she lifted her face up to the sun. Every part of her seemed to be stretching out from the shrunken, compacted version of herself. Suddenly, she halted, almost with a cartoon skidding noise. "Wait. *Roommate?*"

"Don't worry, he didn't see you. He works nights. Cab driver."

She looked maybe 2 percent more relieved. We walked down narrow, winding streets, passing by gnarled banyan trees with air roots hanging down above us like curtains. The streets were steep and Lucky took her time—being careful with her steps and absorbing her surroundings, taking in every detail. The autumn cold snap had stayed through the night—the morning air was chilly and felt cleansing as we walked through it.

We finally arrived at a small, nondescript restaurant located on the ground floor of a slightly dilapidated building covered in bright signs. Because it was so early, it was nearly empty, with a lone old man sitting at a corner table reading a newspaper.

A skinny woman with permed hair approached us with menus and spoke in Cantonese. Lucky and I both held up our hands in a universal gesture of, "Sorry!"

She responded with a flat "Good morning," handing us a couple laminated menus, and waved us toward a table by the windows. Classical music was playing in the background as we sat down in the squeaky vinyl chairs, the glass top of the table bouncing light into our eyes. Lucky was framed by calendars hanging on the wall behind her, the sun hitting her so that only her mouth was in light, the rest of her face obscured in shadow. It was the perfect shot. Lonely, vulnerable.

"Wanna eat an old-ass egg?"

I shook my head. "Excuse me?"

She held up the menu with a wide grin. "You can get your congee with a century egg!" Genuine excitement exuded from her as she pointed to a photo on the menu of what looked like an inky orb of evil.

"Sure," I said, smiling back at her. It was pretty adorable to see how some of her personality quirks were actually real and not drunken antics. "It looks kind of rad."

"You've never had one before?" she asked.

I shook my head. "No. I guess I'm proving to be a boring Hong Kong resident."

But instead of showing disdain, Lucky's face cracked wide open into a smile, and the surprise of it made my breath catch in my throat. "I've never tried it, either. But I've always wanted to."

Even when she pretended to be "normal," Lucky had a star quality. The kind of quality that made people's breaths catch in their throats. *Don't let her charm you, Jack. Stay focused.*

When the food arrived—porcelain bowls full of steaming porridge topped with our marinated eggs—I no longer had Lucky's attention. Her eyes locked onto her bowl like a tractor beam. I wouldn't have been surprised to see the food get absorbed into her face.

And while she only had eyes for her food, I slid my phone out of my pocket. Under the table, I turned on the camera. When she dipped the long plastic chopsticks into the rice, lifting the bowl up to her face, I dragged the phone up toward the edge of the table, ever so slowly. And at just the perfect angle, I took a quick shot of her as she moved the bowl from her face. The light was still perfect, falling sharply on her features, dissecting half her face into shadow.

If she stuck around, this could be a story about a K-pop star escaping the confines of her life. Doing what she wanted. Like eating a local breakfast in a tiny restaurant tucked away on the busy streets of Sheung Wan.

I put my phone away before she could catch me in the act. But she still wasn't paying any attention to me, instead gazing worshipfully at the congee. "My God." Her voice hit this low register that sent a jolt through my entire body. But then she held her spoon up in the air and exclaimed, "You are sooooo deeeeeeelicious!" She sang the words—expertly and clear as a bell. Obviously, she was joking around, singing to a bowl of porridge. But the caliber of her voice . . . It was like watching Serena Williams play tennis when you never watched tennis. One look at her playing against normal human beings and you knew you were witnessing something special.

I don't know why I was surprised. Maybe because I always thought of K-pop stars as manufactured performers rather than actual singers. But sitting in front of me, serenading a bowl of porridge, was a true vocalist.

"You have a nice voice. No wonder you're in that choir," I said while glancing down at my food.

There was a beat of silence on the other side of the table as I poked my porcelain spoon into the hot and gelatinous porridge. "Thanks," she said quietly, her effervescence suddenly bottled up again.

I worried that I might have scared her off. But when I looked up she was shoveling more food in her mouth, her eyes closed blissfully.

"Fern, you *love* congee," I said with a laugh, breaking my boiled egg apart with my chopsticks.

"Bless this food and bless you for bringing me here," she murmured as she wiped daintily at her lips with a tiny, thin paper napkin. Her face was flushed from the warmth of the food, or maybe it was from the pure joy of enjoying a quiet meal, undisturbed. I wondered how far-reaching her celebrity-life limitations were.

"It's good," I said between mouthfuls. And it was. Charlie had been trying to get me to wake up early enough for breakfast congee for months, but this was the first time I'd done it. The right motivation was all it took, apparently.

"What do you like about being in choir?" I asked her.

She took another bite before answering me. Her expression was incredibly composed even as she chewed. She was trying to figure out what to say. "It's . . . a way to share music with an audience."

"Is it music you feel passionately about, though?"

I thought the question might make her choke on her food, being as direct as it was. But she only frowned slightly. "You seem to have an opinion about church music."

If "church music" was subbing for K-pop in this conversation, then yeah, I had an opinion. "It doesn't seem personal. It's music that's . . . for everyone."

Her eyes lit up. "Music for everyone. You say that like it's a bad thing. But I find it to be a very cool thing. People are so divided in the world, you know? It's a miracle to offer something that so many can all agree to like."

I blinked. I'd never thought of pop music that way. "That's . . . so insightful."

"Wow, don't look so surprised," she said with a snort, back to goofy Lucky again.

When every morsel of congee and egg was devoured, Lucky reclined in her seat and lolled her head back. "That was the best breakfast I've had in months." The strangeness of the words landed with a thud between us. We both seemed to avoid looking at them, neither of us willing to acknowledge the weirdness of their shapes. I politely ate my porridge, taking the occasional sip of tea.

Suddenly she bent forward, sliding her elbows across the table until her cheek rested on her right palm. "So, what's *your* story?" she asked.

Her proximity made me choke on my food. Without moving her torso, her left hand snaked over to my cup of tea and pushed it closer to me. I took a big swig of it and it scalded my throat. When I recovered, I placed it down on the table with a gentle rap. "My story?"

"Yeah, how old are you?"

Koreans always got down to business—age first. Where did we stand in the hierarchy of seniors versus juniors? "How old do you think I am?" The teasing words came out of my mouth so swiftly, like some practiced creep.

Lucky was not amused. "Who cares what I *think*? What's the truth?"

Hm. She wasn't one for beating around the bush. "I'm eighteen. I graduated last June."

There was a flicker of something like jealousy behind her eyes. "High school? Here or in California?"

"Here."

"Where in Cali are you from, anyway?"

"LA."

She straightened up. "I knew it. Me too. I'm from LA."

"For real?"

"Yeah! I grew up there, in Studio City."

She *was* a Valley girl.

"Cool, I'm from La Cañada." It was a suburb north of downtown, near the foothills of the Angeles National Forest. A suburb filled with giant trees and kids taking tennis lessons, headed for Ivy Leagues. It was strangely serendipitous, both of us growing up in such placid suburbs, finding ourselves sharing congee seven thousand miles away.

"Wow. What a coincidence, don't you think?" she asked, her chin slipping back down into her palm, her dark eyes staring up at me.

Everything she did was kind of perfect, and it didn't seem practiced somehow. But she was a performer. Maybe the beauty of her performance was the belief that what you were seeing was real.

And it was kind of a weird coincidence. One that made me uncomfortable. I wasn't the one being interviewed here. The less she knew of me, the better. "Where do you live now? Seoul?" I asked, taking a sip of tea, extremely aware of how close her forearms were to my fingers.

Another moment of silence as her mind whirred, strategizing, already thinking five steps ahead and making decisions based on where she wanted to land. "Yes. I moved there a few years ago."

I nodded. "How old are *you*, then?" Seventeen. She was seventeen.

"I'm also eighteen."

My hand stilled over the teacup. Liar. "You are?"

"Yeah. Why, do I look older?" Her tone was teasing now, and I suddenly felt a flash of heat in my cheeks. Why did she get the upper hand so often when I was the one who held all the cards?

Time to flip this. My fingers brushed against her arm, ever so casually, as I moved the teacup a little. "Not old. But you look like you've seen some life." My eyelids were lowered. I felt downright *coy*.

And there it was. A sharp intake of breath. Vulnerable-celeb-looking-for-someone-to-see-her-loneliness mode initiated. But then I heard a peal of laughter and my eyes flew back up.

Her cap was pushed so far back on her head that I saw all of her smooth forehead, straight eyebrows, and clear brown eyes. "Is this how you get girls?" she asked, tapping my wrist with a long, tapered peach nail. "Because, I get it. Woo, must knock them off their feet."

And for maybe the first time in my entire life, I couldn't muster any words.

"Check, please!" Lucky called out, holding up a hand. Totally in control.

CHAPTER SEVENTEEN
LUCKY

IT WAS IMMENSELY SATISFYING TO SEE THIS LOVELY-faced jerk look flabbergasted for even a second.

I took a moment's pleasure in it as I waved down the server for our check. I looked at Jack with a lazy, all-too-comfortable speed. "You can pay, right? I don't have my wallet. S-o-o-orry."

How great did it feel to be *that* girl? The bratty, spoiled first date getting her way? I never, ever, ever got to behave this way. Being a diva was not a part I was allowed to play.

Jack's eyes sparked for a second before he shook his head, reaching for his wallet in the back pocket of his jeans. I couldn't help but notice the way he moved. Fluid, self-assured. I had noticed it last night, even in my haze. The way he slid down onto the low bar stool next to me. His swiftness at shielding my body when we hid in the dark street.

How he sprang up in that pile of blankets even while half-asleep. That stretch of forearm as he reached for the check.

Get a grip, Lucky. My attraction to this guy was unsettling. Yeah, he was good-looking. But how many celebrity paths had I crossed in the past couple years? Some of the most gorgeous people in the world. The absolute elite of hotness.

I wondered if it was simply timing and circumstance. He didn't know who I was. That was a big deal in and of itself. It changed the dynamic from every other guy I had known, immediately.

Until I spent so much time with someone who didn't know who I was, I didn't realize how much I missed it. The luxurious normality of it. So that every reaction from Jack—flirtation, interest—was merit based. It was because of *me*. Not my fame, not because he wanted something.

When you were famous, it didn't matter what you looked like, what kind of stuff you were actually made of—grit, kindness, intelligence. Everyone wanted a piece of you. They were willing to tolerate any behavior if you shined some of your light on them. To warm them, to make them feel part of something special.

After he paid for breakfast, I felt a melancholy settle in. I didn't want this feeling to end. Only an hour earlier I had wanted to book it back to the hotel, to make sure I wasn't caught. And now . . .

Now I had tasted the joy of a carby breakfast and wanted more.

Jack pushed his chair back and stood. "So what kind of punishment is in store for you? Are they going to make you recite Bible verses?"

And as he stood over me, hands tucked into his back pockets, expression expectant and full of good humor, I felt a pang of regret. At having to lie to him. At the circumstances that made regular things impossible.

"Something like that," I muttered. I actually had no idea. I'd never done anything to get punished before.

"What's their plan today, anyway?" he asked as I finally got up from the table.

Hm. "Practice," I said. It was true.

"On a gorgeous day like today?" he asked, stretching his arms out in a wild gesture. "What a waste."

It *was* a waste. How many nice days had I spent inside fluorescent-lit dance studios?

"Well, you're already in trouble. Why not take it further?"

I startled. "What?"

He shrugged. "Let me show you around Hong Kong. Church choir practice sounds thrilling and all, but . . . would you be in huger trouble if you got in a couple hours later?"

It would be absolutely stupid and selfish of me to do this. It was already eight o'clock—my absence was definitely noted by now. Joseph was probably losing his *mind*. Ren was most likely combing through the entire city, breathing fire.

And to get into that kind of trouble for a day with this guy? This random, smooth-talking stranger?

It was a fairy tale, a dim idea dreamed up by a tired girl who hadn't had a day off in weeks. Months.

Years.

I deserved a day off.

"Okay, Jack. Let's do it."

CHAPTER EIGHTEEN
JACK

HOLY CRAP. IT WORKED. I TRIED TO KEEP MY EXPRESSION neutral when, inwardly, I was aggressively pumping my fists in the air.

When Lucky ducked in the restroom, I sent Trevor a text: **I have a huge story. Spending the day with K-pop star Lucky. She has no idea I know who she is. Stay tuned.**

While looking at my phone, I noticed a few missed texts from my parents. They asked how I was feeling, if I needed anything. Guilt seeped through me as I texted back saying I was fine and needed a couple days at home.

My dad responded with: **Don't forget we have a meeting Monday morning. Set two alarms so you don't sleep in like last time.**

Ugh. Monday felt light-years away. The thought of waking up early to go to a bank meeting? Made me want this scoop more than ever.

Then my little sister, Ava, texted: **You're lying about being sick, right?**

I smiled. Ava was the only one in my family who knew how much I hated this internship. How this gap year was an excuse to stave off college for as long as possible.

Why would I lie about that?

She sent me a poop emoji. And then: **Can you come over and help me with my geometry homework?**

Ava needed my help with her math as much as I needed help with tying my own shoelaces. She was about five thousand times smarter than me, and unlike me, would probably do all the great things that good Asian kids were supposed to achieve. It ran in her blood, she loved it.

But I knew she missed me, and this was her way of asking me to hang out.

Do you want to fail geometry? How about we get noodles soon, instead?

YES 🍜

When Lucky came back out to the restaurant she caught me smiling. "What?"

"Oh, nothing. My sister's trying to con me into taking her out to eat."

"You have a sister?" she asked.

I felt uncomfortable at having revealed that slice of personal info. "Yup. Anyway, ready for a day of romance and adventure?" I waggled my eyebrows.

She made a face. "Dear Lord."

"You love it," I said easily, opening the door for her. With the entire day ahead of us.

CHAPTER NINETEEN
LUCKY

AGREEING TO THIS DAY TOGETHER WAS EXHILARATING, but also made me want to throw up. Kind of like being on an amusement park ride—one of those giant Viking ships that swing forcefully, making you scream with excitement when your stomach drops, but then leave you suspended in space just long enough for you to start panicking about what's ahead.

Yeah, like that.

The streets were bustling now and people were everywhere. I tugged on the brim of my cap, tilting my face down, and buttoned up my coat so that the collar hid my mouth and chin. If Jack thought this was weird, he didn't show it.

He had his phone out as we hovered in the doorway. "Well, Fern. It's your day. What do you want to do?"

Oh. He was giving *me* the choice.

I hadn't ever planned a day in a foreign city. Every minute of my life was scheduled down to the second. Even ten-minute breaks for snacks and the bathroom. Like a preschooler.

"Um. Can we walk around here? I like this neighborhood." The thought of walking around a cute neighborhood with no plans thrilled me.

"Sure."

As we walked around, something familiar about our surroundings made me slow down. "Wait. A. Second." I registered the neighborhood we were in. There were peeks of familiar skyscrapers between the apartment buildings around us. I walked rapidly until I came to a street sign. Queens Road. I recognized that name.

"Jack!" I yelled. "We are *not* ten miles from the city! We're basically right by my hotel!"

Instead of looking, I don't know, ashamed, Jack laughed. "Yeah. I lied to you."

I wanted to scream. But took a deep breath and stared at him instead. "Why?"

He didn't answer right away, which further rankled me. After a few seconds, he shrugged. "I didn't want you to go."

I tried to stop the blush creeping up my neck as Jack strode on ahead, leading the way.

We had stepped out into a cacophony of sound. Salespeople in crammed stores calling out in Cantonese, the sound of honking cabs, the persistent beeping noise of the crosswalk signals—obeyed by people crowding intersections, because a wrong step off a curb would get you plowed by a cab in seconds. I was surprised by how different it felt from Seoul—it was more like New York City, but with extra chaos and layered improvisation.

It was hard to keep calm around so many people. And Ren could be around any corner. If they were searching for me, it would be kept hush-hush, too. My managers would definitely cover this up for as long as possible.

Once, when one of the singers in Joseph's biggest boy band, Prince 3, went missing for a weekend (with a girl! To Hawaii!), they had a total media blackout about it. Because the only thing worse than one of your artists sneaking out (with a boy!) was a scandal. And for me, the timing would be disastrous since I was about to make my *Later Tonight Show* performance. I needed my fandom at its strongest, for their support to help push me to this next level of my career. Or that's what my management label claimed, anyway.

I felt slightly guilty about how worried they must be, but it didn't override my desire to have this break. For once, I wanted to think about myself. Not my family, my managers, or my fans. I didn't want to be driven by obligation or guilt. I wanted to be driven by *me*. To take advantage of this free day I managed to carve out for myself.

But still, I had to be careful not to be recognized or found.

With this paranoia hovering over my every move, I found that following Jack weaving through people kept me calm, like when I focused on Ren in crowds of fans. My eyes stayed fixed on his dark green shirt, the sleeves rolled up. I didn't know I liked boys in rolled-up sleeves until today. Yes, this was decidedly something I liked.

We were hiking up quite a lot of stairs. I glanced down at my slippered feet. "Hey, Jack. Can we stop by a shoe store or something?"

He paused to glance at me as I trudged up the stairs behind him. "Do I have to buy your shoes now, too?"

"Calm down, Cheapo. I'll pay you back."

"*Cheapo*? I'm fronting this day of whimsy," he said. Despite his words, he flashed me a smile. "My luxury apartment must have given you the wrong impression. I'm actually a starving artist."

When I reached him, I put my palms together under my chin, a praying pose. "Pretty please? They don't even have to be nice. Only . . . not ugly."

"Where's the nearest Target when you need one?" he grumbled. But then his eyes lit up with an idea. "All right. Follow me, Slipper Peasant."

We walked a few more blocks and I noticed the businesses getting hipper. Dry goods gave way to coffee shops and boutiques. Young people strolled around, taking photos. I saw more than one girl posing with her latte strategically, either taking a selfie or being photographed by some patient dude with a tripod. The Instagram game here was strong.

"Give me a second," Jack said, stopping in front of a particularly hip boutique before slipping in.

I gazed around at my surroundings, feeling nervous at being left alone. A movement behind a bush caught my eye.

A cat!

It was a big tuxedo cat with green eyes, its tail stubby and face dirty with gray smudges. I crouched down, cooing at it. One of the things I missed most about my life back in the US was having pets. My parents' Pomeranian was a hot mess, but it was nice to have a little furball around.

The cat came up to me, rubbing its sturdy body against my legs as I petted its fur. It sprang away the second Jack stepped back outside, opening the storefront door with a loud bang.

"Hey, Fern. Come on in," he called out. When I stood up, he glanced over at the retreating cat. "You might want to be careful. The cats here are fleabags."

"He didn't mean it," I crooned to the kitty. I walked over to Jack reluctantly and waved goodbye to the cat.

Once inside, I glanced around at the tiny store, which was empty save for an intimidating cool Asian girl behind the counter. The walls, floors, and furniture were all stark white, the merchandise sparse and artfully displayed.

"Fern, this is my friend Lina. She'll hook you up with some shoes," Jack said.

Lina, with the monochromatic wardrobe and delicate forearm tattoo, walked out from behind the counter and glanced down at my slippers, her eyebrows raised. "Do I wanna know?"

Suddenly, I was aware of how visible I was to this random stranger. I stepped back, closer to Jack. "Um. Long story," I replied, my voice quiet.

"What size shoe are you?" Lina asked. Her friendly tone made me relax some.

I told her and she went into a back room, coming out a few minutes later. "These should work," she said, carrying a shoebox.

I sat down on a bench covered with a sheepskin throw. When I opened the box, a pair of black sneakers were nestled in tissue paper. I recognized the brand and my eyes widened. "These aren't cheap."

"Well, they're kind of a loan," Jack said, flashing a smile to Lina.

She rolled her eyes, leaning against the counter and tucking her shoulder-length bleached-blonde hair behind her ears. She had a nice face with strong features—a straight, slightly large nose and dark, expressive eyebrows.

It was one thing to feel indebted to Jack. But to this random girl? I wasn't comfortable with it.

"I can pay you as soon as I get back to my hotel," I said stiffly, pulling the shoes onto my feet. In Korea, I had all the top fashion brands throwing things at me. It'd been a while since I'd had to think about buying clothes.

She smiled at me, then raised an eyebrow at Jack. "No worries. Jack's handling it."

I stood up and closed my eyes blissfully. "Ooh. Arch support. I forgot about you."

Jack laughed. "Those shoes are blushing."

I flushed at that. "Uh, we'll take them," I said.

We were outside a few minutes later and I was happily bouncing in the shoes. "Did you guys date or something?" I blurted out.

A sharp ray of sunshine slanting into the alley hit the planes of Jack's face. "What?"

Why did I ask that. "Just wondering. You guys seemed . . . close," I said, feeling embarrassed for even bringing this up. Way to be jealous, Lucky.

With his head tilted toward the sun, he blinked one eye closed and looked at me. "It's not like that."

That should have been reassuring, but his vagueness annoyed me. Lina had acted kind of weird. Maybe she liked him and he didn't realize it? I frowned. Boys were the worst. "I'm going to pay her back for these shoes, you know."

We reached an intersection and people crowded around us as they waited for the walk signal. Jack sighed. "You don't have to worry about it!"

"Listen. I know I met you whilst wearing hotel slippers, but I don't need pity shoes from random girls."

The light turned green, but Jack didn't move ahead, not being navigation-bossy as he had been all morning. Instead, he stared at me. "Whilst?"

"Yeah, whilst!" I huffed, moving ahead to cross the narrow street. Jack was right behind. "Sometimes you speak English *real* weird."

"Are you implying that because you lived in the United States for a handful of years more than me, you speak better English?!" I stopped walking and faced Jack as I stepped up onto the curb.

"No, I'm saying you speak weird. Like, all formal."

We skirted past a group of schoolchildren in knee socks and caps. "I don't have a lot of people to speak English to. Maybe I've picked up some expressions from my historical romance novels." As soon as I said it, I had regrets. Bracing myself for the usual judgmental comments about "bodice rippers."

But Jack didn't say anything rude or judgy. He furrowed his brow and asked, "Did you feel awkward moving to Korea? Like, did you feel Korean enough? I often feel so . . . *American* here."

I was surprised by this sudden change in topic. Jack seemed so confident all the time. Unflappable. But I understood what he was saying.

"It was stressful at first. People made fun of my accent." I remembered the cliques of Korean girls that had formed in the dorms, how me and a girl from the Philippines, Carolina, had been ostracized and forced to form an alliance even though we had nothing in common and actually got on each other's nerves.

"Is your Korean really good now?" Jack hopped down some steps to avoid stepping on a discarded tissue.

I sidestepped the offensive paper. "Yeah. Once you're there, it's like . . . the mother tongue returns in full force."

He laughed. "Does that feel good? To speak Korean well?"

"Hm. I guess it does? You grew up with a lot of other Asian kids, right?" I asked.

He nodded. "Yeah. Like, half my school."

"Same," I said, chewing on my lip in concentration. "So, I felt very Korean? Like, I'm connected to these roots, I have no identity issues! But then I got to Korea and felt like . . . an alien or something. It made me so embarrassed that I didn't speak Korean that well."

"Like it was a reflection of your bad upbringing or something?" he asked.

"Yes!" I pointed at him. "Exactly that!"

Jack shook his head. "My family went to Seoul last year and when my sister couldn't speak Korean very well to a cab driver he started like, berating my parents. Saying they should have done a better job."

My mouth dropped open. "Wow. Rude."

"Right?" Jack shoved his hands in his pockets as he walked next to me. Our elbows bumped with the movement. "Anyway. My mom gave him an earful, of course, but I still felt a little ashamed. Like a bad Korean kid."

I let out a short laugh. "That's kind of the low-key feeling all Korean kids have. Guilt—the greatest motivator."

He smiled. "Truth. I'm always feeling . . . guilty for wanting the things I want."

"What do you want?" I asked, looking at him intently. I was so curious, because sometimes the guilt of wanting to be free from K-pop obligations was so intense that I felt like I couldn't breathe.

"I want . . . I don't know." His voice was quiet and he looked down at the sidewalk.

"Come on, say it," I said, bumping my hip against his.

He didn't answer right away. "I don't want the things my parents want for me. And beyond that . . . I'm not sure yet."

Hm. In a weird way, I had no idea what that felt like. I'd known what I'd wanted since I was six. I didn't know what to say. But after a few moments, I finally said, "I know what it's like to have expectations put on you." Not by my parents, but he didn't have to know that.

He looked over at me and I felt a jolt of energy pass between us. Not flirty or anything—a connection of some kind. I never got to talk to anyone about stuff like this. Korean American kid stuff. No one really understood this part of me in Korea.

And it felt good because I didn't have to lie. In a weird way, I could be a true version of myself as Fern.

CHAPTER TWENTY
JACK

LUCKY WAS TURNING OUT TO BE A GREAT LIAR.

Here's the thing with good lying: You don't take risks by getting bogged down with details, making things complicated and tying yourself up in some web of deception.

You selectively tell truths.

Then when you're saying what you're saying, you exhibit the very real signs of truthiness. Like Lucky was.

We walked down Hollywood Road, a busy thoroughfare that took us from Sheung Wan back to Central, where we had met last night.

An ancient banyan tree grew out of the side of a cinder block wall, its roots snaking over the crumbling concrete all the way down to the sidewalk. Lucky reached up and touched the stringy roots hanging off the branches, giving them a tug.

From behind, I took a quick photo.

The photos from the shoe store turned out great—Lucky reaching over to tie her shoelaces, looking at her reflection, expression thoughtful as she contemplated her shoes, these tools of comfort in a life so full of restraints. Ooh, that was good.

LUCKY STEPS OUT

My phone buzzed. Trevor had finally gotten my message and texted back: **Are you serious? I got a tip that Lucky went missing last night.**

I grinned and texted: **She was with me.** I knew it was slimy and misleading, but it was also catnip for someone like Trevor. He responded immediately: **If you're telling the truth, this could change everything for you. Follow that asset, get that story.**

Yes. *Yes.*

Lucky stopped ahead of me and sniffed the air. "What is that?"

The air was tinged with telltale smoke. "Oh, we're right by Man Mo Temple. That's the incense people burn."

We walked up ahead to an open gate, beyond which were two ancient one-story buildings set inside a small concrete courtyard. It was packed with tourists buying bundles of incense sticks and lighting them in various altars, filling the entire block with smoke.

When I first moved to Hong Kong, I was struck by the incongruous image of this old temple plopped right in the center of a busy intersection, a few feet away from a street full of cars, hipsters, and grandmothers. Now I walked by it like, ten times a day and barely noticed it. Just a building from the nineteenth century straight chillin', that's all.

Lucky looked at me for about half a second before skipping inside, headed toward the stalls carrying the incense.

A LUCKY PRAYER

I followed her inside, where the noise of the street was muffled and replaced with softer, more hushed noises: matches lighting, feet shuffling on the stone floor, the quiet snap of a camera. It was packed with tourists, and the air was thick with smoke from the incense.

I found Lucky watching an older woman light a giant pack of incense. Her delicate hands gripped the sticks firmly as she stuck them into a large gold urn filled with ash. After the incense was properly placed, the woman clasped her hands to her chest and stared into the flames, eventually closing her eyes, her eyelids paper thin and almost translucent.

"What are you going to pray for?" I whispered as I sidled up to Lucky. My phone was ready to capture it, whatever it was.

Her gaze not moving from the old lady, Lucky thought about it for a second.

"I'm not actually praying. I'm being respectful of other cultures," she whispered.

"So you're not religious?"

She cut me a glance. "Nope."

"Even though you're in church choir?"

A moment passed and we both stared at the lady, the lie hovering over both of us. Finally she said, "I used to be religious. That's how I started out in church choir. But I do it mostly for the singing now."

I nodded. "Gotcha."

The lady left and Lucky lit her bundle of incense—holding the lit match over the ends, expertly lighting them before the flame reached her fingertips.

"Well, if you were the praying type, what would you be praying for?" I asked.

Lucky spread the sticks of incense out in a tray full of ash on an altar facing a golden deity statue. "I guess . . . I would wish good health for my parents."

Korean media training at its finest. "Pft. Okay."

She glared at me. "What!"

"That is complete crap. What would you actually pray for?"

Lucky ignored me, clasping her hands to her chest, like the old lady had done. She closed her eyes while her lips moved, silently offering words to the magical sticks.

I took a photo.

When she opened her eyes I slipped my phone back into my pocket.

"I prayed for an upcoming performance to go well," she said. "It's kind of . . . a big deal."

Aha. "Why is it a big deal?"

We walked over to a wall full of small drawers—cremated ashes. Lucky's fingers drifted over the red trim on the square drawer faces, tracing the paintings of radishes on each one.

"If it goes well, then we might make it to this next level of our, um, competition," she said.

"Oh, cool," I said. "That's exciting, right?"

She stared at the drawers intently. "Supposedly. But I can't seem to get excited about it."

I looked at her sharply. "Why not? Isn't it your choir's big break?"

"That's what everyone says but maybe I like things the way they are?" she said in such a low voice that I had to strain to hear it.

The incense-thickened air made it hard for me to see, too, and I waved my hand in front of my face. "If you want things to stay the way they are, then why did you pray that it would go well?"

My voice was louder than I meant for it to be and Lucky shushed me before grabbing my sleeve and pulling me over to a quiet spot—an empty area underneath lanterns decked out with red banners and giant incense coils.

I tried to ignore how much I liked the familiarity of the movement.

After glancing around to make sure no one was listening to us, she said in a loud whisper, "I prayed for it to go well because I still want good things for the choir. For everyone else who's so invested in it."

I stilled, taken aback by the honesty of that answer. "But what about what you want?"

She contemplated me for a second before countering my question with one of her own. "What do you know about Buddhism?"

"Uh. I know it involves . . . Buddha?" Where was *this* coming from?

She laughed, then covered her mouth quickly. "Buddhism is pretty interesting. It's all about the path to liberation—to be free of things like earthly desires, to be free of *craving*." She was fluttering her hands in the air, punctuating the whimsicalness of what she was saying with graceful movements.

"What's so bad about craving?" I asked with an easy smile. But I was serious.

Her mouth scrunched up slightly, unsure if I was teasing. "Sometimes it clouds your decisions. Like, you're driven by the wrong things."

I glanced at her sharply. "What are the 'right' things?"

"I don't know. Um, doing good things for the world? Humanity? Desires not born out of selfishness and ego, but like . . . something bigger?"

"That sounds super boring," I said.

She laughed. "Shut up."

"I'm serious!" I tried to keep my voice down. "Because even if you're living your life so selflessly, *why* are you doing it? Isn't it ultimately to feel good about yourself anyway? So then you come back full circle to this idea of being 'selfish.' Like it's a bad thing."

"I couldn't disagree more," she said, her face tilting up to me, fully visible under her cap. "I don't think doing good things is selfish. That's so Cynicism 101."

That stung. "Thanks."

She shook her head. "It's true. Jack, there is actual goodness and badness, you know that, right? Like, there's a life that is quality and there's a life that is . . . empty."

"Trust me, I know," I said quietly. "But I think you're applying like, morality to measure quality."

"How am I doing that?" she demanded.

I stared at her upturned face, the earnestness of her expression. Did she truly find her life empty? I couldn't believe that. She was at the top of her game. A job people would kill for. A job that people who worked in banks dreamed about.

My question rang through the quiet temple: "Who says a quality life can't have some selfishness in it?"

CHAPTER TWENTY-ONE
LUCKY

WE GOT KICKED OUT OF THE TEMPLE.

"Jack! Look what you did!" I said, holding back laughter.

His eyebrows shot up. "What *I* did? Okay, Chatty Cathy."

"You chatted more than me!"

"Let's agree to disagree," he said mildly, the late morning sun hitting his hair, making it glow. I would kill for that volume.

He glanced down at his phone then. "Hey. Are you hungry?"

"Always." The wistful tone came out before I could help it. "We don't get to eat that much in church choir," I clarified.

"When you travel, or all the time?" He asked.

I was careful with my words. "We're encouraged to be healthy. All the time." What an understatement.

"Well, today's the day to screw 'healthy.' You're in Hong Kong!"

He put his hands on his hips, thinking for a second. "Ooh. Are you a fan of bao?"

"What's that?"

He clutched his chest with exaggeration. "What's bao? Just the most delicious food. Stuffed buns usually eaten for breakfast, but I basically live off of them."

"You got me at 'bun.'"

He walked us to an inconspicuous train station entrance set into a gray brick building. We walked down a dimly lit stairwell until we were hit with the bright lights of an underground mall bustling with people and subway signage.

With so many people rushing around me, I tensed. And it was the oddest thing—the second I did it, Jack looked over at me.

Then grasped my hand.

My eyes flew up to his.

"Don't lose me," he said easily, as if this was a normal thing he and I did. As if those words weren't insanely *hot*.

His hand was warm, the skin rough. I remembered when we held hands last night—running through dark alleys. It felt like forever ago.

Before last night, I'd never held hands with a guy. And here I was, doing it for the second time with this guy I barely knew. The feel of my hand in someone else's—a *cute* someone else—filled me with a giddiness that embarrassed me. It was only holding hands.

I couldn't get a read on Jack as we maneuvered through the crowded train station mall. Was he holding my hand in a boyfriendy way? Or as a friendly, platonic tour guide? Did boys hold hands with girls platonically?

And *did* I want something more than a platonic tour guide?

We stopped in front of a counter manned by a sulky Asian teenage girl in an apron. Above her were photos of various steamed buns, brightly lit from behind.

My mouth watered even though it hadn't been that long since we had that decadent congee. "I want one of each."

"Are you serious?" Jack asked, his voice high-pitched.

"Yes. One of each, please."

"What am I, a millionaire?"

I laughed. "Do you exaggerate *everything*?"

Jack paused at that, a surprised expression crossing his face for a second. "What do you mean?"

"You use a lot of hyperbole."

He grinned. "I've *never* in my entire life used hyperbole."

I relished this back-and-forth. When was the last time I could joke about *hyperbole* with anyone around me? Even though I was near-fluent in Korean, more sophisticated conversations confused me, which frustrated me to no end. "I'll pay you back for everything. I promise." A silence settled over those words and I added, "Also, I'd like milk."

After ordering six bao, a small carton of milk, and a water for himself, Jack led us out of the station and back outside.

The bun was hot in my hands, and I peeled the thin paper wrapper off of it impatiently, burning my fingertips in the process. I hissed and stuck them in my mouth.

Jack shook his head. "You have to wait for it to cool off."

"Never," I said, already biting into it. The hot pork filling scorched me, but it was so, so good. Slightly sweetened chewy dough paired with the sugary, caramelized pork—that perfect combo of sweet and salty. Pure heaven. I kept eating, the roof of my mouth burned for life.

We approached a particularly busy intersection with curved roads and older buildings crowding the space, groups of suited business people out for their lunch breaks. For a second I felt like I was in London, but when we crossed the street and rounded a bend, suddenly the traffic was gone and we were engulfed in tropical plants, the shade of giant trees cooling us off immediately. We were on the edge of a hillside bordering a park, and to the left of us was a small canyon with more dense, dark green foliage.

I marveled at the surroundings, my head bent far back so I could see the tops of the trees. "Wow. I almost forgot that Hong Kong is so tropical."

"You're lucky to catch us on a cool day. The weather's been hellish. Like, Florida on steroids," Jack said as he swung the bag of buns and drinks between us.

"Humidity," I said sagely. "The literal worst."

"Literally."

We laughed and in the quiet of the shaded road, I felt kind of shy. Aside from this morning in his apartment, we hadn't really had a moment alone. "It was so hard for me to get used to humidity after living in LA. I was like, what is happening to my hair?"

He grinned. "Yeah. This summer almost killed me. But my skin looks *great*."

I looked at him. Yeah, his skin and everything else looked pretty great. "Do you miss LA?"

"Do I miss the dry summers, you mean?" he said.

A cab passed by us, a streak of red against the green of the trees. I shook my head. "Yes and no. I mean, do you miss living there? Like, America?"

"Not that much," Jack said. "I did at first, but . . . I don't know. Hong Kong is cool."

I waited for him to elaborate but he didn't. I finished up the last of my bun. "It *is* cool here. But don't you miss not being a foreigner?"

"That's what's cool about Hong Kong. A lot of us are foreigners. I don't really stick out or anything."

In Korea, when I was still an obscure K-pop trainee, I had loved how invisible I was, how easily I melted into Seoul. How it felt to be in a place where I was a part of the history.

But now? Now I stuck out.

"I get homesick," I admitted, wiping my fingers on my jeans. I almost said, "I miss my family," but caught myself quickly. Jack had no idea I didn't live with my family. That would be weird.

But I did miss them. More than dry summers or easy communication in my native language. I missed fighting with my parents and sister over what we wanted to watch on Netflix—taking so long to pick something that it was inevitably bedtime when we finally came to a decision. I missed my mom yelling from the kitchen when she opened the fridge and food toppled out because my sister and I had shoved things in there haphazardly. I missed my dad not believing me when I said I'd checked the mail, watching him ramble down the driveway to double-check and then ignoring me as I gloated. I missed the fear of my sister's fastidious wrath when I borrowed her clothes and got a stain on them—hiding out in my room when I heard the inevitable scream from hers.

But I couldn't say all that. Instead, I said, "I miss In-N-Out."

Jack smiled, a flash of white in the cool shadows. "Yeah, me too." He walked alongside me in silence for a while, then asked, "When did you move to Korea?"

"When I was thirteen."

"How was that? I mean, that's a hard age."

It was really hard. But I had moved because of my own desires, unlike kids who were uprooted by their parents. Like Jack. "It was hard at first, but . . . I was kept pretty busy, so. I didn't have much time to get homesick."

"That busy church choir life?" His voice was teasing and I cursed my past self for trapping myself into this church choir nonsense.

I let out a feeble laugh. "Kind of. I took a lot of music lessons, dance, all that. And then I joined the choir and it became . . . more serious. A time-consuming hobby."

"So, you've been singing for a long time?" he asked as he hopped over a lumpy portion of sidewalk where massive tree roots had disturbed the concrete.

"Since forever." I smiled, remembering the many home videos of me singing as a kid. At the dinner table, clutching a white plastic rice scooper in my small fists and closing my eyes as I crooned old Whitney Houston songs. In the bathtub as my toddler sister lolled around in the background, oblivious to my made-up love ballads.

Jack smiled, too. Almost as if he could see what I was remembering. "Do you want to do it, I don't know, professionally one day?"

We were walking in a patch of sun and the heat made me uncomfortable. "Um, yeah. Maybe." I glanced at him. "Am I being interviewed or something?"

"No," he replied easily, stepping back into the shade. I followed. "I'm curious," he said.

Something occurred to me then. "Hey, are you in college? Didn't you say you graduated last spring?"

He shook his head. "No, I'm interning at my dad's bank right now. Taking a gap year."

"Oh, cool. Like, a break, right? Where do you want to go to college?"

This time he was the one to take a long pause before answering. "I don't know yet."

"To go into banking, though?" I asked.

He made a face. "God, no. It's only to keep my parents off my back while I'm doing this gap year."

I thought back to our earlier conversation, when he said he didn't know what he wanted. "Well, if you had to pick right now, what would you want to do?" The question bothered him, I could tell. He crossed his arms, the bag of bao bumping into his thigh. "I don't know what I want to do. I grew up in a suburb where everyone was on this path to achievement. And now that I've lived here? I don't feel that pressure anymore. It's like I can see clearly. And college seems so small."

Path to achievement. I knew what he was talking about. My talents were discovered and nurtured from an early age, and my parents had done everything within their power to keep them flourishing. But that path was forged by *me.* My parents were happy to help because they recognized my drive and knew I wouldn't be happy until I got to where I wanted to be.

So I was supposed to feel grateful. Grateful that they supported me, that I got chosen by my management label, that my girl group was popular, that my solo career took off, that I was the biggest name in K-pop right now.

Instead, I felt guilty. Because that gratitude was really hard to summon nowadays.

He continued, "I don't get it. We can't think creatively beyond like, college and a job and marriage and kids? It's so depressing."

I had a feeling Jack didn't truly understand that word. "What's so depressing about it? It's a luxury to have those options, Jack. It's why your parents and my parents uprooted themselves to start new lives."

He was quiet for a second. "I get that. But I also think there's a spectrum of things that make people unhappy. Even if it was comfortable—that path was making me feel dead inside."

I remembered the dead look in my eyes at my latest performance. Jack seemed so confident in himself, about his life. But that comment there—it revealed the same yearning that I had felt for months. I thought it was the hamburger that got me out of my hotel room last night. But, if I was being truthful with myself, it was this. The yearning.

And Jack had it, too. He wanted something more. Something different.

"I know what you mean," I said softly, crumpling the paper wrapping of the bao tightly into my fist. "You can't help what you want."

The sharpness of Jack's look startled me and I choked. Hard.

Jack stopped and pounded my back. Also hard. Like Korean-mom style. "Do you want some of your milk?"

I nodded, embarrassed as I watched Jack set the bag on the ground and bend down to fish the milk carton out of it. Crouching, he unwrapped the straw and poked it into the carton before handing it to me.

He had even bent the straw.

"Thank you," I said, taking a giant swig. Once I had annihilated the drink, I crushed it in my fist and made a satisfying "Ahhh" sound.

Watching me from his crouched position, Jack started laughing. "You really enjoy your treats."

"I do."

He got up. "Well, we're almost at the park, we can finish the other buns there."

I skipped ahead. "Ooh. *Romantic.* A picnic in the park."

He laughed, then jogged to catch up with me.

CHAPTER TWENTY-TWO

JACK

THERE WAS SOMETHING MORE THERE. MORE THAN JUST a homesick K-pop star.

You can't help what you want.

She clearly missed her family, her home. America. So, what was so irresistible and compelling about being a K-pop star that kept her so far away? Was it pure narcissism, basking in adoration?

If I kept digging, I'd have something more here than a sexy celebrity profile.

I watched Lucky practically skip ahead of me.

She was enjoying this day.

I had to shake off the uneasy feeling of being, you know, a horrible human being. Lucky was surprising me, but I had to keep in mind what she was: a product. She knew it. She chose to be a part of the nightmare that was the K-pop machine. In my research last night, I found out all about the messed-up conditions in their training, the draconian nature of their contracts. Anyone who wanted fame that badly would be fine with more publicity.

Plus, this was a thrill for her. An escape. I was essentially doing her a favor.

We were headed to Hong Kong Park, a sprawling, lush park set into a hillside right in the middle of the Central district. There was a giant crowd near the base of the park and we had to weave through it.

"What is this crowd for?" Lucky asked as she did that thing again—of compressing her body into a smaller version of itself.

It occurred to me that her people might be looking for her. That she wasn't only hiding from fans, but her management, too. I pushed myself into the crowd to get closer to her, using my body to keep her somewhat shielded. I didn't want her to get caught, either. It would be the end of the story.

I replied, "Oh, it's for the tram. It takes you up to Victoria Peak."

Her eyes lit up. "A tram? Ooh. What's Victoria Peak?"

I was already calculating the cost. It was at least eighty Hong Kong dollars for each of us. But man . . . that photo at the peak would be *killer*. I'd ask Trevor to pay me back for all expenses later.

"It's the highest mountaintop in Hong Kong and it has amazing views of the city." I looked at the giant line of tourists and shuddered inwardly. "Do you want to go?"

Her smile hit me like a ton of bricks. It was the smile I had seen in her concert videos, the full wattage reserved to stun anyone in its path. The smile of someone who is worshipped. When she wasn't shrinking into herself trying not to be discovered, she was the most confident person I'd ever met. Someone who was keenly aware of her own power.

"I would *love* to go!" She was already scooting herself to the end of the line.

We stood in the sun and it felt good. Lucky seemed uncomfortable in close quarters with everyone, but the tourists around us were absorbed in their own conversations, and after a while, she relaxed. I did, too, feeling more and more certain that Lucky would stick with me for the rest of the day.

An entire day with her. Undercover. This was too good.

It was a good time to finish our bao, and I scarfed one down, the filling having cooled off some.

The line moved forward, and Lucky looked deep in thought.

"Thinking about your next meal?" I asked with a grin.

She widened her eyes. "I wasn't, but now you've got me thinking all sorts of things."

"Oh, God."

"Actually. I was thinking about our Buddhist conversation earlier," she admitted. "You asked me something. Can't a quality life also be selfish?"

I shook my head. "No, I said can't it have *some* selfishness?"

She waved her hand. "Okay. Well, I've been thinking about it. Yes, you can have selfishness. But there's a balance. If you're always driven by ego, narcissism . . . what you create at the end of the day, what you've built, isn't that meaningful."

Like Lucky's body of work? Her fandom? Interesting.

"But isn't that all art? It's driven from ego and it's okay! People love it, they want it. You should be proud. I mean, as in, people should be proud of what they create, even if it's driven by ego!" Holy crap, that was close. "It's not something that should make you feel ashamed."

"I'm not ashamed," she said, quick and defensive.

132

Careful.

"I'm using 'you' in the general sense," I said. We were both quiet, sitting with our lies.

"You sure have a lot of opinions about art," she finally said, shooting me a smile. "Are you an artist?"

I thought of my camera back at home. I would have killed to have it with me today, but secrecy was the name of the game.

"Nah," I said easily. "You'll be surprised to know that I, a male, am merely very opinionated." Even though I loved photography, I always hesitated to call myself an artist. Something about it felt, I don't know. Presumptuous. I was a guy with a camera. That's all.

Lucky laughed. "What about you, then? What would you pray for in that temple? If you were a believer?"

I crumpled up the paper wrapper of my bao to avoid answering right away. "Hm. I don't know. I've never prayed for anything before."

"What?" she exclaimed. "Not ever? Not even when you were a kid and you were scared of getting in trouble or something? No, 'Dear God please don't let my mom see the grape juice stain on the carpet.'"

"Grape juice?" I made a face.

"You know what I mean," she said as the line moved and we both shuffled ahead. "Don't avoid the question."

I shrugged. "I don't remember praying. And I really don't know what I would pray for." It was true. When I watched everyone in the temple offering up their prayers or wishes or whatever it was, I felt so detached.

"What about getting into the college you want?"

"I don't know which college I want to go to," I said.

She shook her head. "I don't get that. I have a list of wishes a mile long."

That didn't surprise me. I also suspected she made sure her wishes happened. Like being a famous performer.

"*And*, I am being selfish today," she added with a raised eyebrow. "Ditching choir duties and everything to hang out with *you*."

"See? Selfishness is a good thing," I said, happy to ease the mood. Something about this conversation was unsettling and I didn't want her to get to me. I had to stay in control of this, our interactions. *She* was the one being observed.

Lucky shot me a dubious look and I said, "I'm serious! Because you'll have this break, this nice day. And then you'll go back to choir, fresh with . . . energy. Bring the entire mood of the choir up."

She let out a snort of laughter, her arms crossed as we shuffled forward. "Like, I go into practice doing cartwheels, high on carbs."

That made me laugh—suddenly and very loudly.

Lucky beamed at me. "I like making you laugh."

The words paired with her smile did all sorts of weird things to me. I cleared my throat, suddenly aware that the plastic bag of bao was empty and I had no more weight to swing around in my hands. "I have a terrible sense of humor."

"Well, if you don't laugh at my jokes, then yeah. Agreed." She turned around then, her hair whipping through the air. I watched her watch the crowd in front of us, as she stood high on her toes to assess the length of the line ahead.

Something was looser in Lucky's limbs. Direct in her gaze. Seeing her like this—scrubbed of her glamorous persona and getting more comfortable with me—I could almost forget who she was. Almost.

CHAPTER TWENTY-THREE

LUCKY

I WAS PRETTY SURE I WAS GOING TO DIE ON THIS TRAM.

Why wasn't everyone else on this jalopy losing their ever-loving minds like me? People were jammed into this wooden antique toy, excited and taking selfies and pressing their faces against the windows as we crept up a nearly vertical mountainside. Visions of cables snapping and the tram plummeting down amid the screams of the trapped humans inside made me sweat.

I pressed my hip firmly into Jack's side and then glanced up at him. "Hey. Don't get any funny ideas," I said.

Jack held on to a pole and didn't move a muscle in response. "Yes, I got the memo the first three times you said it."

His arm was grazing my hair and I felt a pleasant warmth radiate off his body. Even when sweating in an overheated tram, Jack didn't smell bad.

In fact, he smelled good. Really, terribly good.

Lucky. Do not have your sexual awakening on this tram, please. Today wasn't for *romance*. It wasn't for some thirst liberation.

It was for me.

Who says a quality life can't have some selfishness in it? Despite the cynical feel of Jack's mini lecture, I couldn't help but turn these words over and over in my head.

When did I start to feel discontent about being "Lucky"? If I truly thought about it, maybe for a year now. And ever since then, I had been enduring it, not speaking up when I was tired or unhappy. All out of this idea of being "good." A good idol to my fans. A good daughter to my parents. A good client to my managers.

But was it possible to have both? Freedom *and* this career?

When a bracing wind whipped through the cracked-open window of the tram, I let myself take a deep breath and focus on the views rather than my jumbled thoughts. And the sheer terror of the physics-defying tram ride.

We were creeping up a lush ravine—ropey trees and foliage enclosing us on both sides. Every once in a while there was a break in the trees, and I saw the Hong Kong skyline, the glimmering harbor waters, the pastel-hued apartment towers.

The tram lurched suddenly as it came to a halt and my body slammed into Jack's. I grabbed a handful of his shirt to keep myself from falling.

"Wha-what in the world?" I stammered as I straightened myself up, trying to use incredulity to disguise my fluster at being so inappropriately smushed up against Jack.

But the fluster only grew, exponentially, as he rested both of his hands on my shoulders and steadied me. "You okay?" The crisp matter-of-factness of that action, that question, rendered me incredibly useless.

"Yeah, fine. Why did we stop?" I adjusted my jacket, my voice cool.

He pointed out the window. "More passengers." There was an actual tram stop on this hillside angled at a barfy forty-five degrees. A sheltered stone bench that looked ancient marked the stop, and three people in business attire boarded the already-crowded tram.

"I didn't know this was a commuter tourist tram," I grumbled as we got more smushed.

I was so distracted by my proximity to Jack that I didn't notice my hat was pushed off my face until I caught a glimpse of my reflection in the window. Before I could adjust it, I felt a tap on my shoulder. From the reflection, I could see it was a young woman. She was staring at me with her mouth slightly dropped open.

Blast.

I looked up at Jack but he was staring outside. The finger tapped me again and I stepped hard on Jack's foot. He yelped, then looked over at me. "*What?*"

My heart was about to straight-up Astro Boy rocket out of my chest. I had watched enough K-dramas in my life to know what I needed to do.

So I slipped my hand onto the soft skin on the back of his neck and pressed my body to his. Hips bumping, torsos grazing. I saw his stunned expression for about half a second before I squeezed my eyes shut and pressed my lips to his.

CHAPTER TWENTY-FOUR

JACK

THE FIRST THING I NOTICED WAS THE COOLNESS OF HER lips.

You expected lips to be warm.

The second thing I noticed was the awkwardness, the uncertainty.

I leaned into it by instinct—when a girl kisses you, you kiss back!—and her hand shifted from my neck to my hair, her fingers pushing into it.

Damn.

Her lips were seamed shut, almost pursed, and kinda smashing into mine.

I had seen the girl tapping on Lucky's shoulder. I knew why she was doing this. Diversion tactic.

So we had to do it right.

I pulled back, slightly, so that she relaxed her lips. I reached up and grazed her jaw with my fingertips. Her eyelashes fluttered before I pressed my lips to hers again, softly. Moving over them slowly. Her mouth matched mine in response, with a gentle intake of breath.

That little sigh sent a jolt of crazy feelings through me before her hands clenched in my hair and on my waist. But I kept my touch light, barely holding her face, keeping the kisses soft. Like feathers. Petals.

CHAPTER TWENTY-FIVE
LUCKY

WHEN I HAD LAUNCHED MYSELF ONTO JACK'S LIPS, A tidal wave of embarrassment and panic crashed over me. I hadn't given myself even a second to think it through before I kissed him.

But the mortification had disappeared the second Jack took over.

Everything was so soft. Gentle. I found myself melting into the kisses, feeling every overthinking piece of me float away.

So, this was what it was all about. The pages and pages in my romance novels. This was the feeling of getting a good, thorough kissing.

It was my first kiss.

With a complete stranger in front of other complete strangers. But it didn't matter. All that mattered was *him*. Everything else disappeared and I was absorbed into pure feeling. His lips on mine, his hands on my face.

I understood now why the proper ladies in my books threw caution to the wind and got swept up by those hot scoundrels.

Jack was guiding me with each touch and I couldn't get close enough. I dropped my hand from his neck to his back, pulling his body in, feeling the warmth envelop me. The second I did it, something switched, and his kisses weren't so soft anymore. His right hand slid from my jaw to the nape of my neck and his other hand pressed into my lower back.

Scratch that—*this* was what it was all about.

CHAPTER TWENTY-SIX
JACK

KISSING THIS GIRL WAS GOING TO KILL ME, AND I couldn't stop.

And then the tram stopped. With a teeth-grinding halt. And it all ended as quickly as it happened.

When I opened my eyes, I was staring right into Lucky's. Wide, startled, and dilated to full black.

The shoulder-tapping girl was long gone and everyone was getting off the tram. They moved around us like water. My hands dropped from Lucky, heart pounding.

I took a deep breath, trying to regain some of my senses. This was not a part of the plan. Flirting, yes. Kissing, though? And feeling like *this* after kissing her?

Totally, 100 percent not anticipated.

Her cheeks were pink and getting pinker by the second. I could see her trying to think up a phony explanation. She couldn't hide it because her defenses were so completely blown.

I knew why she kissed me. Somebody recognized her. But I had to pretend like I didn't. I pulled myself together because I had to create a diversion for her diversion.

Knowing that I was being a total ass, I let a shit-eating grin stretch across my face. "Was that your first kiss?"

Whatever explanation she was trying to cook up flew out the door. Her mouth dropped open and the color in her face deepened from a pale pink to red. "Pardon *me?*" she sputtered.

I cocked my head, the universal sign of patronization. "Wasn't it, though?"

She stood stock-still, staring at me with arms hanging down by her sides. For a few seconds I wondered if she was having a stroke.

"Yeah, it was my first kiss! *What of it?*" she finally yelled.

What.

The tram was empty now and it was just me and her and the weight of her words surrounding us.

"Wait. What?!" It was my turn to sputter.

She glared at me. "Happy?" Then she tore out of the tram, jumping off the steps, feet landing hard on the pavement before she stalked off.

I stood there for a second until I heard someone clearing their throat. The conductor. The young dude shook his head at me. "Smooth move."

"Okay, creep!" I blurted out before chasing after Lucky.

First kiss. I was Lucky's first kiss. I had joked because she had seemed so nervous, and I thought it was because of the situation. Teasing her was only supposed to distract her.

Way to go, Jack.

I saw a green cap bobbing in the crowd, headed toward the visitor center sitting at the base of the peak.

"LU—" *Crap.* "FERN!"

She didn't turn around, of course. Fern had only been her name since last night. I pushed through the tourists streaming into the center until I got to her. I resisted reaching for her. "Fern!"

"Excuse me, *who* are you?" Her voice was icy and her eyes fixed on something in front of her. We were shuffled along into the visitor center.

Think, Jack. "Hey, sorry. I didn't mean to—"

"Be a cad?" The words flew out as quickly as her head swiveled. I resisted flinching visibly. Damn, she could be scary.

"Yes. Er, a cad. I was teasing . . . I didn't realize . . ." I stumbled over the words. This lack of cool was very disconcerting. *Smooth the situation over, Jack. Smooth it!* "I would have said it to anyone! Not because of how you kissed." Okay, the *least* smooth thing you could have said. The least!

Her look of disgust confirmed this. "Why, thank you. Thank you, oh experienced lover."

The word "lover" almost made me laugh, but I stopped myself. An awkward silence fell between us as we walked into a narrow but tall building encased in glass. Escalators led to various levels filled with souvenir shops and attractions. One sign near us pointed to the "Sky Terrace."

Lucky stopped in front of the sign, then looked at me. "What's the Sky Terrace?" Her voice was flat, still annoyed at me.

"We can skip it. It's so touristy. You can still see great views from other parts of this area."

She stared at me, her mouth a straight line like that one emoji.

144

Those tickets were another fifty Hong Kong dollars or so. I closed my eyes. All right, I had my credit card. If this story panned out, I'd get my money back and then some. "Okay. Fine. Let's do it."

"Thank you," Lucky said, voice still cool, but her step lighter. She was excited.

After I got the tickets, we took the escalators up to the terrace in further silence. She kept her cap lowered on her face and crossed her arms. This melancholy was bumming me out and suddenly the only thing I wanted was to get her out of it. Her smiles from the morning felt like a faded dream.

Jesus. Faded dreams, flower petals, and feathers? What was going on? *Stay focused, Jack.*

When we reached the terrace, a cold wind kicked up around us. We were at the very top of the peak with 360-degree views of the city. I hadn't been here since I first moved to Hong Kong, and forgot how cool the view was. If you could squeeze between the people pushing against the railing.

Pulling her hat down to obscure her face, Lucky made her way to the edge, wriggling between people and leaning her body against the railing and glass partition. We were on the side facing the city, tall apartment towers shooting up around us like something from Minecraft.

I took a shot of her from behind, her hair picked up by the wind, her body bent forward, reaching for something. The staggering skyline in front of her.

When I managed to make my way next to her, she kept her face resolutely away from me, looking at the view. I was Lucky's first kiss. I felt like a jackass but I felt something else . . . honored and happy?

No, this was bad. On so many levels. No kissing the subject, Jack.

Also, I wasn't supposed to know why she kissed me. What was she going to say about it? I had to unfreeze this situation, even if it meant being a pest.

"So, do trams normally put you in the mood?"

"What!" She turned to me quickly, mouth agape.

Gotcha. I unleashed the smile that my sister Ava called, with disgust, *The Devastation*. Like it was a ship. "I'm not complaining."

She glanced around us, as if everyone and their selfie sticks cared about this conversation. "*No*. Trams don't . . . get me . . . in the *mood*."

I didn't say anything. The less I said the better, probably. I wanted to see how she would lie her way out of this one.

"I was . . . curious." And she looked me straight in the eye when she said it. I felt a jolt because, again, her lying skills were amazing. She picked the one truth. And knowing that the whole "Quick! Kiss a Stranger!" move could have meant something more than a diversion?

I swallowed, and it was the most difficult task of my life, getting that saliva down my completely dry throat. "Curious?"

She nodded. "I'm curious about a lot of things."

Another dry swallow. "Yeah?"

She peered at me from below her cap, and her lips curved into a smile that sunk *The Devastation* in one quick, brutal shot.

CHAPTER TWENTY-SEVEN
LUCKY

THE FACT THAT JACK KNEW THE KISS WAS MY FIRST freaking kiss was *the worst thing in the world*. The embarrassment about killed me, and I needed to assert myself. Smoldering K-pop video queen stares? Check. Jack's reaction was exactly what I had hoped for.

The truth is, the Lucky who oozed sexuality and confidence onstage was a total charade. Not every part of me used to be that way—I was goofier, more girlish than vixen. But now, so much of me was Lucky-the-fantasy that I wondered where she ended and I began. The line had become so blurred, and it was only today that helped put it in focus again—the contrast between Lucky and me had never been sharper.

Spending time with Jack, running around somewhat anonymous in a foreign city—there was something about that, you know? That put all of *LUCKY!* in relief against Fern.

And . . . *what was that kiss*?

Whatever I was expecting, it was not that.

I must have been looking at his mouth then, because Jack sucked in his lips self-consciously. I pressed my palms onto the metal railing, willing myself to cool off, looking at the view in front of me instead.

He seemed to believe my "I was curious" explanation. I'm sure lots of girls were *curious* about what kissing him would feel like.

It was a clear day—the smog inching in had dissipated somewhat, and the lush green hills, razor-sharp buildings, and pristine waters of Victoria Harbour were practically sparkling. Beckoning.

"Want to try something fun?" I asked, feeling that streak of impulsiveness again.

Jack tapped the railing with his hands, keeping his eyes on the view, too. "Do I want to know?"

I pulled him away from the railing and walked us toward the center of the terrace, on a concrete platform. "You're going to spin me around while I close my eyes and point. We're going to go wherever I land."

"What if you land in the middle of the water?" he asked, completely nonplussed and his mouth already quirked into a smile. He was so game. For anything. He didn't care that any of this was totally wacky. He had zero expectations of me.

It was such a good feeling.

I covered my eyes with my left hand and pointed straight ahead with my right. "Then we go to the water."

A second of silence passed before he reached for my shoulder and waist. "Okay." His voice was low and very close to my ear. Something fluttered in my stomach and I sucked in a breath. Bastard.

And then I was turning counterclockwise, my feet shuffling, my body hitting Jack's at certain points. Laughter bubbled out of me. "I'll tell you when to stop!"

He didn't answer, but kept spinning me, and finally when I felt a wave of nausea I cried out, "Stop!"

Jack's hands stilled me instantly, firmly holding me into place. When I opened my eyes, I followed my pointed finger to a random spot on the mass of land across the water.

"Kowloon," he said with a furrowed brow. "I know where to take you."

I raised an eyebrow. "It has to be where I pointed."

"Close enough."

We were on a ferry.

It glided through the water, quiet and slow. I took in a deep breath of salty air and let it out in a loud, gusty *pfffft*, leaning so far over the railing that my feet lifted off the hardwood floor.

I felt good, but one glance at Jack told me that I was the only one. He was sitting down in one of the seats, an old wood bench lacquered over in black paint, and his face was pale.

"Are you okay?" I asked.

He nodded his head with a grim smile that was all, "Carry on."

I sat down next to him. "Are you seasick?"

The word "seasick" made him gag slightly. "Oh, sorry!" I patted his arm. "This thing is barely moving, you must be super sensitive."

He gave a small nod, closing his eyes and breathing deeply.

"Why did you want to take the ferry if it would make you this sick?"

After a few seconds, he answered, his eyes still closed. "Because I thought you'd like it."

That lodged a warm little nugget into my chest. Yeah, this was a guy who dragged a washer up three flights of stairs for an old lady. I looked at him, the handsome features of his face. Smooth brow, serious eyebrows, a straight-up *sensual* mouth.

Did you kiss me like that because you actually like me?

"I do like the ferry," I said.

Another deep breath. "Good."

Everything about Jack was charming and magnetic and the overall effect was setting off alarm bells.

But this wasn't a normal situation. In a normal situation, I would be cautious. But today? Today was today. The usual rules did not apply.

I would eat all the buns, all the rice, all the sweets. And I would grab every bit of heat, sweetness, and fun with this guy. I'd leave as quickly as I came and the memory would sustain me for whatever was ahead.

So I threw caution to the wind on that ferry. "And I like you, too, Jack."

Saying those words out loud was an insane release. I wasn't nervous about it—it felt right. Easy. I stared at him, waiting for some comical reaction, like his eyes snapping open and his body boinging out of the seat like, "Wha-ha-ha?!"

What I didn't expect was his eyes to remain closed and a horrible smirk to appear on his face. I could punch that perfect face of his.

"Hello?" I poked him in the arm.

His face slackened immediately and I regretted it. "I'm going to let this reaction go because you're near death," I mumbled.

Finally, he said quietly, "I'm not near death." His eyes opened and he gazed at me. Heavy-lidded, tired. It shouldn't have been hot but it was. "I know you like me."

I imagined heaving his body into my arms and tossing him over the side of the ferry like a sack of rice.

"Don't look at me like that," he said with a laugh. "You kissed me. I figured you wouldn't kiss someone you hated."

My face felt hot, again. "Well, there's an ocean between 'hate' and 'like.'"

"Is there?"

Something about seasick Jack made everything he said sound oddly sage. His gaze was still on me, hyper-focused now. "Why is it that in rom-coms people always go from hating each other to like, ripping each other's clothes off?"

I pulled my coat tighter around me. "There shall be no ripping off of clothes. Calm down, sir."

His hand reached out and tugged at my sleeve. "Don't worry. I can barely move right now."

"Good."

"So why is it, then? Why is hate so hot?"

I squirmed. Jack with a depleted battery was still lethal. "I don't know! Maybe because hate means you feel something strongly. And people you're not attracted to don't bring out anything that strongly. It's a whole lot of nothing."

I thought of the many polite interactions I'd had with various K-pop guys in Korea. None of us were supposed to date, of course. But there were hookups and covert dating. It was all very romantic for the ones who did it. But I never did.

When I met these guys, I discovered that what we brought out in fans was so separate from who we actually were. So, then, when we met it would be awkward because we felt that expectation: that two attractive people were supposed to culminate into something fiery. Fueled by the adoration of thousands. Millions, even, for some of us. But it'd be this cold, strained thing.

Today, though, after a few hours with this stranger, this guy who I knew wasn't telling me the full truth about himself, I felt it. The thing. I understood how you could go from wanting to punch someone to kissing them.

It was chemistry, for sure. But it was also the way I remembered him taking care of me last night. His genuine pleasure in my enjoyment of this city.

Goodness. I was actually falling for this guy.

"So you feel strongly about me, then?" Jack asked, still touching the sleeve of my jacket. His fingernail got caught on the shirt underneath and when he pulled his hand away a strand of thread unraveled from it, the fabric puckering.

I huffed. "Yeah, I strongly feel that you are *annoying*." I tried to pull my arm away to yank the hanging string off, but he held my wrist up to his face, examining the thread.

"What are you—"

His gaze moved from the thread to my eyes. And without looking away, he brought my wrist up to his mouth, placed the thread between his teeth, and pulled.

The thread broke off and fluttered to the floor.

CHAPTER TWENTY-EIGHT
JACK

I WANTED LUCKY TO STOP TALKING ABOUT HER feelings. But after that piece of thread fell to the floor, the look in her eyes wasn't something I was anticipating.

Her pupils turned black black black, filled her entire eyeballs almost. The heat in them almost knocked me over.

A voice crackled over the speakers as the ferry stopped with a gentle bump. Nausea came up in waves; whether it was from the movement or the look in Lucky's eyes, I don't know. I wasn't prepared for the depth of feeling in them.

"Let's go," I said, dropping her wrist. Because I was confused by my own feelings, too. Guilt mixed with, well, being flattered.

We both staggered up and got off the ferry, ending up at a port across the street from giant buildings filled with super-high-end stores. Everything in Kowloon was larger than life.

I walked ahead of her, trying to sort out my thoughts with every brisk step. When we reached the crosswalk, I jabbed at the walk button and felt my head ache with every ring of the crosswalk signal.

What. *Ding.* Are. *Ding.* You. *Ding.* Doing.

Earlier today, I felt like I knew exactly what I was doing. The mission was clear: Get the photos. Get the story.

But now? Now everything was all muddled. I was Lucky's first kiss. She trusted me enough to do that. She had told me she liked me. The matter-of-fact confession had shocked me, but I had hid the feeling. Self-preservation had kicked in.

I needed to ignore feeling pleased by it. And I had to stay focused. Despite the guilt. I could *not* fall for this girl.

We crossed the street. I glanced behind me to make sure she was close. She was, keeping her head down, her body turned inward again.

It wasn't a good feeling. This shaking of my confidence. Feeling like I crossed a line somehow.

"Do you want to know where we're going?" I asked after a few silent minutes walking past the long lines for Prada, Hermès, Gucci, etc. Lucky shrugged in response to my question.

Today felt like a tug-of-war between me feeling good and feeling like a jerk. And now, after she told me she liked me, after being her first kiss . . . I knew that I couldn't keep doing this to her. Celeb undercover or not, she had no idea why I was going hot and cold today.

Story or no, she didn't deserve it.

"I'm taking you to a movie theater with a bookstore. I think you'll like it."

She nodded, concentrating on keeping her face hidden as she dodged the crowds. I reached for her hand and held it tight. Sending reassurance through the firm grip. Even if she didn't know that I knew why she needed it. Even if it made her like me more. Made *me* like *her* more.

The hand-holding relaxed her and she smiled at me. "So that's where my pointing led us? To a bookstore?"

"It's special," I said. "You'll like it. Old movies are always showing at the theater. It's all very . . . romantic." I muttered the last word.

But Lucky was back to her feisty self. "Pardon? *Romantic?*"

I laughed, and it felt so right to be holding her hand at that moment. "Yes. Romantic."

"Well, you *do* strike me as a romantic guy. Reacting the way you did to me telling you I liked you." Our hands swung between us.

The crowds started to thin, and the buildings transformed from sleek glass behemoths to older apartments with businesses on the ground floors. Kind of like in Sheung Wan but way bigger. There was a lot of construction going on, bamboo scaffolding encasing entire buildings. Men in jumpsuits teetering on ladders as they worked at impossible heights.

As we walked I thought of what Lucky said on the ferry. That she liked me. There was a Korean word for that sort of confession but I couldn't remember it.

"Hey, what's the word in Korean? When you confess your feelings for someone?" I asked.

"Gobaek." She paused. "Isn't it interesting that Koreans have a specific word for that? Because we understand that even saying you like someone is meaningful. In America, the moment is sealed by like, sex or some dramatic love confession. But in Korea, 'I like you.' That's a big deal."

155

"Wow, you're being very subtle about this right now," I said, with a smile, so she knew I wasn't bothered by it. "I get it, girl. It was important."

She shoved me with our clasped hands. "Well, is it though? We're not going to see each other again."

We both knew this was true from the beginning. But hearing it said out loud . . . Some invisible clock in my brain started its countdown.

There was still so much to learn about Lucky. How and why did she get into K-pop? I hoped I had enough time to find out.

"You don't know that we'll never see each other again," I said lightly.

She glanced at me as we walked by a store packed floor to ceiling with pots and pans. "We live in different countries."

"Within the manageable continent of Asia."

"Are you saying," she said with a laugh, "that you would visit me in Korea? After one day together?"

I shrugged. "You never know what the future holds!" It was meant to be glib but Lucky's expression was serious.

"I know my future," she said in a calm voice, resolute but also resigned.

"Church choir forever?" I teased.

We let go of each other's hands to step around an old lady sitting on a stool, fanning herself on the sidewalk.

"Something like that." Lucky reached for my hand again. "When you commit to something like choir, you commit to a life that's kind of different from everyone else's."

She had to know that sounded weird. But it was also vulnerable. So I let my guard down, too. "I hope I get to see you again."

The words were out there in the world and I couldn't take them back.

She slowed her steps and didn't look at me right away, as if turning the words over in her mind. Examining them.

My palm grew sweaty in hers.

CHAPTER TWENTY-NINE
LUCKY

SERIOUSLY, THOUGH, WHY WAS IT SUCH A BIG DEAL TO show me that you like me, Jack? The slickness of his palms really drove the point home. This is the most noncommittal fling you'll ever have, bucko. Thank your lucky stars.

"Cool, now we can acknowledge the *suffocating* sexual energy that you've been giving off all day," I declared.

He laughed, almost running into two guys pushing a cart full of metal rebar. "You're the one giving me hornball eyes," he responded.

I thought of the warmth from his fingers as he pushed them into my wrist, the flash of his teeth before he bit into the unspooling thread. This shameless jerk. "You mended my clothing *with your mouth*. Don't even."

I waited for a blush but it never came. Instead, it was that stupid, slow smile. "It was a matter of practicality."

"Oh, shut up." But I smiled back, and there we were. Two smiling fools, holding hands, walking down a busy street. This was something I dreamed about. The love songs I sang, the bumping and grinding, the moon eyes I made—it was all hinting at this feeling.

As we walked, I noticed a lot more women in hijabs, schoolboys speaking Arabic, and halal restaurants the farther we went. "Oh my gosh, can we get good shawarma here?" I asked.

Jack nodded. "Oh yeah."

Even though we had eaten our weight in bao, my stomach grumbled. I was never able to satisfy my Middle Eastern food cravings in Korea.

We stopped by a small storefront lit by fluorescent lamps and run by an older South Asian man wearing a loose cream-colored button-down shirt. Jack ordered us a couple sandwiches and we ate them at the metal counter, facing the street. I was adding up today's costs in my head, keeping them stored away so that I could remind Ji-Yeon to get Jack paid.

Delicious. The lamb fat dripped off my chin. It was perfect, a balance of crisp and tender. Paired with crunchy pickled veggies and a rich tahini sauce. I didn't bother wiping the fat off and didn't mind that Jack watched me eat with undisguised interest.

"You're kind of a pig," he said affably.

"Truth." I peeled back the foil wrapping on my sandwich. "I rarely get to eat like this. So, YOLO, right?"

He was quiet for a moment, munching on his sandwich. "Are you on a diet?" He looked uncomfortable after he said it. "Sorry, that was a rude question."

"It's okay. I brought it up. Yeah, I'm on a *diet*." The bitterness of the word scraped down my throat, resting like a rock in my stomach.

I had been careful with how much of my real life I revealed to Jack. Subtle things dropped here and there, trying not to lie too much. "I don't remember when I wasn't on one."

The second I entered training school, I, and everyone else, was put on a diet. We were weighed every week, equally judged on that as we were with our dance skills. And it's not like it was a secret. The public acted outraged on your behalf, about things like the "one cup" diet (everything you ate for the day fit into a tiny cup). There was always a temporary discussion about eating disorders when someone had to drop out of a group to go into rehab.

But then it was forgotten. The management labels laid low until the coast was clear. And then all the old rules were enacted again.

And, honestly, whose fault was it? Starving teenagers marked for life with eating disorders that would never leave them? Was it the management labels and entertainment companies? Or was it the insistence on a standard of beauty in the culture?

A girl has to be pretty more than anything else, my grandmother would say, so matter-of-factly. In Korea, strangers felt comfortable commenting on your appearance from "Wow, you're tall!" to "You need to use more moisturizer." In America, it was a lot more undercover, but it was there. Women and girls were held to different standards *everywhere*.

So was it any surprise that when you reached a level of stardom in Korea, you were expected to be the most perfect version of yourself that you could be? There was no hiding that.

You got used to it. And then it felt normal.

At least it felt normal until you were around food. Eating like a regular human being made me realize—wait, this was *not* normal! *Food is freaking delicious, my God!*

160

"I'm glad you get a diet break, then," Jack said mildly, taking a sip from a paper cup full of sugary soda.

I smiled at that because he didn't expand on it. Even when well meaning, anyone having an opinion on other people's eating habits got my hackles up.

A couple of boys in soccer gear walked by the window and waved at us. I waved back with a smile, not worrying about being recognized at that moment. I wouldn't normally venture outside of touristy spots in any city I visited. I barely left hotel rooms. The ironic terribleness of that was those central tourist spots were where I was most likely to be spotted. So I was this helpless prisoner stuck in my (literal) glass tower, being fretted over while at the same time worked like a horse.

I don't know if it was a false sense of anonymity or what, but here in this regular neighborhood, I felt like I could really, truly relax.

So relaxed that I burped. I stared at Jack after doing it, daring him to make some comment about how unladylike it was. But he merely burped in response. We cracked up, which earned us a stern throat clearing from the café owner.

It wasn't only the neighborhood and the anonymity that made me relax, I realized. It was also Jack. Everything was easy with him. Comfortable.

We finished our sandwiches and stepped back outside, the afternoon sun casting a rich yellow glow on everything.

There were an awkward few seconds when we started walking. My fingers twitched, reaching out toward his, in some clumsy, ghostly movement.

The butterflies, the giddiness at these moments always struck me as eye-rolly when I watched them in K-dramas. Like, get over it, you touched *hands*, my God get a *grip*.

But I got it now. When I reached for his hand, I felt that tumult in my chest, the flip-floppy hyperventilating movement in my lungs. He reached for mine last time, but it still felt uncertain and, I don't know, vulnerable? To reach out for his hand this time.

And then a flash of sunlight beamed out from behind Jack's silhouette, and he clasped my hand before I could his.

CHAPTER THIRTY

JACK

AT WHAT POINT DID LUCKY'S PRETENDING BLEND INTO reality?

This day wasn't just thrills for some spoiled pop star—it was a break from a life that she didn't enjoy anymore.

The guilt that had been a tiny ember was now firmly smoking into a warning.

She had eaten that shawarma with such gusto that I couldn't stand digging into her terrible eating restrictions further. Instead, we were walking in sunshine holding hands.

I was going to have to say goodbye to her at some point. My hand gripped hers harder.

When we stepped into the bookstore, an airy space inside an old eighties-era mall type building, the air-conditioning hit us.

"Jack!" A petite Chinese girl in a red beanie and pleated pink skirt waved at me from behind the register, where she was perched on a rickety wood stool.

I smiled and waved back with the hand that was clasped with Lucky's. "Hey, Sissi!"

Lucky glanced between us with an uneasy smile. Jealousy was pretty cute on her.

"Sissi, this is Fern. Fern, this is Sissi. The best bookseller in the city."

Sissi rolled her eyes and pushed up her round-framed glasses. "You're full of it. Hi, Fern. That's a nice name."

Lucky smiled and ducked her head down. "Thanks."

Crap. I hadn't planned on introducing her to anyone today—totally birdbrained to bring her here, where people knew me and might be curious about this girl I brought in.

But there wasn't any recognition on Sissi's part. I couldn't imagine Sissi listening to pop music, to be honest. She played anime soundtracks, exclusively, over the bookstore speakers.

Lucky dipped into the bookshelves, disappearing quickly.

Sissi snapped her fingers. "Oh, Jack! That book you ordered finally came in." She shuffled around under the register looking for it. "It was very hard to find. Here it is!"

I took the large book from her and eagerly flipped through it. It was a rare collection of photos by Fan Ho, a Hong Kong–based photographer. Probably the most famous Hong Kong photographer, really. I flipped through the glossy pages, already getting sucked into the black-and-white images—shirtless men lined up along a street waiting for steaming food, the small figure of a woman walking between the giant shadows of buildings, sunlight filtering through an alley and hitting the stooped back of an old man. I could look at these all day.

"This book isn't cheap," Sissi said as she craned her neck to look at the photos with me.

I nodded. "I know. I saved up for it, though." I paid her and then went looking for Lucky, excited to revisit the book later.

I found her settled on the floor in the poetry section, reading a slim volume. I snapped another picture of her. She was sitting with her knees bent, holding the book up to her face as she rested her elbows on her knees.

It reminded me of those old photos of Marilyn Monroe curled up with a book. Moments where she was so absorbed in her reading that she was able to shed her sexpot image for a brief moment, to drop the act and be some version of herself that she hid from the public.

"What are you reading?" I asked as I crouched down next to her.

She was engrossed already. "Mm. A poetry collection by Gwendolyn Brooks. I get a lot of song inspiration from poems."

Both of us froze. I tried to keep my voice light. "Oh, do you also write your own music?"

She closed the book and tapped it against her knee. "I do."

She did? Probably not the stuff that was popular. In my research last night, I found out that her managers hired top hit makers for that.

Every new bit of info was more intriguing than the last.

"That's so cool. Um, is it about . . . God?" I asked.

She stared at me and then we both burst out laughing.

"I'm being serious!" I said.

Lucky was laughing so hard that people nearby threw us dirty looks. She covered her mouth and after a while was able to wheeze out, "I don't live for church choir, Jack."

I picked up the book she had dropped in the process of laughing. "So, you write for yourself?"

She nodded, not self-conscious or shy about this at all. "Yeah. I like it. I'm good at it."

It wasn't arrogant or anything. Just . . . a person who knew who she was. Envy trickled through me, icy and sudden. It was rare to see someone my age so sure of herself.

"Maybe one day I could hear one of your songs," I said.

She raised an eyebrow before standing up in one smooth, athletic motion. "In this fantasy future where you visit me in Seoul?"

Before I could respond, she reached down and tugged me up to standing. I was surprised by it, she was stronger than she looked. When I stood, we were facing each other—very close.

I pushed the book into her chest. "Did you want me to buy this for you, too?"

She glanced down at it. "Nah. I already have a lot of copies."

"You were reading stuff you've already read?"

"Yup. When I like something, I *like* it." She turned around, headed to the café, and for some reason those words quickened my pulse, made me feel overheated.

Before I could recover, Lucky hollered from across the bookstore, near the adjoining café. "Can we get some of this food?"

I laughed. "Feed the beast."

"Always."

CHAPTER THIRTY-ONE
LUCKY

WE SAT DOWN TO SOME MILK TEA, A HONG KONG specialty according to Jack. A plate of cookies was brought alongside them, and I grabbed one.

"Tell me about your parents," I said before I bit into it. It was my time to question him for once.

His eyes widened. "Okay, cutting to the chase, I guess."

"It's only a few steps after, 'when and where were you born,' which I already happen to know." Los Angeles. The coincidence of that still baffled me. "What do they do?" I paused. "I mean, if they're both still alive." Why did I even say that? So morbid.

Jack slid his hand over and grabbed a cookie chunk, his hand grazing mine. A tiny firework went off where our skin touched. *Poof.*

He let out a short laugh. "Yes, they're still alive. Well, my mom stays home and my dad is a banker, like I mentioned before," he said, popping the cookie into his mouth.

"Oh, cool. There does seem to be a lot of banking here," I said feebly. Genius observation, Lucky. "So do you like interning at the bank?"

"I pretty much hate it," he said, dunking another piece of cookie into his tea. His tone was light.

"That sucks," I said. "Well, it's only temporary until college, right?"

Before he could respond, he knocked his cup of tea over, the milky liquid pouring to his side of the table, dripping into his lap.

I jumped up. "Oh no!"

Jack made an annoyed sound and stood up, wiping his shirt off where the tea splattered. "Sorry, I'm gonna go wipe this off," he said as he pushed his chair away from the table.

"Okay." I reached across to mop up the tea with a napkin and was joined by Sissi, who came over with a rag.

"Thanks," I said to her with a smile.

She nodded in response. "Hey, maybe he needs a new shirt?" she said, half question, half statement. "We have some nerdy literary shirts in our gifts section."

"Ooh," I said, tapping my fingers against each other. "I'll go take a look."

The gift section was pushed back into the corner of the shop, as if the shop were reluctant to hawk non-books among its precious literary tomes. I sifted through a rack of soft cotton T-shirts emblazoned with vintage book covers, illustrations of glasses, cats, etc.

I wanted to get him something embarrassing but it had to be the *right* kind of embarrassing. Something caught my eye then. It was one of those black-and-white ampersand name shirts:

Jo &

Meg &

Beth &

Amy

I snorted. Perfect. If he got the *Little Women* reference I would faint. And then marry him, let's be honest.

I held it up and waved it at Sissi, who gave me a thumbs-up from across the store. Heh heh. The bathroom was down a narrow hall lined with mops and lockers. I knocked on the door.

"Hey, Sissi said you can wear one of the shirts here. I picked one out for you."

The door opened and Jack stood there with the bottom of his button-up soaking wet with water and soap suds. He peered at the shirt in my hands. "Let me see it."

I held it up right under my eyes, the cotton brushing against my mouth. "Cool, right?" My voice was muffled behind the shirt.

He stared at it, bewildered. "Who the hell are those people?"

He raised his eyebrows at me and I pushed the shirt into his chest. "Only the four coolest women ever."

"I don't even want to know," he grumbled as he started to unbutton his shirt.

I stared. "What are you doing?"

"Changing?" He kept his eyes on his shirt as he continued to unbutton.

Keep your eyes on his face. "Well, okay, Magic Mike." That made absolutely no sense and was embarrassing and weird and revealing way too much about the exact way his undressing was making me feel right now.

Laughter made his eyes crinkle in the corners as he looked up at me. I was paying such close attention to his eyes right now. Two spherical organs nestled into a skull. That's all. Like, nope, not gonna look below those eyeballs. Just keep starin' at the eyeballs.

"Are you trying to see into my soul?" he asked. His body was shifting now, he was taking off the shirt.

"Yeah. And I see a black void. Congratulations, you have no soul." And try as I did to stop it, my gaze shot down to Jack's shirtless torso.

Are you freaking kidding me? Good *gravy*, he was pleasing to look at. All lean, corded muscles and smooth, tanned skin. I wanted to throw the shirt into his face in frustration.

He took the shirt from me. "Thanks."

I narrowed my eyes at him. "Stop trying to be . . . seductive."

"What! You're the one standing there while I change."

"Don't say 'thanks' like that."

"Like *how*?" He pulled the shirt on.

"All . . . *thanks*." I tried to make my voice low and liquidy like his but it was pretty much impossible. That voice was patented and preserved forever by the Jack School of Undercover Hotness.

What am I even . . .

The hallway felt claustrophobic—hot and, somehow, the air was thick.

Jack folded up his button-up neatly and tucked it under his arm. "You're so hot and bothered by this entire situation."

The words "hot and bothered" were really too much. I actually *fanned myself* with my hand. "Well! I mean!"

He stood there, waiting for me to say more, but I couldn't and instead started laughing. He tried not to laugh but I reached over and poked his abs (which I now knew were pretty rock hard) and made him.

As we walked back to the café, he draped his arm around my shoulders and the ease of it was so pleasant I couldn't keep the smile off my face.

When we sat down, I noticed a book sitting by the plate of cookies. "What's that?"

He glanced down at it. "Oh, a book I ordered."

"About what?"

"Uh, a book of photos."

"Really? Cool," I said, looking down to see it. "Can I see?"

He handed it to me. "It's an old collection of photos by this photographer I like." His voice was so mumbly that I barely understood him. He was being shy about this.

I flipped through the thick pages of the book. "Wow. These are amazing. It's Hong Kong, right?"

Jack nodded. "Yeah, the photographer is Fan Ho! Arguably the most significant Hong Kong photographer." His words were clearer now, animated and lively.

"Wow, you must be a big photo buff, then?" I asked, looking through the photos. They were beautiful—a glimpse into everyday, old Hong Kong.

"Yeah, I guess you could say that. It's not a big deal." Jack leaned forward, his discarded shirt a cushion for his elbows. "Change of subject. What do *your* parents do?"

God, that question felt like a million years ago. A million years before seeing shirtless Jack ago. I closed the book.

"My parents? Oh." I stalled, trying to think of something. But then, why lie about this detail? It would mean nothing to him, he of zero K-pop knowledge. "My mom's a paralegal and my dad's a teacher."

"What does he teach?" Jack leaned forward, propping his face into his hands.

"Middle school algebra."

"Nice. Are you good at math?" Jack asked with a smile, as if he already knew the answer.

"Are *you*?" I asked in response.

"Well, shouldn't we both be good at math?"

I smiled. "Give me a break. No one thinks that anymore."

He raised an eyebrow. "Hi, did you *not* grow up in America?"

"I mean, the math thing—that was the least of my problems."

"What were the bigger problems?"

It was weird—we were in this very public place, but suddenly it felt so intimate. "Um, I don't know. I always felt quite separate from other kids my age." It was true. I was so focused on performing as a kid.

My pulse quickened then; I could feel my heartbeat at the base of my throat. It happened to me when I got anxious. It occurred to me that I wasn't sure when I'd be back in my hotel room, back to my meds. That made me more anxious, so I subtly dropped my hands onto my lap under the table. Then I took my right index and middle fingers and placed them on my left wrist, feeling for a pulse.

"How were you separate?" Jack asked, oblivious to any weirdness.

I felt it then, the gentle beat under the thin layer of skin. It calmed me immediately and I counted the first few beats in my head. *One. Two. Three.* After a few seconds it would slow down and that would help.

"Oh. I had to stay home and watch my younger sister a lot, so I didn't have many friends to hang out with after school and on the

172

weekends." That was true. But I also had all my dancing and singing lessons.

"You have a younger sister?" He smiled. "So do I."

That made me smile back. I could imagine him with a sister to pester. "Oh, yeah, you mentioned her. What's her name and how old is she?"

"She's twelve. And her name's Ava."

Jack and Ava. I liked filling in these negative spaces of Jack— watching them fill up to form a complete person.

"Cool, my sister's fifteen and her name's Vivian. She's a total jerk," I added with a laugh. "Is yours?"

He shook his head. "She's actually kind of . . . a saint. And driven and smart. She's going to do something spectacular one day. Which is good, so my parents can have one reliable kid."

"One?" I asked. "You also seem driven and smart."

An appalled expression came over his face. "Take that back!"

"What? You don't want to be smart?" I laughed. My pulse was now at a normal pace and I pulled my hands back up to the table, reaching for my teacup.

"I'm *fine*. But I definitely don't have my life figured out like Ava does. Her like, patronus or whatever, would be a spreadsheet."

Tea went up my nose and I choked. "Shut up."

He grinned. "I'm funnier than her, though."

"I doubt it," I said, dabbing my face with a napkin.

"Anyway. I'm kind of . . . messing around until I figure it all out," he said with a shrug.

"That's okay," I said. "Not everyone can be Ava."

"Or you," he said pointedly. It was complimentary, and my cheeks warmed. I'd hit every record in K-pop stardom, and having this guy compliment me casually made me turn into a beet.

173

I tapped the photography book in front of me. "What about photography? Seems like you must like it if you special order books."

He shrugged again. "I do like it, a lot. But it's not . . . exactly a career path for me. Art, I mean."

It took everything in my power to keep my lips sealed. To not blurt out, "I am the living embodiment of making art a career!"

Instead I cupped my tea. Waited a few beats before I asked, "Well, what is your path, then?"

The question seemed to dislodge something in him. The confident swagger left and an uncertain hunch in his shoulders was all that remained.

CHAPTER THIRTY-TWO

JACK

IF ANYONE ELSE HAD ASKED ME THIS, I WOULD HAVE A BS answer ready, while being inwardly annoyed by the question. But coming from Lucky, it felt different. I wanted to respond to her, even if my answer wasn't all that great.

I cleared my throat to break the conspicuous silence. "Well. That's the thing. I don't have a path and I'm okay with that."

She nodded. "Yeah, we're young. That's okay."

But I could hear the strain in her voice. To remain neutral. I knew what Lucky did to get where she was. At the age of *thirteen* she had decided what she wanted to do with her life and she did it. Someone like me—aimless and unsure—was a mystery to her.

"I do some photography work on the side," I said cautiously, suddenly needing her to know that I wasn't someone without *any* interests.

Her eyes lit up. "Really? So you *are* a photographer! What kind of work do you do?"

Quick, Jack. Something completely unrelated to the media . . . something safe . . .

"Weddings."

She exclaimed, "Oh! That must be nice. Witnessing love over and over again."

It was like she punched me in the chest. Because what I did was the opposite of witnessing love. It was witnessing adultery. Someone popping into rehab. Decadence and excess. People either at the lowest point in their lives or at their worst.

"It's a job to get by," I said with a shrug. Feigning nonchalance. But as I said the words, it occurred to me that with this story, this could turn into more than a job to get by. That I would be committing to rising in the ranks of tabloid photojournalism. And only yesterday, that had felt exciting. And now? It felt flimsy. I shifted in my seat uncomfortably.

Lucky munched on a cookie thoughtfully before she spoke. "Well, then maybe you can build your portfolio with these wedding photos and apply to photography programs!"

I could see the gears turning in her brain. She was already envisioning some future for me that allowed me to have dreams. I swallowed hard at the lump in my throat. No one had ever been excited for my future before.

"My parents won't be down for that," I said. "Can you imagine Korean parents paying for you to study photography for four years?"

Confusion clouded her expression. "Yeah, I can?"

Right. Her parents probably helped pay for her entrance into K-pop. It wasn't cheap—all the training before you were even signed on to a label. Vocal coaches, dance classes, the works. Not to mention all the travel abroad.

I sighed. "Well, some of us don't have the progressive-thinking kind of immigrant parents. Mine are very firmly in the camp of, we work this hard so you can have a stable future. No-nonsense."

Lucky frowned. "But stability doesn't have to be some path you don't want. Who says photography can't be stable? You could do the wedding stuff and do the kind of photography you want on the side."

I smiled. "Have you ever seen that *Onion* headline? 'Find The Thing You're Most Passionate About, Then Do It On Nights And Weekends For The Rest Of Your Life'? That's probably what I'm destined to do."

"Well, that's bleak," she said with a huff, dusting the cookie crumbs off her hands. "No one says it's *easy* to turn your passion into a job. You just have to believe you can do it."

There was something bothering me in this pep talk right now. Not only the slightly self-righteous delusion of it. But what it meant coming from *her*. If she believed in this, why was she with me today?

She was avoiding something.

I looked her in the eye. "What if you turn your passion into a job, and it stops giving you joy? Haven't you ruined something you used to love?"

I held my breath. I was pushing it.

Her face transformed. A kind of cold wall went up in her expression and her shoulders pulled back. An aura of aloof untouchableness dropped like a curtain over her entire being. It was startling. This was Lucky with the media.

"Well, I don't know. You should cross that bridge when you come to it, right?" Her voice was cool, her expression neutral.

Something felt lost then. No more warmth, no excitement. No

belief in me. I regretted having to ask her that question, at having ulterior motives for it.

I knew this was a job, but I couldn't lose her now. I needed to salvage the situation.

"Want to watch a movie?"

CHAPTER THIRTY-THREE
LUCKY

JACK WAS SOMEONE I RECOGNIZED IN MY INDUSTRY. Someone with drive, smarts, and natural instincts. But also someone who was sabotaging himself out of fear.

He found excuses not to do the thing he wanted to do. I wanted to shake him, to show him that he could. I didn't know what kind of photographer he was, but that was almost beside the point. The one thing I'd learned from four years in K-pop was that hard work trumped talent on any given day.

I wanted to dig in deeper, but his last question froze up something in me. It was almost like my skin turned translucent and he could see everything inside and for the umpteenth time that day, alarm bells were going off.

I simply couldn't figure out *what* they were warning me about.

"A movie?" I asked.

"Yeah, the theater's next door. They'll have popcorn." He grinned.

Hm.

He shook his head at my hesitation. "I was kidding. How in the world could you possibly eat right now?"

"I'm a scientific marvel," I said, already getting up.

Jack tied his still-wet long-sleeved shirt around his waist, paid for our food, and left his book behind with Sissi for safekeeping before we walked next door to the theater. Since it was only three o'clock or so, the evening crowd hadn't arrived yet. I skipped in, excited to see what was playing, but stopped in my tracks.

"*No way!*" I screeched.

"What?!" Jack asked, alarmed.

I pointed at the poster in front of us: *Wong Kar-wai Movie Marathon.*

"Can you *believe* it?" I said, going up to it to run my fingers over the beautiful face of Tony Leung.

"Wow. A Wong Kar-wai movie playing in Hong Kong. Miraculous," he said drily.

"A Wong Kar-wai *marathon* at the *one* movie theater we happen to be in when *you've* never seen one of his movies!" I refused to let Jack tamp down my enthusiasm. "Let's see which one's playing."

The next movie, in twenty minutes, was *In the Mood for Love.* Unreal.

"You are so lucky!" I rhapsodized as Jack purchased the tickets. "This is like, the OG. Everything I know about Hong Kong? This movie"—I jabbed the poster for emphasis—"God, Maggie Cheung and Tony Leung are like, these untouchable, beautiful beings."

"They look exactly the same today as they did in this movie," Jack mused as we stood in front of the poster again.

"Asian don't raisin," I said.

He threw his head back and laughed for so long that I got embarrassed. "Have you never heard that before?" I asked.

"No!" he said when he finally got ahold of himself. I was pleased to have introduced something new to him. And I was glad to make him laugh so hard.

We got some popcorn and went into the theater, picking seats right in the middle. The theater was still lit up and the rows of comfy leather seats were mostly empty.

"So, why do you love his movies so much?" Jack asked as I picked the butteriest bits of popcorn to eat.

I munched for a few seconds while I thought about it. "I don't know . . . they're so lovely and moody. The soundtracks are perfect. The characters are flawed and mysterious." I sighed happily. "And also . . . they're kind of sad."

"Sad?" he asked, settling back into his seat, his head leaning against the leather and his gaze sliding over to me. A heavy pitter-patter beat all the way down my ribs.

"Yeah, sad. A lot of times they're love stories about people who . . . aren't meant to be. You know from the beginning that they're not going to end up together."

"Doomed love?"

"Yeah."

We were quiet, and I knew he was thinking what I was thinking.

At the end of today was a goodbye. Anything that could grow

between us would be gone within hours, ephemeral and faded before it could even begin.

We were like the stars seen from Earth—a memory of something that was already finished.

The lights dimmed, the curtain rose, and Jack reached over the armrest to hold my hand, our fingers greasy with butter and salt.

CHAPTER THIRTY-FOUR

JACK

HOW I SAT THROUGH A MOVIE WITH THIS GIRL'S HAND in mine was beyond me. Every once in a while I would feel her eyes on my face, and when I glanced at her, she would be looking at me expectantly. Waiting to see if I had the right reaction to whatever was on screen. A favorite scene probably. It was annoying and cute at the same time.

"So, how did you like it?" she asked the second the lights turned on.

"How did I like what?" I asked, only half-kidding.

Honestly, though, I could hardly concentrate on it. A dark room, romantic soundtrack, sexy scenes? It was a lot.

She made a face at me. "I don't like to be teased."

"You need an older brother, clearly."

"Actually, I *don't*," she said before punching me hard in the arm, then running up and out of the theater before I could react.

When I caught up with her, she was slipping into the restroom. I paced outside, thinking about how much I had revealed to her in the café. Was it because I wouldn't see her after today? That even if she found out about the photos, I would be old news? A jerk she once hung out with in Hong Kong.

Or was it . . . because it was her? Because something about *her* specifically made me want to tell her about all sorts of things? No one in my life took my photography seriously. But in the few hours she had known me—she could tell it was important to me. That it was something worth pursuing.

"I've peed so many times today," she proclaimed as she walked out of the restroom.

And it was the strangest thing. That TMI proclamation, like her other unexpected bursts, made me realize something: I liked Lucky, too. A lot.

I liked her confidence in who she was balanced with a healthy dose of good humor. Not taking herself too seriously when she could have been this unbearable out-of-touch superstar. I liked how she thought I could turn photography into a job. That she even cared about it. I liked how she reached out for my hand all day.

"Cool, good job," I said, trying to smile through the sheer terror of this realization. This complicated everything to the billionth degree.

"It means I'm well hydrated. My trainer would be proud," she said. Her expression froze as soon as she said it.

"I don't drink enough water," I responded smoothly, draping my arm around her shoulders, so that we could both ignore the fact that she had a personal trainer. Like all normal teenagers did.

She was at the perfect height for arm-draping. Every part of her seemed to fit just right with me. I felt pulled to her like a magnet. A magnetic puzzle. God, I was poetic.

She made me want to be poetic.

When we stepped outside, the sun was starting to set. Perfect. "Let's head to the harbor," I said, walking us out of the courtyard. There was a playground nearby, part of the neighboring apartment complex. Tons of kids crawled around the equipment, unsupervised yet safe. For a big city, Hong Kong was very safe. The CCTVs everywhere probably helped with that.

We headed back toward where we began, walking by people strolling the streets, grandparents with children, the hazy light golden on every window, every treetop.

Lucky was content to walk nestled into me and I was content to let her.

It felt right to ask her then, during this quiet moment, "What do you like so much about singing?" I had asked about why she liked choir earlier in the day—but I still didn't know what she actually got out of singing. Of performing.

She was contemplative, but she stayed at my side. "Hm. That's an interesting question."

Something about that was crazy flattering. I asked *interesting* questions!

A breeze ruffled through her hair and a strand stuck to my neck. I pushed it away, and she put her hand over mine to tuck it behind her ear. Something in my chest twinged at that effortlessly intimate touch.

"Well," she said with a wrinkle of concentration between her eyebrows. "There's so much. I love how it makes me *feel*. Like, it actually gives me a high. Or, what I imagine what a high feels like," she said with a snort. "I, uh, have never done that."

I knew I was supposed to be surprised that she had never been high, but I didn't feel like making her lie. My heart wasn't in it right now. "So, that's why you're hungry all the time," I said instead. "Singing-high gives you the munchies."

She hit my arm. "Ha. Anyway. Yeah, it makes me feel good physically. But it's also this act of creating something beautiful out of thin air, communicating everything you're feeling with *sound*. It's magic."

The hairs on my arm stood on end and I rubbed them. "I know what you mean." Photography did that for me. When I captured something special, the image reflected my point of view without any words. I always thought that was magical, too.

She glanced up at me, a flash of self-consciousness flitting across her features. "Also, I'm good at it and it feels nice to be able to share that with the world. I know that sounds conceited."

I shook my head. "No, it's actually refreshing to hear someone own up to their skills."

"Right?" she exclaimed, skipping a little. "Girls are taught to be so self-effacing all the time. Heaven forbid we actually show pride and confidence at something."

"Well, otherwise you lil' ladies might think you could rule the world or something," I said with a tsk.

Lucky laughed, heartily, throwing her entire body into it, dislodging my arm. "It's funny because men are so screwed in the future. You guys have messed up this world."

We dodged a couple of kids dribbling a soccer ball and broke apart for a second before coming back together to hold hands. "We have. And it's going to continue to get messed up," I said.

"What do you mean?" Lucky's face was turned up to mine, the brim of her hat pushed far back enough so that I could see her eyes. They were open and curious.

"I think human history is, in essence, sad. Since the beginning of time, we've been stuck in this cycle of abuse and suffering," I said.

She was quiet for a second. I wondered where she fit into this history. What her life was actually like. Was it glamorous as it appeared on her social media, full of first-class flights and free clothes? Or was it more of a miserable prison? She wasn't here with me because her life was all Instagram vacays. Maybe it was something in between.

"Do you really think we're stuck?" she asked.

I nodded. "Yeah, look at us right now. We've had wars. We still have wars. We *never* stop being terrible."

She made a face. "Yes, I can't deny awful things have happened throughout history. Unspeakable, terrible stuff that still continues to happen. But I think it *does* happen less."

"That's not quantifiable, though." It was so obnoxious of me to say that, but not untrue.

"No, but I have a *brain*," she said, walking quickly ahead. Fueled by self-righteousness, it seemed. "And even without a list of statistics right in front of me, I could say the quality of life and general safety of human beings is, oh, ever so *slightly* better than the dark ages?"

"Ever so slightly," I said with a small smile, trying to keep up with her. "By the way, do you know where we're going?"

"No!" she said.

"'Kay, just checking," I said. "Keep going straight until we hit the water."

"Fine," she clipped. "Anyway. I'm not some Pollyanna. Things are messed up. Human beings are both evolving and devolving constantly.

We found the cure for polio but also we have automatic assault rifles. I get it. But I don't find any value in like, cynicism."

"Are you low-key insulting me right now?" I asked, amused and not offended somehow. I caught up to her so that we were now walking in step, back near the luxury stores, the crowds growing thicker.

"No." She paused. "Maybe. I understand cynicism. I just don't think it's very valuable at the end of the day." She slid an inscrutable glance at me, and I was trying to find a way to defend my jaded worldview when she pointed a finger in the air. "Human beings are messed up. But we are not beyond fixing!"

"Oh my God," I said with a laugh. "What is happening right now?"

"You got me on a roll!" she exclaimed.

"Are you running for president?"

"No. But I could," she said with a huff.

I imagined future Lucky doing great things, even greater things than she was doing now, and it suddenly struck me that I wouldn't see Lucky tomorrow, let alone future Lucky. That this was the only Lucky I would ever see in real life.

The clock would strike midnight, and she'd be gone forever.

CHAPTER THIRTY-FIVE
LUCKY

I COULD BE PRESIDENT.

Once, when I was twelve, I said, "I could be a K-pop star." And I did it.

What happened since then? Why did I, at some point, when *I achieved that exact goal*, stop thinking I could do anything I wanted to do? Here I was, dispensing life-coach stuff to Jack, when I was kind of mired in the same fears myself.

Had I changed? Did what I want from music, from the K-pop industry, change? It didn't matter, though, because the industry would never change.

The energy I felt earlier kind of zapped out of me.

We walked past a Porsche dealership where men in tuxedos were standing outside with trays of champagne proffered to potential buyers. The crowds were getting louder, so we grew quieter.

Then I heard the faint, soothing sound of flutes. It grew louder as we walked until we came across the source: a group of older women in track suits doing tai chi in a giant courtyard surrounded by various fancy stores. A small wireless speaker was playing the flute music at the front of the group where one woman in a raspberry-colored sweatshirt was leading them.

The juxtaposition of these calm older women with the bustling high-end shopping around them was surreal.

And I wanted to be a part of it.

"See you in a few," I called out to Jack before I jogged up to join them.

"What are you doing?" I heard him call out behind me as I stepped into place with the third row of women. No one said anything, but shifted over and made room for me.

I'd never done tai chi before, but I could learn choreography by watching a single pass. Soon my limbs were moving in sync with everyone else's—arms lifting above my head, feet shifting slowly from left to right, my knees bent at a slight angle throughout the whole thing.

Raise arms to chest level, lower slowly. So slowly. Push hands away from body. Bring back gently, pivoting body to the right. Then left. Bend the knee.

Jack watched us with his arms folded and a huge grin on his face. When I turned left and looked over my shoulder at him, he threw me a thumbs-up sign.

I felt so incredibly at peace.

CHAPTER THIRTY-SIX

JACK

IT WOULD HAVE BEEN A PERFECT PICTURE.

LUCKY FINDS HER GROOVE

Golden hour. Lucky surrounded by a dozen older ladies in track suits. She was a head taller than everyone else. And so graceful in her movements, as if she'd been doing it her whole life.

The way she picked up on it—quickly and naturally—made it clear she was born with this gift for movement. She was absolutely comfortable in her body. It was a tool she had fine-tuned after hours and hours of work.

As the light hit Lucky, something was illuminated in my mind. That fine tuning? My dad never did it.

A couple years ago, when I was looking for a basketball in our garage back in LA, I'd found a small pile of literary magazines gathering dust in a corner. The one on top of the pile had a cool black-and-white photograph of a gnarled tree on the cover so I flipped through it. One of the pages was folded over in the corner. It was a spread for a short story called "A Fire in the Valley." The byline was Cameron Lim. My dad. I sat down on the dusty concrete floor and read it, completely absorbed and blown away by the powerful, spare prose. I spent hours sitting there reading each of the stories he had published in the pile of magazines.

Like Lucky, my dad was born with natural abilities. It wasn't only the craft of writing, but also the observational skills of someone who was always examining people and how they worked. Like me. Only I did it through a camera lens.

I always knew my dad was a writer, but I had never actually understood the level of his talent. When I brought it up with him at dinner that day, he brushed it off. "Oh, that was the past." And as I sat there watching him in that giant dining room, with his tie tossed over his shoulder as he dug into his food, there was a sinking feeling in the pit of my stomach. I had a vision of me in thirty years, my kid looking at my old photographs. And feeling like that was the past. Ancient history totally separate from who I was.

Lucky? She was also gifted. But she went after it. So hard. She was someone who took her talent and made it her future.

Someone who threw herself into a group of strangers to try something new. Knowing she could suck, that she could mess up. But doing it anyway because she would keep doing it until she got better. I admired her so much in that moment that it almost hurt.

I should have taken a photo of her doing tai chi. It was almost cinematic. But I decided to save this memory for me. Keep it locked tight so that I could take it out days, years from now. Take it out and turn it over in my mind, remembering the cool breeze and warmth radiating from her smile.

A text vibrated in my pocket. Trevor. **Hope you get a sunset shot. Take her to the harbor.**

It should have made me feel smug, that I was already ahead of Trevor, that I had the instincts for the right photo, the right story.

Watching Lucky as she closed her eyes and moved to the music, feeling at peace in this messed-up world? With Trevor's text on my phone?

It made me question what I was doing. Made me question everything.

CHAPTER THIRTY-SEVEN
LUCKY

"BE CAREFUL," JACK CAUTIONED AS I STEPPED ONTO the beautiful old sailboat.

We were at Victoria Harbour right as the sun was setting and the water was undulating in gold and orange.

Jack was helping me onto an old "junk" boat refurbished for tourists. There were a few people on the boat already and I glanced around, nervous about being recognized again. But most of the people were taking photos of the spectacular views, not concerned with us.

The boat was driven by a lady who looked as old as time but had the energy and zing of a teenager. "Neih hou, Jack," she said in greeting as we stepped on.

"Neih hou, dím a?" Jack said, handing a couple of bills to one of the crew, a young guy in a T-shirt, impervious to the cold.

She grinned widely, her tanned skin stretching to accommodate the hugeness of her smile. "Hóu hóu," she said. Then she glanced at me and said something else to him in Cantonese. Jack held up his hands and laughed in response. She chuckled deeply, starting the engine.

We went upstairs to the top deck, snagging a couple of upholstered seats with great views. "I didn't know you spoke Cantonese," I said as Jack sat down next to me.

"Not that well," he said. "Most people here can speak English, but I like to butter up Mrs. Hua because she's the only driver who doesn't make me seasick. Well, not *that* seasick."

"I can't believe you're getting on a boat twice in one day," I said as I closed my eyes and let the breeze glide over me.

"I have to give you the full Hong Kong experience," he said. When I opened my eyes he was watching me with a strange expression. Was he going to kiss me again?

How soon was too soon to kiss again, anyway?

But it didn't happen. We sat there silently with him looking at me, the sound of the waves lapping against the boat as it started to move, repetitive and lulling.

"What?" I asked after a few more seconds went by without any kissing.

"You were good at the tai chi back there," he finally said, his lips hitching up into a smile.

I laughed. "Thanks."

"You're good at a lot of stuff."

The sun was almost gone but the words warmed me. "Yes, I'm great at eating and tai chi." I felt nervous from his attention. Jack payed *such* close attention to me. It was unnerving but also incredibly pleasing. It was a type of attention that I should have been used to as a celebrity, but felt totally new when it was with a boy I'd kissed and held hands with all day. I guess this was what it might feel like to be in a real relationship.

I understood. How it was like a drug. Intoxicating and all-encompassing. I'd been floating along in that feeling for the past couple hours.

"You're also good at a lot of things," I said, turning to him, my arm draped along the top of my seat.

He shook his head. "Not like you."

"Jack, I learned to get good at a lot of things," I said. "Hours and hours of work. This is a job."

Blast. Church choir was my job?!

Luckily, Jack didn't seem confused by that. He was too busy concentrating on breathing like he did on the ferry to dodge nausea. "So, I asked you earlier. Does it still bring you joy?"

A chill went through me. I stared into the skyline alongside the water. The buildings reflected brilliant colors from the setting sun. "Yes. And no." Those three words unpacked something in me that I had been keeping tightly locked away.

"You talked about why you liked singing. Do you still feel that?"

Twenty-four hours ago I had been on a stage, singing. And I remembered feeling the euphoria. But it had been mixed with something else. Weariness. Dread.

"I feel it. But it's been a little polluted," I answered carefully. Not sure when everything I was saying could turn into something that no longer made sense for a girl in a church choir. "Something's changed but I don't know what it is or what to do about it. So I do nothing."

"And stay miserable?"

I looked up at him sharply. "I'm not miserable."

He untied his green shirt from his waist, pulling it on as a cool breeze whipped over us. "You were running from something last night."

It was true, but I didn't like it being so obvious. "I was hungry."

"Yeah, I remember," he said with a smile. "But you straight-up panicked when I tried to get you back to your hotel."

The moment in the alley came back to me. When Jack was about to call me a car, moments before I passed out. It had freaked him out.

"I didn't want to say goodbye to you," I said.

A silence passed between us. Then Jack snorted. "Give me a break."

I laughed. Always on the same wavelength. "I guess we're both avoiding things, then?"

"I'm not avoiding anything," he said defensively.

I raised an eyebrow. "Gap year?"

"Excuse me. I'm using this year to gain real-life experiences before I become a coddled college kid."

"Give *me* a break," I said, pushing him.

A family nearby looked over at us and I pulled the brim of my hat down.

Jack adjusted his position so that he was blocking me. Phew.

"Actually. I don't think I'm going to college," he said.

I startled. "Oh," I said, not sure how to respond. "Why not?"

"I don't think there's any point," he said, exhaling, as if he'd been holding in this information forever.

As a K-pop star who was barely getting a high school education, I couldn't really say anything. But something nagged at me, regardless. "You're too smart to think that."

He made a face. "Only college students are smart, then?"

"No, of course not," I said. "But I think that saying there's no point to going to college is one of those overly simplistic statements that people say."

"Wow," he said, straightening up and visibly annoyed. "Maybe I'm one of those simpletons."

"That's not what I'm saying!" The friction between us was not what I was hoping for on this sunset boat ride. I sighed and decided to start over. "Why do you think there's no point?"

He was still tense, his hands tightly folded in his lap. "College is archaic. It's no longer relevant to getting what you want in life. Look at people like—"

"Please don't say Steve Jobs, ghost of Steve Jobs," I said with a smile.

Despite being rudely interrupted, he grinned and went on. "Yeah, Steve Jobs. But also like, a billion other people out there. We're all stuck in this mind-set of what's normal and expected. And it's kind of . . . unevolved."

"Okay. But that comes from a place of luxury, you realize?" For so many people, college was an unachievable dream. For K-pop stars, college meant a potential end to your career, your relevance.

He sighed. "Of course this is coming from a place of luxury. I fully understand that. But part of this privilege *is* having other options? And I'd rather explore those. Life is short, Fern. Why waste time on something that's not a sure thing?"

I stared out into the water, reflecting the fiery red sky now. The sun was low, dipping below the horizon, hazy from the smog but still gorgeous. Life was short; he was right. I felt like we were somehow having the same argument all day and I wasn't sure how to break out of it.

"Nothing's a sure thing, Jack."

I thought being a K-pop star, the best K-pop star, meant something. I don't know. Fulfillment, happiness. But not only was the goalpost always moving, you found out that the stuff that made up your dreams could be dark, hard, and lonely. And if you complained, if you stopped, it was like you were quitting. And I wasn't a quitter. My family hadn't spent four years FaceTiming me on their birthdays and New Year's so that I could give up.

I also knew that *The Later Tonight Show* would be a turning point. If all went well, maybe I'd have more trips to the US. Nothing was ever promised, but I still hoped. I needed to hold out for a bit longer, and things could change.

He shrugged. "Maybe not a sure thing. But there are certain things that are patently true: Money gives you security and freedom. Life is easier with it. And there are much faster ways of making money than going to college."

When you're a K-pop star, you don't make money right away. It's a long process, where you have to earn back the money the company has spent on you, to make their investment worth it. But even after that, even after being at the top, you're scrambling to stay there. "I think you're putting too much faith in financial security," I said.

Jack threw his head back and laughed. Hard. "Said nobody ever."

I smiled even though this conversation made me kind of sad. Jack, with all his confidence and intelligence, was afraid to go after something he cared about. Holding on to his cynicism like a lifeboat.

We bobbed on, the sun completely dropped into the ocean, the air suddenly sharp with cold.

CHAPTER THIRTY-EIGHT

JACK

WHEN WE GOT OFF THE BOAT, WE FOUND OURSELVES surrounded by people.

"Oh crap, it's almost eight," I said.

Lucky drew in closer to me, away from everyone else's bodies. "Why is that an 'Oh crap'?" she asked.

"Because it means the light show's about to start. And every tourist in Hong Kong will be joining us here." We were at the Tsim Sha Tsui Promenade, one of the best vantage points to watch the light show.

Her entire body perked up, forgetting about the strangers around us for a moment. "What light show?"

We faced the water, where everyone was lining up on the concrete pathway. "See the buildings across the harbor? That's the Hong Kong Island side, and all the buildings will light up for us to watch with some music."

"Cool!" She tucked her hair into her coat and pulled down her cap.

"You're okay with being in this crowd?" I asked, uneasy. "It can be suffocating," I added hastily.

Indecision stalled her for a few seconds before she shook her head. "I'm fine. I can't miss out on this, right?" And with that, she was already headed toward a spot against the railing.

Yet another good photo op coming up. I had taken a couple great ones on the water, with the sunset blazing behind her, her face at peace. It was all very magical. That is, until we started that testy conversation about college.

Lucky squeezed into a crowd of people and something about that made my skin prickle. This could be a bad idea. People poured in from the subway station, and it was so crowded I could barely make my way to her. It was ground zero for tourists. Maybe even more so than the Peak tram. And the light show wouldn't start for another few minutes.

"Hey, want to get something to eat while we wait?" I knew food was the quickest way to distract her.

"Yes, please," she said. "Is there food here?"

"Yeah, I think there are some egg waffle stalls out here." I touched her elbow to guide her away. We approached a stall parked along the street, farther away from the crowds. The relief I felt as soon as we were away from everyone surprised me. Seeing her in crowds made me nervous. Scared for her physically, but also I wanted her to stay happy. Our day was so dependent on all these delicate mechanisms working perfectly to keep things running smoothly.

We got our egg waffles, a Hong Kong version of a regular waffle with crisp edges and soft "bubbles" in the middle. As suspected, Lucky relished hers.

"Ugh. Yum," she said as soon as she finished, licking the crumbs from her fingers. I was still working on mine and she stared at me.

I handed it to her. She finished it within seconds. "I love all Hong Kong food," she declared as she tossed the napkins into a trash can.

"I think you love all food."

She laughed, her teeth showing, her face glowing. God, she was ridiculous.

"LUCKY!"

The single word pierced through the air, cutting her laughter short, cutting all circulation to my heart.

A group of teenagers was next to us, pointing and whispering. One of them screamed out again, "It's LUCKY! AHHHHH!"

And then as quickly as her laughter was squelched, she was surrounded. I had never seen anything like it. A swarm of bodies rushed to her, their screams and cries filling the air. Their phones out snapping photos. People were touching her, reaching for her.

She was swallowed up within seconds, like a lone rock washed over by foaming waves, and I couldn't see her anymore.

CHAPTER THIRTY-NINE
LUCKY

MY SENSES WERE JAMMED. ALARMS WERE GOING OFF, wailing throughout my body.

I was trapped in a crowd of people that felt like it came together to form one organism of pure chaos. Pushing against me, pressed into me. Hands reached for my hair and my clothes.

"Jack!" I screamed, covering my face with my arms. When a stranger's clammy hand reached for my wrist I yelled, "Please, let me go!"

I was going to pass out. I was going to die in this crush of bodies. All I could think over and over again was that I brought this on myself. That my stupid impulse to have this special day was going to get me killed.

"Lucky!" someone cried into my ear. "Can I get a hug?" My head whipped toward the voice. It was a man, his arms reached out for me.

Every part of me recoiled, and when I spun around to get away from him, my hat tumbled off and I could only watch as it rolled away—trampled immediately.

I closed my eyes and yelled out one more time.

"JACK!"

CHAPTER FORTY

JACK

I RAN TO HER. PUSHING THROUGH THE BODIES. Unthinking, staying focused on her voice.

"Jack!" I heard her yell again.

I couldn't find her; I couldn't reach her. Adrenaline pumped through me as I shoved people aside. It wasn't only the group of teenagers anymore—it was dozens of people. People who had heard her name and come running. I could almost feel her terror, the panic woven through the chaos of the crowd, reaching out to me.

Nothing mattered anymore except getting to her.

"*Move!*" I yelled. "Out of my way!"

"Jack!" Her voice was so close. I stepped on something and when I looked down, I saw that it was her hat. A panicked energy coursed through me from seeing the familiar green object trampled, propelling me forward, moving people effortlessly.

Finally, my eyes found hers and I saw the fear pulsing in them. "Lucky!" I yelled, going to her, not thinking about using her real name. I saw the fear transform instantly into shock.

But her hands still reached out to me and I grabbed them, swiftly and tightly. I pulled her to my chest and she tucked herself into me, popping her jacket collar up toward her face.

The light show started, the music soaring into the night air, but the crowd still followed us. The neon beams tore through the fog of the harbor, the buildings taking turns dancing with every color of the rainbow.

Her entire body was rigid against mine, her breath hot against my shirt. My arms kept her close and I whispered into her hair, "I got you."

Now I had to get us out.

CHAPTER FORTY-ONE
LUCKY

HE CALLED ME LUCKY.

He knew.

He knew the entire time?

Or was it only this moment, when the fans found me?

The need to get out of here, to escape this, was stronger than any of my questions. I kept my eyes on my feet, the usual shuffle-o-concentration to get through the crowds. This time, Ren wasn't here with his team to threaten people.

But I did have Jack.

We were still surrounded by fans screaming and chasing us, and I was about to lose it when Jack said, "Ready?" I lifted my gaze from my feet to what was directly in front of us—a row of electric scooters with restaurant logos on them. Delivery scooters.

Before I could say anything, he was pulling me toward one and I climbed on it, glancing back at the group of people taking photos and reaching out for us. Jack yelled at them to back off and then jumped on in front of me. "Hold tight," he said.

If I wasn't so terrified I would find this over-the-top. Like, a scooter ride through a foreign city—are you serious? Was Jack Tom Cruise? Also, were we *stealing*?

With a sudden jerk, we were riding away from the crowds and I gasped, grabbing him around the waist before I could go flying off the scooter.

We wound through the narrow street, the fans growing smaller behind me along with the flashing of the light show, and it was so, so exhilarating. Without my hat, my hair was whipping everywhere, and I saw Jack bat it away from his face.

"Do you know how to drive one of these things?" I yelled.

"Sure!" he yelled back. "Well, kind of!"

We swerved around a couple crossing the street and they screamed as we drove by. Oh, God.

"*I* know how to drive a scooter!" I yelled. "Pull over!"

"What?"

"PULL OVER."

I felt his hesitation and I pinched him, hard. He finally parked on a side street. I slid off and motioned for him to scoot back. He grinned, his hair sweaty and stuck to his face, and then he did as he was told.

I sat in front and grasped the handles. "Hold tight," I said in a low growl, mimicking him. He laughed and did just that, his arms wrapped around my waist, his hands holding his elbows so that he was folded around me like an animal plushie with Velcro paws.

We pulled into the main road again, and I was careful to stay with traffic, following behind a particularly confident and competent taxi. "Where are we going?" I hollered.

"I'll navigate!" he yelled back.

So I followed Jack's directions, turning right here, left there, shooting down an alley. Colorful neon storefronts blurred by in a dizzying rainbow streak, and the delicious smells of food wafted over us in quick bursts. One second you'd get a whiff of salty grilled meats and then suddenly it was the sugar-laced scent of egg waffles.

Through it all, Jack's arms stayed hooked firmly around my waist, steady and strong. He leaned into me, pressed against my back. He surrounded me with warmth and a sense of security, even as I wondered if he had been lying to me the entire day.

Riding through the city like this, the wind in my face, the sound of the motor buzzing—I was able to focus on the acute feelings of this very second. Not thinking back and not thinking ahead.

"Let's pull over here," Jack finally said, his voice close to my ear. We were in front of a vintage shop lit up with small twinkle lights.

"This is it?" I asked as I parked curbside.

"Yeah. You need a disguise."

Oh, right. I felt the top of my bare head after we got off the scooter. Jack crouched down to look at the name of the restaurant on the side of the scooter. "I'll call the number to let them know where the bike is," he said.

"How did you even turn it on without a key?" I asked.

He shrugged. Suddenly, I wanted to throttle him. The adrenaline from earlier had died down and I felt rage replace it.

"Who *are* you? Did you know who I was this entire time?"

There was a split second where I could tell he was going to lie to me.

Again. But the hesitation turned into defeat, his eyes tired and his shoulders drooping. "I found out last night after you already passed out in my bed."

"Last *night*?!" I screamed. A woman walking by us did a double-take and I covered my face with my hands. I couldn't be spotted again so I walked into the vintage shop, the brass bell hanging on the door ringing as I entered.

Michael Jackson was playing quietly in the background and incense was burning, wafting over me aggressively. Incense was putrid enough on a *good* day.

I nodded to the owner in quick greeting and feigned perusing a rack of nubby cardigans when Jack walked in, the bell signaling his arrival.

He came over to me immediately. "Hey. I'm sorry."

I ignored him as I flipped through the sweaters, the skin of my finger-tips already drying out from the wool.

"I found out last night, but I swear I didn't know who you were until you were already at my place. And then after that . . . well, I kind of wanted to play along with the fantasy day you wanted." His voice was soft, and while I wanted to cave and be okay with everything, I couldn't. I was so comfortable with him and that comfort was because I thought he liked *me*. Not Lucky.

But it had been Lucky all along. Shame burned through me and I moved away from him, browsing through the clothes, my hands shaking. The exhilaration from the scooter ride was completely gone now, and I was standing here in some vintage shop with a guy who had lied to me all day.

"Lucky," he said. The name was new and unfamiliar coming from him and I hated hearing him say it.

I stared hard at the rack of sweaters. "I want to murder you right now."

He stilled. "Okay. Fair."

I flipped through the sweaters with a viciousness that the frumpy wool cardigans didn't deserve. "I feel stupid and betrayed." My voice was quiet, barely heard above the music.

His hands stopped mine from flipping through the hangers. "Don't feel stupid. I was lying to you. That's not your fault."

I looked at his hands. Part of me wanted to snatch mine away in a huff. But another part of me felt soothed by his touch and I was irritated by it.

"You're a good liar."

"So are you," he said.

That got an involuntary smile from me. "Yeah, I am, right? That's what happens when you're . . ."

"Famous?"

It was kind of embarrassing to say out loud. "Yeah." Then I looked at him, hard. "I can't trust you anymore."

He flinched. "I understand. But Lucky, I . . . I like you. Those feelings are real. Even if you can't trust anything else."

It was something people said in movies a lot. And as a viewer you were on their side, like, oh my they got themselves in *deep* with this but we know they love each other! Screw it all and throw caution to the wind and love him back!

But when you're on the other side of that? Nothing's that clear.

I shook my head. "I don't know if it makes up for it."

He moved his hand from mine and ran it over his face. Which was pale and drawn. "It's not an excuse. It's . . . the truth."

We stood there staring at the clothes, silent. Tension hung in the air as some old Céline Dion ballad filled the store. The earnest love song totally at odds with what Jack and I were going through.

"Tell me one thing," I finally said. "Did you agree to hang out with me because you knew who I was? Would you have suggested it if I was just Fern?" My voice shook as I looked up at him. Meeting his eyes, wanting to get to the heart of all of it.

CHAPTER FORTY-TWO
JACK

I KNEW IT WAS THE MAIN REASON WHY I DECIDED TO
spend the day with her. But I was attracted to her from the moment
we met, if I was being honest. K-pop star or no, I brought her to my
place because there was something between us. I had felt concerned
about her but also curious. As a guy.

So I told the one truth. "I don't know."

She let out a breath in frustration, but something seemed to ease
in her posture.

Watching Lucky get swarmed like that had done something to me.
The protectiveness I had felt over her today—as this celebrity who
would get me what I wanted—had shifted into something else.

"The thing is, until I saw you get mobbed, I wasn't fully aware of
what it actually meant for you to be this K-pop star." I took a breath,
feeling myself tense up at the memory of it again. "I found out last

night, yeah, but I don't listen to K-pop. No offense, but I'm not familiar with your music or fandom or anything."

That earned a shadow of a smile from her. "And when I saw you stuck in that crowd, I felt fear. Like a real fear that I haven't felt in so long. I wanted to . . ." This was going to be embarrassing and I looked down to say the words. "I wanted to be the one to save you."

Her silence went on forever. I felt myself drowning in it. Realizing that I had messed up. She wasn't going to let it go.

CHAPTER FORTY-THREE
LUCKY

IT WAS SWEET AND VULNERABLE OF HIM TO SAY THAT. But it was also maddening. I didn't like Jack because he rescued me. Because he was a shield. I had Ren for that.

I liked him because he saw me. He seemed to *care*. Not only about me, but about the people in his life—his family, his cranky landlady.

Also, he made me laugh and fed me.

I lifted my chin. "I like to think I don't need to be saved."

His head snapped up, his eyes on mine in a second. Searching for something—that little give he was hoping for. I didn't want him to see it. But it was there.

"However. I did need it then," I admitted. "I was putting myself at risk all day. I mean, I have a full-time bodyguard, do you know that? He watches my door when I *sleep*."

Jack shook his head. No, he couldn't know that. And even though I was furious with him, I still wanted him to know. To know me.

"Well, thank you for saving me. In that moment."

He blinked. Afraid to respond. The first time I had seen Jack so totally off-balance, not in control, since we met.

"Don't thank me," he finally said, his voice raspy. Fairly racked with remorse.

I reached for him, touching his arm lightly. "I want to thank you. And I want to grill your ass."

He laughed, and the sound filled the entire store with this palpable relief. I could feel the desperation from both of us to hold on to the feeling that had been keeping me afloat the entire day—the illusion of being a normal person.

His fingers trailed up to my wrist, pushing under my jacket sleeve to touch the skin underneath, then stayed there, right on my pulse. "I don't ever want to see you get mobbed like that again," he said. There was so much intensity there that my blood rushed out of my head and into my toes.

Then he smiled and added, "And I get why you were so insistent on wearing that hat."

"You only need one person to recognize you. Then the jig is up."

"Well, we better get you a proper disguise, then."

We flipped through some other racks of clothes, Jack pulling out one ridiculous thing after another—a sequined robe, velvet overalls, a furry skirt. I decided on a giant lavender sweatshirt instead, and handed him my coat so I could try it on.

"Has that ever happened to you before?" he asked as I pulled the sweatshirt on over my shirt.

"Has what happened before?" I said as my head popped out of the sweatshirt, hair staticky and sticking up everywhere.

"You getting swarmed."

I nodded. "Yeah, a few times. The first couple times freaked me out so bad that I refused to leave my apartment for weeks. But the worst time was with Vivian."

"Your sister?"

I patted my hair down. "Yeah. She was visiting me in Seoul, by herself." It had been a big deal for my parents to send her over. The tickets were expensive and my sister was still pretty young. "We were at this amusement park, which I realize now was a bad idea. But Vivian had wanted to go so badly. And I was recognized there. It was awful. She got hurt."

"Oh no. How?" Jack asked, holding my coat in his arms. Like a patient boyfriend shopping with his girlfriend.

The visual was too much. I looked away from it. "A fan grabbed at her and she fell forward, onto her chin. She needed stitches."

Jack winced. "Ouch."

Seeing Vivian's startled face before she hit the ground was the worst moment of my life. Spending a car ride with her while she cried, clutching Ren's rolled-up jacket to her bloody chin, was the second worst.

I nodded. "Yeah. Ouch."

"Hey."

I looked up at him.

He frowned, a deep groove appearing between his eyebrows. "You can't feel guilty about stuff like that forever."

Jack's ability to zero in on my thoughts was unnerving.

"Easy for you to say," I said, laughing hollowly. "There's this thing about being famous. It shines light on people around you, but it can also hurt them."

"With great power comes great responsibility?" he said, the corner of his mouth lifting in a sort of half smile.

Cute nerd. "Yeah . . . except . . . the power part isn't there." I knew how it sounded. Complainy. Ungrateful. Like, boo hoo poor little famous girl. I pulled at the sweatshirt and turned around to look in the mirror.

"I think you need some glasses," Jack said as he looked at my reflection. I looked back at him through the mirror. He gave me a thumbs-up sign and I couldn't help but smile.

We stood in front of a rack of plastic frames. Retro town. He turned the rack, making it creak loudly.

A pair of turquoise cat-eyes caught my eye. "Ooh, let me try those."

I pulled them on and peered into the small mirror sitting on the counter. They were cute, but more importantly, they obscured a big chunk of my face.

"Let me see," Jack said.

I faced him and he nodded. "Cool."

"Don't make some gross hot-librarian comment."

"Excuse *me*. I was going to say you looked unattractive."

I laughed as I pulled my hair back from my face, surveying my reflection to see how different I could look. "Glasses aren't unattractive."

"On you they're hideous. Sorry to say it."

"Thanks," I said, still grinning.

"You're welcome." He winked.

We grabbed the glasses plus a new baseball cap (black! Even more camouflaged than before!) and the sweatshirt. I gave the owner my trench as an exchange for everything—his eyes went wide when he saw the Burberry tag. "But this is worth way more than what you're buying!"

"Actually, it's the other way around. You have no idea," I said as I pulled the sweatshirt on.

He shook his head but held up the coat to admire it. I tucked most of my hair under the cap, leaving enough to look like a bob, and pulled the hood of the sweatshirt up close to my neck. Final touch, the glasses.

"Well?" I asked Jack as we stepped outside.

"Well, you look pretty bizarre."

I grinned. "Perfect."

"Want to go eat?" he asked. "Night market style?"

"Now you're just seducing me."

We walked down the street, our hands swinging between us, not holding each other's yet. I wasn't sure if we had hit reset on everything or what. In my new outfit, with the newfound revelations between us, it did kind of feel that way.

CHAPTER FORTY-FOUR

JACK

WE WERE GOING TO MONG KOK, A BIG MARKET DISTRICT in Kowloon. It was going to be crazy busy there but Lucky was pretty well disguised. And I felt like she needed to see it. It was a risk, but everything about today was. Why stop now?

With every step we took, I wanted to reach out and pull her closer to me. To have our hands touch. Something.

A part of her had drawn into herself again. Although her curious energy was still there, excited to see and touch everything, she was different. Wary and subdued.

I couldn't blame her. Something like relief had flooded me as soon as she knew I knew. It wasn't exactly how I wanted her to find out, but I was glad it was out there. And her reaction had been better than I thought it would be.

Well, her reaction to one part of the story. My phone had buzzed in the shop.

Info is leaking out about a Lucky sighting at the light show. What happened?? We better not get scooped.

A part of me wanted to toss my phone into a trash bin and forget the story, forget the hustle for once. But this would ruin all the work I had done the past few months—building Trevor's trust. Without the job at the end of all this? Nothing.

So while Lucky was walking ahead, I texted him back: **We managed to escape. Getting photos at Mong Kok. Don't worry.**

We could hear and smell Mong Kok before we saw it. An endless maze of stalls filled streets lined with stores, selling every kind of good at the bustling Ladies' Market—mostly touristy souvenirs crammed into the small spaces, the wares hung along the metal frames of the stalls. Walking through was slow going, with people stopping to shop and take photos.

I kept close to Lucky, hovering over her obnoxiously. She didn't seem to mind. Despite her new disguise, she looked nervous and walked closer to me.

"Wow. This is intense," she said.

"Yeah, it's definitely a tourist favorite. But you can't leave Hong Kong without having seen it," I said. "We're about to enter the food market. There's so much good stuff to eat there."

She was already walking ahead of me to get to the food stalls—led by her nose, it seemed—a poised figure even in an oversized sweatshirt. That's what I had been noticing about her since we met: Some people have a star quality. They radiate something otherworldly. It's not only that they're attractive, there's a magnetism and presence. And Lucky had it.

Doing the work that I did, I didn't get starstruck. In fact, the closer to celebrities you got, the more they lost their luster. Star quality or not. They showed some petty or unkind behavior that made your soul shrivel up. Like Teddy Slade and Celeste Jiang yesterday. Nothing like seeing a guy in his bathrobe cheating on his wife to tarnish that luster. After enough incidents like that, I had become immune to their glamour. They became another story to chase.

Obviously, this was different. *She* was different. And the weird waffling going on in my head right now was super unpleasant.

"Jack!" Lucky called out to me, waving her arm to beckon me over to her. She was at a seafood stall, pointing at some crabs in a plastic tub. "Totally fresh. Should we try them?"

"Hm." I stared at the small blue crabs, their claws banded with tape and crawling over each other. Just trying to live. How could I explain to her that picking out my seafood when it was alive depressed me? Without looking like a total sheltered American weenie?

"You don't like crab?" she asked.

One of them fell over and ended up on its back. The other crawled over it, trapping it. Tragic. "I'm allergic to shellfish, actually."

She frowned. "That is so sad." To my relief, she moved on, and when she did, she reached behind her to hold my hand.

A tiny jolt of excitement ran through me. As I wrapped her fingers in mine, I felt a surge of hope. She reached for me first. Was I earning back her trust?

Did I deserve to earn back her trust?

"Are you allergic to dumplings?"

I looked at the plump row of sheng jian bao she was pointing to. "Mmm, no, I love these."

"Good! They'll go perfectly with stinky tofu!" Lucky ordered some and I caught a whiff of the pungent tofu before I saw it on the menu.

Lucky was such an adventurous eater that she made me feel like a conventional bore. And maybe I was, to an extent. Today was the first day I'd run around the whole city like this. Everything was so much more fun through her eyes. She soaked in every experience, every molecule of it.

We grabbed a few other eats—a stick of fried pork intestines, curry fish balls, and egg tarts.

"Let's go find a spot to sit," I said, trying to balance all the food in my arms. A few minutes later we came across a group of low tables with colorful plastic stools scattered around them.

We were surrounded by people, but no one was paying any attention to us. Lucky was relaxed; the disguise seemed to be working. I wished we had thought of it earlier. We ripped into our feast messily with our bare hands, using almost the entire box of tissue paper that had been placed in the middle of the table.

"So. I have some questions," I finally said as she finished inhaling some pork intestine. I figured the best time to get answers was when she was full and happy.

She nodded. "I'm sure you do."

I leaned forward on the small table, our knees touching, my elbows pushed close to her. "Why are you doing this?"

"Eating pig innards?" A smirk.

Despite wanting to lunge across the table and kiss that smirk off her face, I resisted. Stick to the story. "Lucky."

"Jack." She moved her arm across the table and stuck her index finger into my cheek. Making a dimple. "Our names both have *ck* sounds in them."

"Wow, you're *really* avoiding the question," I said with a laugh, her finger still poking into my cheek.

She pulled away. "I know. I wasn't sure why I was doing this at first. But now, I think the simple answer is . . . because I want to?" The noises around us grew louder and I could barely hear her. So I scooted closer. She smiled and scooted closer, too. "Yeah, I wanted to. Today's my last day before everything."

"Everything? Because you're going to be on *The Later Tonight Show*?"

She raised an eyebrow. "So you know about that?"

Heat flooded my face and I could only nod in response.

"Yeah, *The Later Tonight Show*. The *everything* of becoming a Western K-pop star. If I succeed, it's going to be next level crazy. The stuff that I find intense about my current situation is only going to get so much worse," she said, her words picking up speed. "And if I fail? That'll stop the Lucky train right in its tracks. *Poof* goes the top spots everywhere, endorsements dropped, my managers will move on to the next shiny thing." It was pouring out of her. Everything. The entire story.

Her stool scraped against the ground, her body moved back. Giving space to all the words.

I clasped my hands under my chin. "So, first. Let's assume you succeed wildly. What's so nuts about your current situation? Other than the fact that you're some huge star. I don't know much about K-pop."

A long time passed before she answered. "My life is not my life." That soundbite, Jesus. Perfect. Her expression grew stony. "My life is scheduled down to the minute. It's been that way since I was a kid. Because it was what I wanted to do, I was happy to forgo the normal kid things for it. But I thought, at one point, I'd get a break. I keep thinking, *When I get this,* or that, *or reach some other thing, I'll have that freedom.* But it never *comes.* And I'm freaked out that it never will." Her voice cracked and her posture tensed.

I reached over the small table and tugged on her sweatshirt sleeve. Reaching for her. She instantly came in closer, pushing her hand out of the sleeve to hold mine. Like a reflex.

We were so into each other it was ridiculous. It never failed to surprise me every time I noticed it.

"I'm sorry," I said. It was the only thing I could say. And I meant it. About her life, the difficulty of it. And for today. For the lies I told, for the lies I was still going to tell.

She took a deep breath. "And it isn't only that. It used to be so fun for me. But somehow, even though I'm doing the same thing—recording albums, doing concerts, videos, et cetera—it's changed. I don't *like* it that much anymore." Her hands left mine and picked up a tissue, twisting it into a skinny rope. "I know I'm an ingrate to complain. This was my dream, what's my problem?"

"It was your dream?" I asked. I realized I had no idea how she got into this. Why she did it. The church choir subtext only told me part of the story.

"Yeah, my parents didn't make me do it or anything. Every K-pop star you see out there? We're the same. Incredibly obsessed with becoming a performer since we were young. So, I trained for years as a kid, then auditioned. K-pop labels have satellite offices or auditions in other countries to find talent. They came to LA and I was determined to make it," she said, smiling at the memory. "Believe it or not, I'm a ham."

"Super hard to believe."

She kicked me playfully under the table. "Anyway. I drove my parents crazy with the obsession but they supported me, ultimately. They paid for vocal lessons, dance class, drove me around the city, and came to every meeting once I got signed. The day I got signed was . . . wow. It was a dream and I felt like, well, the luckiest girl in the world."

It was clear how much passion she had as a kid. Still had. It made her glow as she talked about it. And it confused me—her unhappiness in finally achieving her goals.

"Maybe you need to reevaluate what your dreams are," I said. The words surprised me—but I realized I had been thinking about this all day. Turning over her unhappiness and her fame in my head. As if they were inextricably connected with each other. I had assumed she was unhappy because she was forced into this. But she had wanted it at one point.

Lucky cocked her head. "What do you mean?"

"I mean, maybe you lost track of everything once you got on the Lucky train," I said, my voice higher, energized. "Maybe you can still have a version of this life. On your own terms."

A faraway look fogged her expression and I stared at her expectantly. Waiting for her excitement. Instead, her eyes grew distant and she pulled back slightly, barely noticeable. "It's impossible to do anything on your own terms in K-pop," she said, bitterness sharpening her words.

"That can't be true!" I was baffled by her defeatist attitude. "You have power! *You* are the asset to your label." I flinched at that word— that's what Trevor had called her.

"Jack. I'm replaceable. There are, oh, five thousand girls who are waiting to take my place," she said with a laugh. "Younger, thinner, better dancers."

"But you're you. And you're special," I gushed. Oh, God, I was really in it now.

Lucky laughed. "I am?"

"Yes," I said adamantly. I reached for her again. "It wasn't luck that brought you into this."

Her eyes shone bright under her new cap. A full minute passed before she spoke. "Well, then what's the deal with my name?" She smiled.

"Is your name actually Lucky?" I had to ask it.

"Oh my God, what do you think?" She swiped another piece of chicken and took a bite.

"Well, I don't know! What's your real name, then?"

"You can Google it."

"I don't want to Google it! I want to hear it from you, the star herself."

She made a *pfft* noise. "You sound like a journalist."

My stomach fell out of my body. I made a *pfft* noise in response. "You're not going to tell me?"

"Today is a fantasy day. So, you only know the fantasy. And that's Lucky."

There was something so sad about that. I shook my head. "Are you saying that you haven't been you? That you've been Lucky? Because, for me, you've only *recently* turned into Lucky."

She looked thoughtful as she chewed. "I think you're right. Today was a fantasy day *away* from Lucky."

"Are you saying I'm a total fantasy?" I waggled my eyebrows. I was expecting a specialized eye-roll or some kind of withering glance. But instead she blushed.

"I *am* a fantasy?" I couldn't help it.

"Well. Actually, yeah," she said, her face still pink. "I don't get to hang out with guys. Ever. And . . . you're a pretty good one."

It was crazy because sitting across from me was a literal untouchable star. And she was saying that *I* was a fantasy for her. She was probably the fantasy of a bazillion people across the world. And at the thought of *that*, my fists clenched. Like some chest-thumping caveman.

"You're okay, too," I managed to say. What the hell, Jack.

"You know, pop stars need to hear they're hot on occasion," she teased.

That was all I could take. I tipped my stool forward, my body stretching across the table so that I could cradle her face in my hands. Up close, Lucky had freckles scattered on the bridge of her nose and her cheekbones. She had a darker freckle on her chin. Remnants of makeup under her eyes. A very tiny blemish near her nose. Human through and through. Yet.

"You're unreal," I said, my voice so quiet that I could barely hear it myself.

And then my lips touched hers. Finally.

CHAPTER FORTY-FIVE
LUCKY

WHEN YOU GET KISSED LIKE THIS, AFTER A GUY SAYS IN a breathy voice, *You're unreal,* it's very hard to keep your head about you.

Jack was good at this. Truly, he was too masterful. The head tilt was perfect. The soft touch of his hands on my face. The pressure of his lips.

The stalls full of steaming food disappeared. The people sitting on the plastic stools around us melted away. The string of lights hanging over us dimmed. All that existed was Jack in front of me. Jack kissing me. This delicate and hungry exchange of breath. The sweetness and heat of it.

Then he pulled away and looked at me, eyes kind of bleary. "Um, was that okay?"

Lord, did I like, *flinch* or something when he Frenched me? Was I twelve years old?! "Yes! It's so okay!"

But the moment was lost. He looked a little embarrassed as he sat back.

So I got embarrassed. It hit me then how unusual this was—my first kisses being with this total stranger who I would never see again. I guess I had always imagined it would be with my first love.

I know that's some old-fashioned nonsense but when you wait this long for your first kiss you get *notions*, okay?

"When do you have to go back?" he finally asked, clearing his throat.

"I want to stay here until the last possible second," I said, voice quiet.

Jack relaxed. "I want you to stay with me until the very last second, too," he said.

I swallowed, out of nervousness. "I like being kissed by you," I blurted out.

Oh, it keeps getting better and better. Good job, Lucky. I wished my fans could see this. *Idols! They're like you! They don't know how to react to hot guys kissing them and make everything one billion times worse!*

But Jack didn't seem horrified by it. Instead, he did that confident smile thing that made me want to both pummel his body and throw myself onto his mouth.

"I like kissing *you*," he said.

The all-consuming goodness of these feelings was so startling, so real. How in the world was I going to leave this tonight? Not only my freedom, my fantasy day, but . . . Jack?

I had so much I wanted to say to him. To push him more about college. His life. His family. The connections between everything and how it led to him being here. It didn't feel fair that he knew so much about me, and yet remained so much of a mystery himself.

"Well, I'm glad we cleared that up. Kissing: enjoyed by both of us. Awesome," I finally said, after staring at his lovely face for a beat too long. But something else caught my eye.

BLAST. *No.*

It was the distinct hulking shape of the person sworn to protect me: Ren. And a bunch of other security detail with him. They were wildly conspicuous as they stood there in a dark-suited herd, glowering at everyone around them.

I was sure photos of me at the light show had been splashed all over social media by now.

LUCKY AND MYSTERY GUY IN HONG KONG

The thought of someone getting a photograph of us riding off on that scooter, though? That made me smile.

But now was not the time for fond reminiscing. "Jack!" I hissed. "We have to get out."

He instantly tensed up, every part of him alert and coiled like a snake. "Did someone find us?"

"Yes. It's my security. They're here. Don't be obvious, but they're over by the seafood stall where we were earlier."

Barely moving his head, Jack did a casual perusal of the entire market. When his eyes passed over Ren and the guards, his mask of polite boredom didn't budge. He was good.

"Okay, there's a big tour group about to pass them," he said in a low voice, reaching over the table to take my hand again. "In about thirty seconds. When that happens, we book it. Follow me, okay?"

I nodded. While my heart was thumping at the idea of being caught, it was also thumping at the hotness of Jack when he was like this. So very international superspy. It made me wonder about his extracurricular activities.

"You ready?" he asked.

When I smiled in response he frowned. "Why are you smiling?"

"Because I'm waiting for you to say, 'Do you trust me?'"

The frown remained. "I don't get it."

"Never mind. Let's get outta here."

He nodded. "Okay, wait for me to get up and then follow."

With our hands clasped between us, we waited. Then the large group of tourists stepped in front of Ren and the other guards.

Jack pulled me up and we walked directly into another large group of people, his hand holding mine so tight my knuckles were rubbing against each other. I followed him closely as we wove through the crowd. It wasn't easy—people were walking at a leisurely pace, stopping to get food, take photos, and look at souvenirs. I refrained from stampeding over them. When I glanced behind us, Ren was still there. He and the guards had spread out. Shoot.

"Jack, we *have* to get out of here," I said, pulling on his hand with irritation. He was barely paying attention, instead looking down at his phone and *texting*.

"Okay, we're leaving." He looked up and winked at me. As if that would calm me down.

But it did. Sigh.

I followed him through the crowd until we reached a street corner—still in the thick of the hustle and bustle. I looked behind us nervously. Ren was an amazing bodyguard because he could sniff out exactly what he was looking for; he always had a sense for the one weird guy getting too close to me. The uncontrollable teen who might do something she regretted in her frenzy. It meant he knew how to find me, too.

And as my eyes swept over the crowd, I found him. And he was looking at me.

"*No!*" The strangled cry got stuck in my throat as I felt everything slip away. My freedom. Jack. All of it.

But then Jack's voice led me back. "Get ready, Lucky."

I heard the taxi before I saw it—blasting techno music as it squealed to a stop in front of us. The young Asian driver stuck his head out— spiky black hair, tanned face, chiseled features, and a giant smile on his face as he hollered, "Get in, losers!"

CHAPTER FORTY-SIX

JACK

I WANTED TO WIPE THAT SMILE OFF CHARLIE'S FACE.

He was looking at us in the reflection of the rearview mirror, asking too many questions.

"How did you end up with this dweeb?"

Lucky laughed and I poked her as we bounced in the back of Charlie's no-suspension cab. "He took me back to his place when I was unconscious," she said.

"*Lucky!*" I yelped.

Charlie almost crashed the car into a divider. "You mean *our place?*"

Lucky looked at me. "What?"

I dropped my head back against the seat rest. "This monster is my roommate."

Her mouth dropped open into a small O. "Right. Roommate. Cab

driver." Then a strange expression came over her face. "Was there . . .
do you have . . . more than one bedroom?"

Both Charlie and I squirmed. This was why neither of us ever had
girls over.

She stared at me. "Do you guys *share a bed*?"

"Not really," I said at the same time Charlie said, "Yup!"

I took a breath. "We take turns on the sofa and bed. So we don't
sleep in it at the same time! *Not* that there's anything wrong with that."
I held up my hands. "But Charlie is disgusting and I would only share
a bed with a man who had better hygiene. He works nights, as you
can see, so we sleep at totally different times."

The unsettled expression was still on her face. "Okay . . ."

"And you slept on *my* sheets," I said. "We change them."

Relief came over her features and Charlie laughed. "Let's not pretend you're not an eighteen-year-old guy, okay? Plus, he's *American*.
Much worse than me," he said with a wink.

Lucky leaned forward, her head popping up next to his. "I like your
accent."

"Thank you, lovey," he said with the exaggerated British accent he
used to hit on American girls. Her giggle made me harrumph. "I have
to say, it's surreal having you in my taxi right now. Not to be a total
fanboy about it, but I know your music. My ex-girlfriend used to be
quite obsessed with you."

Weird. I knew she was famous, but famous to people in my life? I
guess I had ignorantly not considered it.

Lucky laughed in response. "That's sweet. It's also surreal for me—
being in a Hong Kong taxi unsupervised with two guys I barely know."

Charlie glanced at me in the rearview mirror. "What's the story?

How did you get mixed up with this guy? I got an SOS and then suddenly I've got *you* in my taxi!"

Lucky glanced at me and I answered him, "Well, I found her drunk off her mind on the bus last night. Rambling about hamburgers in Korean."

She hit me in the arm. "I wasn't drunk!"

"Why do you keep saying that? You were completely wasted." It was kind of odd at the time. As I said it now, it occurred to me how dangerous it was, especially given how she was fodder for fans and paparazzi alike. I didn't like it. It made me clammy to think of something happening to her.

"I *was* out of it," she said with a rueful smile. "I had taken my sleeping pills and meds and I should have been in bed." The words came out haltingly, and she looked straight ahead at the traffic.

Both Charlie and I exchanged glances in the mirror.

"What kind of meds?" I asked, trying to keep my tone light, not too inquisitive.

"Uh, it's something for my anxiety." Her shoulders tightened, making her body small again. Willing herself to turn into a pinprick of light.

I touched her back, lightly and out of Charlie's line of vision. "Ah, okay. Well, that explains it," I said brightly. "Interesting time to head out looking for a hamburger."

She looked at me, tucking her nose into the crook of her elbow. Her eyes searched mine for judgment. I smiled at her, keeping my hand steady on her back.

"I was hungry," she said with a muffled laugh, relaxing.

"Have you had that hamburger yet?" Charlie asked abruptly.

"No!" she exclaimed, already excited.

"Let's remedy that, shall we?" Again with the ridiculous British accent.

Charlie made a sharp left, almost tilting the car on its wheels, careening widely. I grabbed on to Lucky, making sure she didn't pitch forward.

"Charlie!" I barked.

"This is typical Hong Kong style, Lucky," he said, his voice proper and didactic. "We'll get you where you want to go. Faster and better." He threw her a wolfish grin.

"For God's sake," I muttered. "Does that line work on all the girls you pull in?"

"You pull in a lot of girls, huh?" Lucky asked as her gaze skimmed over Charlie's pretty-boy face and the intricate network of tattoos that peeked out from his shirt collar and wound down over his ropey arms.

"Bad boy" personified. Ava lost her mind whenever she visited me, unable to look him in the face without blushing.

I scowled. "Hey now. Nothing compared to me."

Both of them cracked up.

We ended up at a popular spot for expats, home to the best burger in the city. I clapped Charlie's shoulder when he parked. "Thanks, man."

He started to unbuckle his seat belt. "You think I'm gonna pass up a burger with *Lucky*?"

My mouth dropped open. "What? You're coming with us?"

"What do you say, Lucky? Am I allowed to join for a quick bite?"

She grinned. "We'd love to have you."

I was *not* into this cute banter. "Don't you have to work?" I snapped.

"I've got my own hours, mate," he said, clapping *me* on the back as he got out of the car.

We walked into the tiny restaurant, filled with colorful stools and graphic murals, finding ourselves a corner booth. Lucky looked nervous in the brightly lit space and pulled her cap down over her hair.

"Luck—I mean, Fern. Look at me for a sec?" I said as I slid into the spot next to her. She turned to me and I tucked a few errant strands of hair back into her cap. Then I pulled the hood up closer around her chin.

She looked at me after I was done. "Good?" she asked nervously.

"Perfect," I said with a smile.

"EH HEM!" Charlie shook out the laminated menu from across the table.

She *was* perfect, though. Not because she was Lucky, the music video goddess, wearing heels that could kill a man. But because she was so excited by the world around her. Because she was making me see Hong Kong through her eyes—a city that, while cool, had felt foreign to me for the past year. She added this warmth to every spot we had visited, a wash of golden light. Everything tasted better because of watching her eat it. Everything looked beautiful because she walked through it.

Jesus. What was I going to do?

CHAPTER FORTY-SEVEN
LUCKY

WHEN JACK LOOKED AT ME LIKE THAT, I WANTED TO throw it all away and stay with him in Hong Kong. Forever and ever, amen.

The desire to call up Joseph and Ji-Yeon to say "Smell ya later" was so intense when I was with him. To imagine myself sleeping in. Having nothing planned for a weekend. A thousand more days like today stretched out in front of me—a glittering sea of possibility.

My chest literally hurt when I imagined it, the longing was so acute and real.

The hamburgers arrived and the scent made my mouth water, even though we had eaten a medley of meats only half an hour earlier. My first bite nearly launched me out of my body and into a heavenly realm of orbiting hamburgers. A toasted bun with substantial bread heft, gooey cheese, caramelized onion, and a thick beef patty that was cooked to perfection.

"Oh. My. God," I said when I could finally speak. "Yes. Yes, *this* is what got me out of that hotel room."

Charlie smiled as he munched on a French fry. "Worth it, right?"

"Worth a giant scandal that might cost me my career? Definitely."

Jack threw me a worried glance. "That's not true, right?"

I shrugged. I had tried not to think about it for the past twenty-four hours. I figured it was one day of rebellion after a four-year streak of model behavior. But now with the leaked photos of me and Jack—I wasn't sure I would come out of this unscathed anymore.

"Don't you know what a tight leash K-pop stars are on?" Charlie asked in a low voice, leaning over the table. "That's true, right? You guys can't have any scandals. And, not to be a total creep, but I know for a fact that your reputation up until today has been squeaky clean."

I smiled. "Yeah, you're not a creep. Most people who like K-pop know this."

Jack made a face like, *Guilty of not being a K-pop fan.* Charlie rolled his eyes. "You and your Soundgarden."

"Soundgarden?" I asked, surprised. Here I was, ready to throw it all away for some guy, and I had no idea what kind of music he listened to.

"Yeah, I'm kind of stuck in a nineties grunge nostalgia thing right now," he said with a sheepish smile. "How original, right?"

"Chris Cornell had a phenomenal voice," I said. "Soundgarden was so distinct during the grunge era because they were a straight-up, no-nonsense, hard rock band."

Jack stared at me. "What?"

Charlie laughed so hard people looked at us.

I sunk lower into my seat but looked up at Jack with a grin. "Do you get impressed by girls who have opinions about music? Get with the times."

He shook his head. "Remember Lina? She's the biggest music snob I know. I guess I'm surprised that you . . . that you would . . ."

I enjoyed watching him stammer for a few seconds. "You mean, surprised that I would know anything about music being *a professional recording artist?*"

"No! I mean—"

"You're not the first person to assume that K-pop artists don't actually know anything about music," I said, annoyed. "Most of us live and breathe music. We don't go through that training because we like the fashion." You could only see these kinds of surprised expressions so many times before it got tiresome, even on cute guys.

Watching us with glee, Charlie sipped on his soda.

"I didn't assume that!" Jack protested, nervously eating a French fry. "I guess I . . . didn't take you for a Soundgarden fan."

I nodded. "Yeah, I like Soundgarden. And Mariah Carey. And Cardi B. And One Direction. And Max Richter. And I could go on and on. Because I love music. That's why I do this."

Jack stared at me in this intense way and I stared back. "What?" If it was possible to smile and frown at the same time, he was doing it.

"Nothing. It . . . it's hitting me now that you are so freaking accomplished."

"It's hitting you *now?*" I teased, even as something lurched in my chest. I'd been praised pretty much my entire life, but hearing it from Jack—*a boy I liked*—well. That was different and new.

Charlie lifted his chin up at Jack. "Hey, you're also accomplished." He looked at me. "Jack's been moonlighting as—"

"*Charlie.* She knows about the wedding photography." Jack interrupted him swiftly and Charlie started. The two shared a silent look between them for about half a second before Charlie got a weird expression on his face and cleared his throat. "I'm gonna throw out our trash. You done, Lucky?"

I handed my tray to him while keeping my eyes on Jack. "What was that?"

"Nothing. Charlie's just being embarrassing. He makes fun of the wedding photography."

"Oh, that's not cool." I frowned.

He shifted closer to me, closing the small gap I had created. His shoulder nudged mine as he stared down at his lap and said, "I actually feel embarrassed talking about it. It's not like anything you're doing. It's a way to make money aside from the internship. It's not a passion or anything." He finally looked at me. "When you talk about music—I can *feel* it. Your focus and your love for it. I admire that and also envy it if I'm being honest."

"Thank you," I said quietly, unsure of how to respond to that sort of flattery. Also, I didn't want to bring up the photography issue again, but why couldn't he see *that* could be his passion?

We left the restaurant and Jack pulled me in close to him as we walked back to the car. With his arm around me, I dropped my head onto his shoulder, feeling immensely satisfied.

I had left my hotel room last night in search of a hamburger. And I had found it.

CHAPTER FORTY-EIGHT
JACK

CHARLIE STARTED THE ENGINE. HE WAS CONSPICUOUSLY quiet. I knew he was catching on to what I was doing. And judging me harshly for it.

His music blasted and while it was loud and horrible, it was also kind of nice. To avoid talking to Lucky, to avoid lying to her. I rolled the window down again, letting in gusts of air, feeling the thrum of the music. Not wanting to think, only feel.

"Where to next?" Lucky asked. "The night is young!" It wasn't quite ten o'clock yet.

Charlie glanced at me. "I don't know. Up to ol' Jack here. Seems like he's the one calling all the shots tonight."

Good one, Charles. Subtle.

As my body thumped with the bass blasting through the car, I had an idea. "Dancing. Let's go dancing."

Lucky looked at me with surprise. "What? Are you serious?"

"Yeah, let's do it." I wanted to be in a space where we could avoid digging into the truth. Where we could forget everything and move ourselves through the night. "Charlie, you know a good spot?"

"You know I do," he said, already peeling out of our parking spot. We drove through throngs of traffic, the crowds getting younger and drunker as we got closer to our destination.

"Do you like to dance?" Lucky yelled at me over the music.

I yelled back, "Not really!"

She looked confused before shaking her head and grinning widely. "We're doing a lot of things differently tonight!"

We reached for each other's hands at the same time.

Charlie dropped us off at a club I'd been to once, in the middle of Lan Kwai Fong—party central for expats in Hong Kong. It wasn't my usual scene, but it was pretty much where you were guaranteed some dancing. And I was hoping Lucky would be less recognizable in a group of expats over locals.

The area was so crowded that Lucky recoiled as soon as she stepped out of the car. "Oh, Lord," she said.

"They play the best music. Don't be scared of the club rats," Charlie said, sticking his head out the window, right arm dangling alongside the door. Lucky eyed the crowd skeptically, and Charlie took that moment to grab me by the arm and bring me in close. "Whatever you're planning on doing, don't," he whispered furiously.

What a time for him to turn into some noble knight. "Don't worry about it," I said tightly.

He got a worried expression that was completely foreign to Charlie's usual happy-go-lucky MO. "I mean it. She likes you. She doesn't deserve it. And more than that—*you* like *her*. I've never seen you like this, Jack. Don't mess it up."

I glared at him. "Mess *what* up? There's nothing after tonight. Today is *it*."

He shook his head but before he could respond, Lucky had whirled around and tugged on my shirt. "There's a good song playing right now! Let's go!" she said, jumping from foot to foot in excitement.

"Thanks for the ride, Charlie," I said, shaking my arm from his grip.

Lucky came over and reached into the window to hug Charlie. "Thanks so much. For the hamburger, for saving us. For everything!"

Then the asshat planted a quick kiss on her cheek and said, "Don't mention it. Have fun. And you're gonna kill it on *The Later Tonight Show*. I can't wait to watch."

She looked surprised as he drove away, honking his horn and waving at us. I resisted flipping him off.

"How did he know about that?" she asked.

"I'm pretty sure he's a fan," I said drily.

"Don't be jealous," she teased as we walked to the end of the long line snaking around the bar.

"How dare you," I said with Lucky's mannerism.

She laughed, throwing her head back. "Well, if you were jealous of every fan . . ."

I frowned. It was true. There were thousands of dudes (and dudettes) who were probably obsessed with Lucky. Who memorized every angle of her face and body. Who imagined kissing her the way I had kissed her earlier today.

"Good luck to your future boyfriend," I muttered. I regretted it the second I said it. The word "boyfriend" clunked down between us, like an anvil. I cleared my throat. "Let's cut this line."

She protested. "No! I don't want to make a scene."

"It won't be a scene." I wove through the crowd with Lucky's hand in mine. When we got to the front of the line, I assessed the bouncer. He looked like he could crush me with one of his meaty fists. But he was fairly young, and seemed stressed out as he tried to keep the line in check.

I pulled out my phone and talked loudly into it. "Jesus Christ, Garrett! Where are you?" Lucky looked at me with wide eyes. I kept talking. "I'm at the club, but I don't see you anywhere. I don't have time for this. The meeting was supposed to happen *now*."

I pulled the phone away from my ear, feigning irritation, and barked at the bouncer, "Hey, is Sylvia in?"

He looked at me in confusion as two girls in short skirts passed him. "What? Who?"

"Sylvia!" I snapped. "I have a meeting with her and my freaking agent isn't here yet."

The bouncer frowned. "I don't know who that is, sir."

At "sir," Lucky giggled. I threw her a warning glance. She composed her features into a serious face. A serious face that looked bored.

"Ugh. Why are we even out here?" she asked in an agitated, lazy drawl. She got the rich-party-kid thing down. I raised my eyebrows. *Good job.*

"Bro, can you let us in already? This is getting ridiculous! Sylvia's gonna lose her *mind*!" I raised my voice. Lucky sighed heavily next to me, crossing her arms and tapping her feet.

Trying to wrangle a group of drunk dudes, the bouncer shook his head. "I can't—"

But Lucky walked up to him and put her hand on his arm. "Sylvia will thank you later." She smiled, using the full wattage of Lucky star power on him. He looked physically stunned for a second before waving us in.

When we slipped into the dark entrance, I pulled Lucky toward me. "You're good."

Her arms wrapped around my neck and she grinned at me, her eyes bright behind her glasses. "That was fun. Do you do this often?"

I didn't answer, reveling in the feel of her body so close to mine, her hands resting on the bare skin of my neck. The energy between us was buzzing and I was about to kiss her again when she jerked her head around and said, "Do you hear that?"

"Wh-what?" I stammered, my hands dropping from her waist.

She tilted her head. "Music."

I heard it then, tinny and echoing from a hallway to our left.

"'Total eclipse of the heart'!"

We looked at each other at the same time. "A karaoke bar," I said with a laugh. "I forgot they have that here. The actual club is downstairs."

She raised an eyebrow. "Well, let's not squander this rare opportunity."

"For what?" I asked.

A mischievous expression crossed her face—the same one that had been coming and going all day. And then she pulled me down the hall.

CHAPTER FORTY-NINE
LUCKY

IT WAS AN AMERICAN-STYLE KARAOKE BAR, NOT ONE
with separate rooms like in Korea. Small groups of people seated in
booths and scattered tables crowded the space. Colorful lights were
strung everywhere and there was a small stage where a middle-aged
Asian man in a panama hat was belting out the rest of "Total Eclipse
of the Heart."

He was both terrible and good, and when he finished, everyone
applauded thunderously. The man blew a kiss into the audience
before traipsing down the steps back to his table, where a group of
people high-fived him.

Something stirred in me.

"Are you sure you want to be here?" Jack asked, shifting his weight
next to me uneasily as we hovered at the entrance.

When we walked in here, I thought it would be fun to watch people sing. But being around people singing again brought a rush of emotions.

I want to make people feel how I felt when I listened to their music.

You can't help what you want.

There's a life that is quality and there's a life that is . . . empty.

Is it possible to have both? Freedom and this career?

Did what I want from music, from the K-pop industry, change?

I need to hold out for a bit longer, and things could change.

It all clicked into place. I wanted to capture that feeling again. The love I had for singing. For performing.

And I couldn't wait around for the perfect moment for change. Life was short.

This day was almost over for me.

"Yes, I want to be here. And I want to sing."

"What!" Jack whispered loudly. "You *can't*."

"Yes, I can." It was time to stop hiding.

I headed to the "DJ," who was set up in the corner by the stage.

"Fern!"

I ignored Jack and gave the DJ my song request. He gave me a thumbs-up sign. "You have one person ahead of you," he said.

Jack was fretting next to me. "Why are you trying to bring more attention to yourself?"

"Jack. It's okay, I'll be fine. Let's go get a drink." I led us to the bar, trying to distract him.

Jack was still tense when I ordered myself a drink. "Are you sure about this?" he asked.

"I'm getting a Coke!"

"I meant, the karaoke." He crossed his arms.

I grabbed the frosty Coke can handed to me by the bartender. "I'm sure, Jack. I promise. Thanks for the soda," I said with a grin before taking a swig, keeping my eyes on him.

He flushed and paid for the drink and guzzled a glass of ice water himself. "You're welcome." Then he reached over quickly and pressed a cold kiss on my mouth.

It was his silent support of my decision and I appreciated it. And enjoyed it.

We watched two women onstage sing along to "Crazy in Love." Then the duet slowly turned into a slow dance and the crowd whooped. They grinned, and at the end one of the women shouted into the mic, "We got married today!" More cheers were had and the bartender uncorked a bottle of champagne.

It was sweet. There was this vibe in the air—I had felt it the second we walked in. I liked this crowd. I trusted this crowd.

Then it was my turn to go up.

I gulped down the rest of my Coke and grinned at Jack. "Here I go." He tried to smile back but I could see the worry etched on his face.

I love you.

The words flew into my thoughts and I almost fell as I stared at Jack's now-familiar face.

Oh my Lord, WHAT?

I stumbled away from him toward the stage. *Lucky. You cannot. You cannot possibly have those levels of feeling for Jack.* I barely knew him! I was . . . caught in the throes of today. The romantic veneer of it. That's all.

The confusion and tumult inside of me calmed the second I was onstage. The heat from the lights, the crowd of faces shrouded in darkness, the microphone resting in its stand in front of me. Even though the stage was tiny, it felt familiar.

And I had the nerve to choose one of my own songs.

When I had gone up to the DJ, the word had tumbled out of my mouth, unplanned. I thought that I was trying to escape Lucky-the-K-pop-star when I agreed to spend the day with Jack. But in all honesty, I was looking for the real version of myself all day. And, as unhappy as I was, the real me was still tied to K-pop.

I needed to test myself right now. Sing "Heartbeat" after everything I had gone through. See how it felt. What was different.

The music started and the monitor lit up with the lyrics. I ignored it, of course.

At first, I sang "Heartbeat" like I had been doing at my concerts— going through the motions. Going on muscle memory, keeping every note perfectly to the way it sounded on the recording.

I found myself doing a compacted, abbreviated version of the dance moves, too, keeping my microphone on the mic stand.

Someone hooted in the crowd. "Lucky!" I could see Jack sit up straight and look at me in shock. Good gravy. Jack didn't know my biggest hit. It made me smile.

A few people tittered.

Yeah, haha, I kinda sound like her, right?

I remembered when this song was fun. And wow, were these dance moves easier in sneakers. My limbs relaxed, my voice grew louder.

When the chorus came in, I grinned because I was going to go for it. These people had no idea.

The choreography here required a vicious hair flip, so I did it, sending my cap flying off, my hair unfurling.

Then I threw off my glasses and shot my signature smile and wink into the crowd, directly at a girl in the front row. I saw her tortilla chip drop onto the table.

And for the first time in over twenty-four hours, I was Lucky again.

The murmurs in the crowd grew louder and people started taking photos. For a split second, I felt panic set in. It was instinctive, I realized. This fearful reaction. I'd let myself get controlled by it, withdrawn from my fans. And my reasons for doing this—for them, for me—had been buried.

I was so done with hiding out. Pretending to be someone I wasn't. Tucking away parts of myself under a baseball cap.

I had been myself and not been myself.

I closed my eyes and sang at full force, using the voice that I used to unleash in auditions. In the shower. In concerts for school, for church. It had been gone for years.

When I opened them, I saw a figure standing in the middle of the flashing lights.

Jack. Watching me, mouth dropped open.

The shape of him was so distinct to me now. The broad shoulders, the loose way his arms hung by his sides, the slight tilt of that head— all as familiar to me as someone I had known my entire life. A day with this guy and he had burned himself into my bones, the stuff that ran through me, the stuff that made me a living being.

He had encouraged me. Believed in me. Made me examine myself, all the fears I had hidden deep inside.

The music was familiar, but this feeling was new. I sang the chorus, the only English words in the song:

I miss our heat
I miss your heartbeat-beat-beat
All the ways I wanted to show you
How to thank you

When I sang them here on this stage, looking at Jack, suddenly it was a brand-new song. And the way I sang it was new. I dropped my voice down a few octaves, entering a husky range that I never got to use. I slowed down the words the tiniest bit, dragging out syllables, finding different meanings in every single line.

His eyes never left my face the entire song; I felt them when I danced across the small stage. I saw them when I looked up.

When the song ended, I didn't dangle my head like a rag doll, a pose that insisted on my vulnerability and submission. Instead I stared out into the audience, directly at everyone. And smiled.

The room erupted in applause and wild cheers. "ANOTHER ONE, LUCKY!"

Jack whipped around, tense, ready to fight. But the crowd wasn't rushing me, it wasn't demanding anything from me except another song. They were with me, and I was with them. A silent agreement between us—this was special. Let's stay right here in this moment, in this place that no one else knows about.

It was a rare moment that they happened to stumble upon. They didn't know how much it meant to me. How much I needed it.

I'd never had it before. This was a different way to connect with people through music. Not through seven million views on YouTube. But in a quiet, dark bar.

I felt elated. Weepy. Powerful at the realization.

So I sang a couple more songs, not caring that people were recording me, probably uploading this to the Internet. Bringing my company and security guards closer to me with every passing minute.

It was worth it to perform on my own terms after so many years of accommodating everyone else.

I felt like I was brought back to life. *Welcome back.*

CHAPTER FIFTY

JACK

I FULLY UNDERSTOOD AT THAT MOMENT, WATCHING Lucky onstage, why K-pop stars were called idols.

As she stood up there in a baggy sweatshirt singing with the confidence of a superstar, she was unearthly. I, a mere human being, felt unworthy to be in her presence. I wanted to drop to my knees and beg for her to stay. Anything to be in the same city with her, on the same *planet* as her. To share air with this creature.

And I had no idea why she did this. But I knew it was something brave. I had urged her to reevaluate her dreams. And as she had done her entire life, Lucky rose to the occasion.

In spectacular fashion.

When she finished, she was looking at me. The cheering people around us turned into a fuzzy mass. I wanted it to be only us two so badly.

I walked over to the stage immediately after the applause died down, trying to get to Lucky before people swarmed her. But they didn't. They watched us as I reached for her. As she gripped my hand and jumped off the stage.

"I think we need to go," I said, my eyes sweeping over her flushed face. Feeling a little shy. Feeling like I was in the presence of someone *famous.*

She nodded. "Yeah, let's go dance."

I startled. "What?"

"There's not much time left," she said simply. Without any of the drama the words insinuated. "They're going to find me now. Let's spend every last second enjoying it."

Something in my chest tightened. A knot of melancholy and regret. Why did she do this if she knew that's what would happen? But deep down, I knew it was selfish of me to think that. Like she had done on that stage, Lucky was taking control of the situation.

Even if she had been loopy last night, she had left her hotel room for a reason. And something about this karaoke performance—I think she found her reason. It was time.

A few people approached us as we made our way out of the bar, but it wasn't scary or aggressive. They were being polite, giving her high fives. Expressing their excitement at meeting her.

One young woman stood up and asked, "Could I get a hug?"

"No," I said, moving between her and Lucky.

Lucky touched my arm. "It's fine, Jack." She shot me a smile, a reassurance that it actually was.

I stepped back, feeling like some kind of overbearing busybody. Lucky stepped toward the girl and enveloped her in a tight embrace.

The girl closed her eyes and whispered loud enough so I could hear it, "Your music changed my life. Thank you."

The two hugged for a few seconds, and I looked away from the intimacy of it. I remembered our argument earlier in the day about living a life that was quality. When she said it, she wasn't talking about her own life. But she didn't realize she was living it.

When we walked away, I held Lucky's hand tighter than before. I saw it now. What her music did. It wasn't simply entertainment. Although that was reason enough to do something. It gave her fans something valuable.

The sounds of the karaoke bar faded away behind us and we walked downstairs into the main part of the club—which was also alive with music. But not the echoey drunk sounds of people singing out of crap speakers. Instead it was the body-thumping, brain-melting beat of sexy dance music. Projecting the sensations and rhythms of bodies out into a room full of people. Everything neon and pulsing.

"Do you want a drink first?" I hollered near her ear to be heard.

She shook her head, her eyes focused on the mass of bodies in front of us. "No, let's dance."

The ocean of people seemed to part for her as she led the way. And I was helpless to do anything but follow her.

CHAPTER FIFTY-ONE
LUCKY

THERE WAS SOMETHING DIFFERENT ABOUT JACK AS I pulled him onto the dance floor. There was something different about *us*. Maybe it was the dark, or the music taking over our senses, or the palpable end of the day looming over us like a gathering cloud.

Whatever it was, I welcomed it with every ounce of my being. Let the sweat drip off my face as I danced and danced and danced. Shamelessly ran my hands through Jack's hair, over his arms and chest. Spun in circles, got low to the floor, got close to Jack. Shuffled away from Jack.

Came back to him swiftly, pulling him close, kissing him now and again. He let me do everything. Let me lead. And he followed, matching my frenetic energy. When I moved across the dance floor, I felt his eyes watching me. Always watching me.

I wanted to dance forever. I wanted to be that person that Jack was watching forever.

I love you.

I love you.

I love you.

CHAPTER FIFTY-TWO

JACK

YES. THE DANCING WAS A GOOD IDEA.

I knew that Lucky didn't know what she looked like. That she was acting on pure feeling. Her eyes closed sometimes. Her hands raised above her head. Her voice singing along when she recognized the songs.

Even in this state of uninhibited freedom, she was a star. Her dancing was different from what I'd see online of her performances. Looser, more offbeat. Yet still unique and graceful and interesting. You could feel her communicating through her body.

People watched her and I felt possessive, hating myself for it. Lucky was for the world. But this Lucky? Today's Lucky was for me.

When her fingers grazed my cheek, when her lips met mine in the dark—I was lost. Unsure of where to go next.

CHAPTER FIFTY-THREE
LUCKY

JACK GOT US SOME WATER. I TOOK A LONG SWIG AS WE stood around a circular high-top table, away from the dance floor. The cold water was the best thing I'd ever tasted in my life. After I finished drinking, I rolled the frosty glass on my forehead, then touched it to my hot neck.

When I cooled off, my senses returned to me and I looked at Jack, who was drinking his water in measured, tidy sips.

I had this sudden flash of him untucking his shirt. Smiling and giddy. In an elevator. "I recognize you."

His eyes met mine as he took another slow sip of his water. "Well, we did make out on the dance floor."

I flushed but shook my head. "No. You were in my hotel. In the elevator."

His expression didn't change, his reaction measured. "Yeah, I was. I think I witnessed you sneaking out of your hotel room."

The buzz from the dancing was still there, but now I also felt unsettled. "Why were you at the hotel?"

He didn't answer right away, his Adam's apple moving as he gulped heavily. "I was working."

I shook my head, trying to make sense of that. "Was there a wedding in the hotel?"

"Yeah. I have to use the bathroom. You okay out here for a sec?" He handed me his glass, fingers brushing against mine. Every part of me was attuned to every part of him.

I was a smidge annoyed but nodded. "Sure."

When he walked away, I stared after him. It was good and fine to forget about things as we danced, but now something didn't feel right. It occurred to me then that he never *really* let his guard down all day, he was always so careful with me. Mysterious in the places he wanted to be. Why Lina agreed to give me the shoes. How he was so good at getting us into this club. Even his interest in photography.

That's when I noticed he had left his phone behind on the table.

I knew it wasn't cool to look through his phone. What did it matter that he wasn't telling me everything about himself? Today was our day and that was it. If he had another girlfriend or was a felon—whatever it was, it wouldn't matter. I should leave well enough alone and keep today frozen perfect in my mind forever.

My hand reached for his phone anyway.

When I looked at the screen, there were a few missed texts from someone named Trevor Nakamura.

Where are you now?

Can you send me some preliminary photos so I can assess the quality of the story?

Story. Hm. Was he also a writer?

I couldn't believe Jack didn't have a lock on his phone. I almost wished that he did. When the phone unlocked easily with one swipe, I went straight to his photos. If there was a secret girlfriend, she would be in here.

Instead, there were dozens and dozens of photos of *me*. From today. Eating congee. Walking through the park. Looking terrified on the tram. At Victoria Peak. Reading a book. At the harbor. Trying on glasses.

Wow, he had been super secretive about taking these. Looking at the day through his eyes, I felt a warmth seep through me. He was a phenomenally talented photographer. Each photo was so beautifully composed, using lighting thoughtfully—whether it was sun or shadow. All through a bit of a besotted lens, if I were being honest. I smiled.

Maybe, like me, he didn't want to forget today. My heart beat quicker. Maybe he had deeper feelings, too. Maybe today didn't have to be goodbye.

The electricity between us on the dance floor had been so intense, I knew it had to mean more.

I was about to put the phone back on the table when another text from this Trevor person popped up.

Lucky's management has been in touch with us—wondering if we've spotted her. If I don't hear back from you soon I might tell them. GET BACK TO ME ASAP JACK.

A roaring in my ears deafened me. The words in the text swam in front of me.

Photos. Story.

What's your job, Jack?

Oh my God.

I couldn't breathe.

Jack's been moonlighting as—

I couldn't think, my senses overwhelmed by the pounding music, the stifling heat of the club, the lights flashing in sync to the music. From everything finally clicking into place.

I couldn't be here.

CHAPTER FIFTY-FOUR
JACK

THE COLD WATER FELT GOOD AS I SPLASHED IT ON MY face. I'd felt overheated for hours. I turned off the rusty faucet with a screech and stared at myself in the bathroom mirror.

Up until a few hours ago, I had been very okay with who I was. And then . . . then it all changed. Not only because we kissed and because she was lighting me on fire every time she looked at me. But because I had been justifying lying to her with this job opportunity.

But now? The job felt so insignificant next to my feelings for Lucky.

What is a quality life?

Stability? Passion? I still wasn't sure about all the details. But I knew one thing: A quality life involved caring for people. Being good to them. Being a good person *for them* in addition to yourself. Like your family. Friends.

Girlfriend.

I dropped my head into my hands, ruffled my hair, and looked up.

Figure it out. You've gotten out of every kind of sticky situation.

When I headed back to our table, I didn't see her. I looked around; maybe this wasn't the right table. But she wasn't anywhere in sight. Was she on the dance floor? I made my way over there, trying to find that lavender sweatshirt in the throngs of dancers. The crowd had thinned and I still didn't see her.

My palms got sweaty, my breathing shallow. Did someone recognize her? Did her security find her?

That's when I saw it. My phone. Sitting on a table.

No.

Shit, shit, shit.

I grabbed it and saw that there were no unread messages, but when I looked at my texts, there were a ton of new ones from Trevor. And they were *read*. The last one had said: **Lucky's management has been in touch with us—wondering if we've spotted her. If I don't hear back from you soon I might tell them. GET BACK TO ME ASAP JACK.**

The world stopped moving.

She knew. She knew and she had run away.

A fear gripped me that made me break out into a cold sweat. She not only knew, but she had bolted. By herself. Distressed.

In the city. By herself and without her disguise. I had a mental image of her being mobbed and the fear grew, tightening in my chest.

I had to find her.

I tucked my phone into my pocket and tried to get out of the club, getting stuck in large groups of people dancing or drinking. The dark sweaty room that had been so hypnotic and full of possibilities minutes earlier turned into a nightmarish maze. Bodies kept pushing and the music was so loud I couldn't think.

But I had to think. Fast. I was only gone for a short while, so she couldn't have gone far. I thought about cats—how if you gave them thirty seconds to get away from you, they found some obscure location to hide in, usually very close but near-impossible to find.

Look close.

When I managed to get out of the club, a chill gust of wind hit me and I took a deep breath. My brain flipped through all the possibilities of where she could be, whirring into different directions for each one.

I scanned the crowds in front of me—mostly hipsters and young professionals.

Food was always a possibility. There were small cafés open up and down the hillside streets. I ran and checked each street near the club—but no sign of that sweatshirt.

There was a chance she was walking back to the hotel. God, there were so many places she could be.

I needed help. I pulled out my phone.

"Stop being so obsessed with me," Charlie said when he picked up.

"Charlie. I can't find Lucky." I tried to keep my voice steady but it came out high-pitched and desperate.

"Did you lose her at the club?" he asked, voice loud as he turned down the volume of the music in the background.

"Yeah, she . . . she saw something and freaked out. When I was in the bathroom. It was only a few minutes ago but she could be anywhere and I don't know—"

"Where are you?" he asked.

Within minutes, the cab appeared in front of me. I jumped into the front seat.

"Well, you're a mess," he said cheerfully.

I dragged my hands down my face. "Thanks. I looked everywhere around the club. I can't find her."

I could feel his stare and sighed. "What?"

"How did she get lost?"

A crowd of people ran out in front of us, one of the girls wiggling her fingers at us through the windshield as she passed. Charlie didn't even notice, he was so fixated on me. I watched the girl strut down the street in a high pair of boots. Like the kind Lucky wore onstage.

"She found out something and . . . left me. Upset, I think."

I could barely hear Charlie's low-muttered curses. "I told you to stop what you were doing, Jack."

"Are you seriously *lecturing* me right now?" I smacked my hand on the dashboard. "She could be lost, or maybe mobbed again. She could be *hurt*!"

"Hurt by *you*."

What in the world! I looked at him in shock. Charlie and I never fought. He never got riled up enough to instigate anything with me.

"You were taking photos of her, weren't you?" That accusatory tone. "For Trevor?"

I nodded curtly. "Yes."

"*Man.*"

"Are you . . . *judging me*?" I said, incredulous.

He started the cab, driving at a snail's pace, which he never did. His eyes swept the streets and I realized he was looking for Lucky. "Yeah, I'm *judging* you. You know, when you started this job, I thought it was fine. Like, get that celeb money. I feel you. We have to hustle. But you know what? Ever since you started that internship, I've heard you complain about the ordinariness of your parents' lives. How you hate working at the bank and wish you could do something more interesting. But then something . . . *extraordinary* comes along, and you mess it up."

I was speechless. What the hell, Charlie? Since when did he care about me complaining? We were complaining buddies! Both of us broke and hungry for something else. It was our bond. I stared at him, my jaw probably scraping the floor of the cab.

"Having a chance to spend a day with a girl like Lucky? It's the magic, the adventure, the opportunity of a lifetime."

"Because she's famous?" I finally managed to say.

He made a sharp turn. "No, you fool. Because she likes you and you like her and that's special."

I wanted to jump out of the car with a "Screw you, dude." But under that impulse was recognition. That Charlie was right. That he had exposed what I had been feeling—like I was a lying piece of garbage who didn't deserve even a second of Lucky's time.

"Well, that's over now," I said quietly. "She's never going to speak to me again. I'm never going to *see* her again."

"Don't worry, we'll find her." His voice was firm, his eyes still searching around us.

It was reassuring even though Charlie was often confident about things that didn't work out.

The chaos of the day hit me like a ton of bricks and I leaned my forehead against the window, staring at the passing scenery, looking for that familiar figure.

Lucky finding out the truth was always a possibility. I had kept pushing back my real feelings for her when the idea started to bother me. I thought it would be okay for Lucky to hate me after today. That she didn't mean that much to me.

But now the thought of it made me want to die.

An actual human tear ran down my face, and I wiped it away before Charlie could spot it. Good God.

All I wanted at that moment was Lucky in front of me. So I could explain myself. So I could feel her warmth and infectious joy. Nothing else mattered.

And that's when I saw the cat.

CHAPTER FIFTY-FIVE
LUCKY

THE ONLY THING RUNNING THROUGH MY MIND WAS, *get away.*

As far away as possible from that bar and Jack and every bad feeling roiling through me right now.

I ignored the drunk dudes as I pushed through the bar-hopping crowds, gasping for air as I tried to hold back tears.

Someone yelled out, "What's the hurry, babe?"

It was nothing. Another drunk loser trying to talk to any girl who walked by him. But the word "babe" stopped me in my tracks. I turned around slowly and stared at the tall guy in the popped polo. He grinned, clamping a cigarette between his teeth.

Don't do anything. Ignore him. So I did, walking away.

"Bitch."

Every part of me wanted to sprint up to him and land a round-house kick to his face. Wanted to tear him apart with my teeth.

But it wasn't smart. A lone girl surrounded by drunk guys. This wasn't the time for that battle. I needed to get to my hotel. So I allowed him to live, the sting of that insult on my retreating back, and bit back tears.

The effort made my throat raw and I barely breathed as I stumbled through the crowd. Everything hurt. And it wasn't because some entitled creep called me a bitch.

Registering Jack's betrayal was so intense that I felt it inside my organs. Felt it eat away at everything good and pure and happy about today.

I thought of how much I had shown him. Exposed. How much I had given him. Not only a few kisses in dark places. A part of myself had been unlocked at some point today. A discovery of so many tiny and big feelings.

And that discovery had led to me risking my entire career with that karaoke performance. The triumph and clarity I had felt earlier was completely gone now. What had I done? What had I done because of some stupid guy? A guy I didn't even know.

The entire day flashed through my mind through a different lens. Everything I had enjoyed and experienced was now dissected and analyzed by a stranger with a camera. Because that's who Jack was to me now.

The streets grew quieter, and emptied out the farther away I went from the bars. The lights lining the steep streets burned yellow and were diffused in the fog that had rolled in from the harbor.

I wouldn't cry. I wouldn't be *that girl* crying in the street in the middle of the night.

Find me.

Even when I hated him, I wanted to see him.

I kept walking without knowing how the heck to get back to my hotel. What was the name of it, even?

Then I remembered who I was.

Be discovered. Then Ren would find me.

I took a few more shuddering breaths and straightened out my shoulders, feeling that familiar and practiced self-control pull me up toward the sky, like a string tugging on the top of my head.

I never cried. There were so many unshed tears when I missed my family. My house. When I was so tired I would have murdered someone to have an extra hour of sleep. I didn't cry then, and I wouldn't cry now.

I knew what I had to do. How to get out of this.

A group of people walked by me and I stared for so long that one of them, a petite Asian girl wearing an olive-green romper, scowled at me. "What are *you* looking at?"

American accent. Blast.

I moved on, smoothing down the front of my sweatshirt and fluffing up my hair. I headed back toward the bar, where it was more crowded, running down a steep set of stairs much too quickly. I dodged a couple making out against a lamppost, recoiling at the romantic scene.

When I reached the main road teeming with the late-night party kids, I stood there and took a deep breath, ready to expose who I was in some massive way. But before I could, something brushed against my leg.

I glanced down and saw a black-and-white cat.

It stared at me with green eyes and I recognized its stubby tail.

"Hey! You're the little buddy from earlier, aren't you?" It had been so many hours since I had seen him in front of Lina's store. Were we that close to it? I crouched down and petted him, setting off a purr machine. He flopped onto his back immediately, his paws curled up and his gaze fixed on something over my shoulder. I touched his downy fur.

"Lucky."

That low, quiet voice settled through the night air—heavy and buoyant at the same time. I glanced up and there he was.

Hands tucked into his front pockets. Hair completely messed up yet still somehow gorgeous. That stupid *Little Women* T-shirt, which fit him outrageously well.

Jack looked miserable and relieved and a million other things.

The cat bounced to its feet when I stood, prancing away from us. I stared after it, not wanting to look at Jack's face.

"Are you okay?"

The words were almost a slap to my face. He didn't care about me. How dare he sound so *concerned*.

"No, I'm not okay." I hated the tremulous sound of my voice. It wasn't from nerves, it was *fury*. "Don't even take one step closer."

There was a beat of silence. "Okay. I won't. Lucky, I'm *sorry*."

He knew the order of things: Ask me how I was doing. Apologize. He was good, that Jack. So good with people. I watched him get his way with everyone today, didn't I?

After a few steady breaths, I was ready to look at him again. His eyes were huge, his mouth tight with worry. *Blast*. Despite everything, I wanted to reach out to him.

"You were using me," I choked out.

Regret weighed him down, his shoulders dropping. "It was more than that."

"Shut up." I whispered it. "Stop lying to me. I'm so tired of it."

"I lied about some things. Not everything. You *have* to know that." The hoarse, pleading tone didn't placate me. It hurt. Everything he said was laced with the possibility of deception and it hurt. So much.

I finally started to cry. The tears spilled before I could stop them, uncontrollable and swift. Jack and all the lights and people around him blurred.

He was next to me before I could stop him.

"Lucky, please. I'm sorry." His hand reached out to touch my face and I jerked away before he could. When I wiped my tears and looked at him, I almost choked.

How dare *he* look wounded.

"You're exactly like everyone else," I spat out. "Using me. I never should have done this. It was a huge mistake because I was being manipulated by you from the first second we met. And now my entire *career* might be ruined over *you*."

"What?" He shook his head. "I know I messed up—but *you* made the choice to leave that hotel room. You can't blame me for your unhappiness."

I flinched. "Excuse me? The only unhappiness I'm feeling right now was caused by *you*."

Everything changed in his demeanor then. He tensed, a frown wrinkling his brow. "Lucky. You have to know that you're super unhappy. You hate your life."

"I don't hate my life!" I exclaimed. "There you go, exaggerating everything to fit your story. Is that the angle you were going for? *Miserable K-pop Star*? How boring. How utterly unoriginal." Venom spewed from me and I couldn't stop it.

His lips pressed into a line and he took a second before he spoke.

"It's the truth. Somewhere along the way, you started to hate this. But you can change that, do things on your own terms. You're a star. *You* have the power. The way you sang at karaoke—"

"Oh my God, you're naive," I blurted out. "You can't change *anything* in this industry. Okay, *Jack*?" I said his name in the most obnoxious American accent I could manage. Turning the energetic, boyish name into something mock-worthy.

"You're too scared to change things!" He finally raised his voice. A few people looked over at us.

I stepped away from him. "You don't know me. *At all*. And clearly, I don't know you. Talk about scared. You're too terrified to try *anything*. Scared of failing at something you care about." He blinked quickly, taken aback. I went on, "So what, is that why you've taken this trash job? As some lowlife *paparazzo*? Because it's easy?"

It was like I had physically pushed him. He staggered back a step. The distance between us growing with every word we hurled at each other.

He held up his hands, as if protecting himself. "Not everyone's born with your *gifts*, Lucky," he said. Even though his tone was measured, the emphasis made "gifts" a dirty word. "The rest of us living down here on planet Earth have to make do with what we have."

"What a load of crap." I laughed harshly. "You think that I didn't sacrifice almost everything to get where I am? It's not a *gift*, it's *work*. That's what you *do* when you have a dream, Jack. When you care about stuff. You *go for it*. You don't take the path of least resistance, and you don't give up!"

Recognition and hurt registered on his face. "Then you get it. Why I did everything so I could get this story. This is my big break, Lucky. I'm sorry. You were never meant to be a casualty of that."

Woo boy. I had to take a deep breath so I didn't scream. People were definitely watching us now. But I didn't care.

"How could I *not* be a casualty of that, you jerk? One, it would throw my career into total scandal! Two, you did *everything* to make me fall for you today." Again, that tremor in my voice. It negated the fury I was trying to use to hurt him back.

I thought I loved you. Even thinking back to those feelings filled me with burning shame. Talk about naive.

He dropped his hands and stilled, staring at me. Eyes searching my face for something. "I fell for you, too. I'm still falling for you. I'll *always* be falling for you."

The words were like butter. So smooth, so welcome. A balm for the wounds he left behind. It killed me to hear them, because I couldn't believe anything he said anymore.

This had to end.

"That's too bad, because I would never fall for a loser like you." The words came out like bullets, and I couldn't take them back.

CHAPTER FIFTY-SIX
JACK

WE HAD BEEN TELLING LIES ALL DAY. SO WHEN WE finally told the truth, it was like dropping a bomb.

Lucky's face was pale when she turned from me. Even though I felt like she had punched me in the gut, I wanted to reach out and comfort her. From the second I met her, I had been trying to make sure she wasn't hurt.

That's when I noticed people taking photos. Videos.

A tingly sense of foreboding came over me. The same feeling I had before she was mobbed at the light show. Lucky was walking away, straight into the crowd.

"Lucky!" I cried out without thinking.

And then the screaming started. "It's Lucky!"

"LUCKY!"

No. Not now.

She turned around to look at me, and I expected fear in her eyes, but there was only resignation.

People ran toward her, and I sprinted to get to her before they did. But I was too late. She was already surrounded. Fear coursed through me because that look in her eye had sent a chill down my spine. She wasn't going to fight them.

I fumbled for her. "Lucky!" Pushed through the crowd.

Suddenly, a strong pair of hands grabbed me by the shoulders and pushed me back. Hard. What the hell? I glanced up and saw a towering man in front of me. I recognized him. It was her bodyguard.

Within seconds, the crowd was broken up, and an army of men in suits had created a barrier in front of her.

Lucky on one side, untouchable.

The rest of us, on the other. Unworthy.

A giant SUV came to a screeching halt in front of us, and the group of men moved as one solid unit, Lucky somewhere in the middle of it.

"Lucky!" I yelled out uselessly. I knew she couldn't hear me past everyone else. I tried to bypass one of the guard's arms, but it was firm and impenetrable.

I couldn't believe it. I couldn't believe this was how we were saying goodbye. I craned my neck to catch a glimpse of her, to make her see me.

I needed to see her one last time.

For a second, as the crowd of men hurried over to the car, I caught a streak of lavender. My breath caught in my throat as the men parted and I saw her step into the car.

And then she looked up, straight at me. Her eyes unreadable, her face a perfect mask of composure.

The door closed, the car drove off, and she was gone.

The bus moved perilously through the streets. I was sitting on the upper level, front row. Like last night.

Also like last night, I had my phone clutched in my hands. This time filled with dozens of photos of Lucky. And a text from Trevor.

Meet me in the office. NOW.

I was being summoned. News had leaked of Lucky out and about in Hong Kong. Being paranoid and controlling, Trevor had demanded I hand the photos over to him in person. Once he saw what I had, I knew he'd offer me the job. There was no way he wouldn't. I'd gone above and beyond.

I had gotten a K-pop star to fall for me. To follow me anywhere. To tell me things.

It would be an incredible exposé, and the timing would be perfect with her American debut.

Too bad my excitement for the story was gone. A numbness had taken over me since I saw Lucky drive away. With Trevor's texts guiding me, I was on autopilot. I knew this was the right thing for my career. That to *not* do it would ruin everything that I had been building for the last four months. I'd have to go to my parents with my tail between my legs.

The bus lurched as it stopped at my destination. Central. Back where it all started. I walked through the wide streets, past glossy department store fronts, under a pedestrian tunnel running between giant buildings—and I saw Lucky everywhere. No corner, no alley in this city was safe from memories of her.

When I reached the office for Rumours, the lights in the lobby were harsh and cold. The security guard let me pass to the elevators.

It stopped on the twenty-eighth floor and the office actually had people in it even though it was past midnight. The celebrity news cycle was real. I walked by cubicles filled with people working late shifts and filing last-minute stories. They barely glanced up as I passed by. One of these cubicles might be mine after tonight.

The thought wasn't reassuring.

I rapped on the open door to Trevor's office, a spacious one with floor-to-ceiling windows with a view of the entire city. It was lit up in rainbow behind the glass, dreamy-looking in the fog. I could barely stand to look at it.

Trevor waved me in. He was on the phone, lounging on a black leather sofa, his expensive sneakers propped up on a glass-topped coffee table. Trevor always had the best shoes and I had admired them. He was in his late twenties, exercised like a fiend, was always on some paleo diet, and had a vintage pinball machine in his office. Trevor was kind of millennial goals.

I stood there awkwardly for a few seconds while he wrapped up the call.

"Hey! Jack!" he finally said after he tossed the phone onto the sofa, bouncing off of it in one agile swoop. "Word on the street is Lucky's back with her people safe and sound. Tell me you got something."

"I did," I said, holding up my phone. "I've been with her for the past twenty-four hours."

He whistled. "Wow, that lady-killer face of yours does a lot of good for us, huh?"

I smiled uncomfortably. "Well, she found out. So. She hates me now."

There was no sympathy from Trevor. His finely sculpted shoulders shrugged in his expensive sweater. "Tough luck. But you got the story, right?"

"Yeah."

"You did good. Maybe I'll even let you write this one."

I looked at him sharply. "What?"

He pulled his laptop over to the coffee table and motioned for me to sit next to him on the sofa. "You were the guy she spent the whole day with, hopefully spilled her guts to. You should be the person who writes this scathing profile, no?"

I sat down. "Scathing?"

"Of course. That's what's going to get us global attention." He tapped on his keyboard, not looking at me. "She's supposed to be this angelic girl-next-door, beloved by her fans. The South Korean *president* confesses to being a fan, too! She performed at his daughter's twelfth birthday party!" He turned the laptop around and I saw a photo of her posing with a preteen girl in braces, both of them making peace signs.

"So, let's see the photos." He held his hand out. I handed my phone to him after a second's hesitation. He plugged it into his computer and the photos populated the screen.

One by one, my day with Lucky was laid out in a tidy grid. Photos of her eating, of her looking, of her *doing*. Her face gilded by sunlight, mysterious in shadow. Happy, contemplative, curious. Each one twisted the knot in my chest.

"Oh, look at *that* one," Trevor said as he jabbed at the one of her leaning over the edge of the Peak, her hair fluttering in the wind, her face tilted up toward the sun. She looked so happy.

"She looks hot. That's an ass shot."

My blood ran cold. "You're not using that one," I clipped out, barely keeping my anger in check.

Trevor made a face. "What? Why not? And also, you have no say in what we use or don't use."

"Isn't this my story?" I kept my voice measured, even as an icy fury gathered inside of me.

Trevor kept scrolling through the photos. "Don't get ahead of yourself. Let's see what you got out of romancing this bitch."

Right.

I yanked my phone from the cable and the photos disappeared from the screen.

"What are you doing?" Trevor looked at me in shock.

I stood up, shaking slightly. "You're not getting these photos. Or the story. Or anything from me. Ever again."

Trevor laughed. "Excuse me?"

Lucky deserved better than this. Her words echoed in my head: *You're too terrified to try anything.*

She was right. I had taken this path because it was easy. It was safe. The work kept me at a distance from caring about anything. I let my fear of becoming like my dad keep me from figuring out who *I* wanted to become.

For the first time in my entire life, I saw things so clearly.

When I walked out of his office, I heard Trevor yelling behind me—that I'd never get work at any tabloid again, that I was *through* in Hong Kong media.

I kept walking.

Out of this office.

Down the elevators.

Through the lobby.

Into the Hong Kong night.

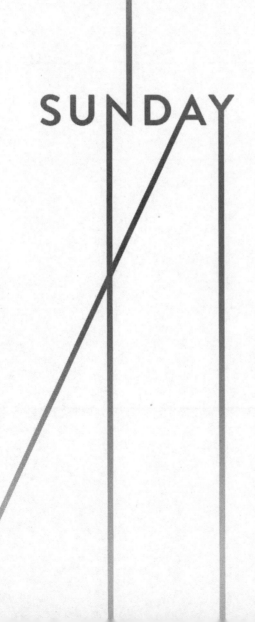

SUNDAY

CHAPTER FIFTY-SEVEN
LUCKY

WHEN I LANDED AT LAX SUNDAY MORNING, THE FANS were waiting for me. They had been anticipating this for months. *The Later Tonight Show* was a red-letter date with its own countdown on my official website.

I was wearing sunglasses along with a baseball cap. Sunglasses to hide the fact that, despite being bone tired, I hadn't been able to sleep on my flight over. And the pink wig was back on.

As expected, I had gotten chewed out by Joseph when I got back to my hotel in Hong Kong.

"*Do you have any idea what you put us through?*" His yelling vibrated through the hotel room. Ji-Yeon covered her ears, her expression surprisingly blasé despite the fact that Joseph never yelled.

"I'm sorry." My voice was almost a whisper.

Ji-Yeon looked at me with concern. "Are you okay? Did anything bad happen?"

She never fussed over me like that and I had bit my lip to hold back tears. I was so sick of crying already. I shook my head. "I'm fine."

"Of course she's fine!" Joseph roared. "She had her day of fun. With a *boy*. Hours before the freaking *Later Tonight Show*!"

The boy. I didn't want to think about the boy. Ever again.

I got a thorough reprimanding from Joseph, complete with threats to drop me from the management label and of siccing higher security detail on me.

When I had finally crawled into bed later, every molecule in my body felt defeated. The day's revelations and discoveries were tainted in something embarrassing and pathetic. I took my meds and fell asleep minutes later only to be woken up at the crack of dawn for my flight.

That extra security Joseph promised was in full effect as I walked through LAX. I drew my baseball cap lower on my head, but it was no use. What was the point of this hat? So I wouldn't get photographed? Everyone knew it was me.

My exasperation intensified with each step I took. First I took off my sunglasses. The crowd roared with screams as I tucked them into my T-shirt.

Ren threw me a look, but didn't say anything.

Then I slowed my walking, taking time to wave to the fans. Behind the barricades, they were holding up signs with my name on them. Wearing my concert T-shirts. Crying.

I stopped in my tracks and Ren bumped into me. "What's wrong?" he asked.

"Nothing," I said. "Give me a few extra seconds." Before he could respond, I walked over to the fans, causing another wave of screams. I reached to give outstretched hands high fives, bumped fists, grazed fingertips. Each touch and connection bolstered me. Zapped into my being. *You did this. You created this. You are in charge of this.*

When we finally reached the gate, a Latina teenager broke free from the barricades, her long ponytail trailing behind her as she sprinted toward me. Ren immediately caught her, almost swinging her up in the air.

"Lucky!" she exclaimed, her brown eyes huge, her hands stretched out toward me as she was restrained by the giant man. "I love you!"

I stopped. And I looked at her. Really looked at her. My Instagram account had so many comments from girls like her.

I love you!

Follow me back!

DO YOU SEE ME?

In the beginning, I had tried my best to like each comment, to respond to some of the questions. But Ji-Yeon handled my social media now, and she blocked followers and deleted comments with a heavy hand.

I looked at Ren and gestured for him to let her go. He did. But not without a deep frown. The girl stood there, so surprised that she had frozen in place.

"I see you," I said, reaching out and giving her a hug. "You want a photo?"

She nodded, unable to speak. Her hands were shaking so hard that she couldn't get her camera into selfie mode.

"Do you want me to do it?" I asked. She nodded again, handing the phone to me with trembling fingers. I aimed the phone so that we were both in frame. "Say kimchi," I said with a laugh. A giggle came out of her and I took the photo right then as she was smiling and comfortable.

She started crying when I handed the phone back to her. "Thank . . . thank you," she managed to say.

How many fans had I seen crying as I walked by them? In the front row of my concerts? I had grown so numb to it. I had grown numb to *absolute adoration that made people cry.*

I smiled at her, my lips quivery as I let myself absorb her emotions. Her feelings. I sang these songs for her a long time ago.

"What's your name?"

Her eyes were wide, her mascara smeared. "Etta."

"You're welcome, Etta," I said, and gave her shoulder a gentle squeeze.

People had hushed during this interaction and the crowd roared back into noise as soon as I started walking again.

"Ren," I said.

He only had eyes for the path ahead of us. "Yes?"

"I'd like to pad in some extra time when we land in airports. I want to say hi to fans."

I expected a protest of some kind, but he shrugged. "Fine by me. I get paid by the hour."

I grinned and pulled on my sunglasses as we stepped out into the LA sunshine.

I was home.

Nothing felt more like home than being stuck in traffic on the 405 freeway. It had been three years since I'd been here, and I tried to gobble up every second of it. Even the traffic.

I watched it through the tinted windows of the car, happy to be home even though it would be brief and I'd only see my family for a day before recording the show tomorrow. After the show, we had to fly immediately back to Seoul to start recording the American version of my album and do a couple of variety shows to discuss my American debut.

The radio volume was low—set on an oldies station I used to love as a kid. Ren and the driver were up front; Ji-Yeon and Joseph in a separate car, headed to their hotel.

I closed my eyes and slouched into my seat, wanting to turn my brain off before the long drive to my parents' house.

Something fell into my lap. My eyes snapped open.

"I forgot about this," Ren said from the front seat, looking at me through the rearview mirror. "That, um"—he cleared his throat—"guy. That guy you were with yesterday. It's from him."

I stared at the large white envelope and the scrawled handwriting on it: *For Lucky*.

Hastily written, slanted script. I felt light-headed and my breathing quickened.

"He found me in the hotel lobby last night somehow. That kid knows his way around."

He sure did.

I tossed it back to Ren. "I don't want it."

He raised his eyebrows. "I think you do."

"Pardon?" I said. "Since when do you even care—"

The envelope was thrown back into my lap. "Trust me. Look at it."

This was *very* out of character for Ren. He looked away then, absorbed in his phone. I picked up the envelope nervously and opened the already-torn seal.

A photo slid out. An eight-by-ten glossy of me. I was on the Sky Terrace looking at the view from Victoria Peak. The happiness in my expression as I looked over the city made my throat tighten up. I didn't want to be reminded of this. My fingers trembled as I held the photo, unable to stop looking.

"You, um, might want to turn it around."

I glanced up at Ren, confused. "What?"

He cleared his throat again and went back to his phone. For Pete's sake.

I turned the photo around. Written in the same ballpoint blue ink:

Lucky,

I took this photo because you looked happy. And I want you to
be happy. I believe in you so much. There isn't a story anymore.

   I'm sorry.

I love you.
Jack

P.S. Thank you. For everything.

MONDAY NIGHT

Los Angeles

TUESDAY MORNING

Hong Kong

CHAPTER FIFTY-EIGHT
JACK

"YOU'VE BEEN DOING *WHAT?*"

I gulped at the incredulity on my parents' faces.

Ava was sitting on the sofa next to them, staring at me with wide eyes. Like, *Bro. What.* She pulled on her long black braid and shook her head.

I took a deep breath, standing awkwardly in the middle of my parents' living room. "I've been lying to you guys and taking photos for a tabloid. As a side job."

"A *tabloid*, Jack?" my dad asked, disgust and disappointment wrapped up in that one word. He rubbed his hand over his eyes, not able to look at me.

Even though I didn't work there anymore, I needed to defend myself. In the past, I had shrugged everything off, okay with letting them think I was some restless bozo. But it wasn't accurate anymore. "Yeah, a tabloid. Because I was good at it."

"Good at chasing famous people around?" my dad asked, throwing his hands up in exasperation.

My mom threw him a *look*. "Let him talk." My dad shook his head but didn't say anything.

I pushed my hair back from my face and stared down at the coffee table. "It was more than sneaking into places and getting what I needed from people. I was able to tell stories through photographs."

I looked up at my parents then. "I want to study photography."

My dad's eyebrows came together, confused. "Well, yeah, Jack, we know you like photography. We didn't spend all that money on your camera for nothing. But now you want to study it?"

"Yes," I said quickly before I lost my nerve. "And I don't only *like* photography, I'm good at it, too." There, I said it. There was something so vulnerable about claiming a passion, a skill. Even though I knew my photos were good, I had never felt comfortable in showing pride in my work. Until Lucky.

I kept talking. "I know it's not practical, and you guys don't approve. When I last mentioned it, you pretty much brushed off the idea. But I'm serious. I've had time to think about it. And I want to use my skills to do interesting work. Not chase after celebrities."

There was silence and I glanced over at Ava, hoping for a friendly face. She smiled at me, still tugging on her braid. "You're the best photographer I know," she said, trying to be helpful.

I laughed nervously. "Um, thanks?"

"You are very good," my mom finally said.

My eyes flew to her. "I am?"

Her expression softened. "Yes! Remember that year Ava's school photos were so bad she cried for three whole days?"

Ava made a face. "Thanks for reminding me."

"Well, Jack did a make-up session. Remember those photos?" my mom asked, her eyebrows raised. "He captured your essence."

I did remember. I had spent an hour with Ava in the yard right before dusk, having her run around, hair flying. Then, in a moment of calm, when she finally caught her breath, I snapped a bunch of photos of her with a blissful and flushed expression on her face. The sunlight soft and warm on her skin as it sank behind the hills.

Relief spread through my body, my shoulders less tense. "Thanks, Mom."

My dad's silence was deafening. We all turned to him. My mom finally poked him in the ribs.

He cleared his throat. "I don't know why you thought we didn't want you to be a photographer. We were worried you didn't want to do *anything*."

I blinked. What?

"Please, Jack. Go for it. It's why your mom and I do *all of this*." He gestured toward the apartment. "I know you don't want this exact life. That's okay. I want you to have the life *you* want."

The sincerity in his voice made me swallow hard, pushing down the lump in my throat.

"You got that?" he asked gruffly.

I nodded. "Yeah. And I'm sorry for slacking off so much with the bank, I—"

He shook his head. "I know you hate it. We wanted you to keep busy so that you wouldn't become some backpacking hippie."

I laughed. "What? Oh wait, you mean like Nikhil at the bank?"

My dad rolled his eyes. "Every rich boy and his backpacking trip of discovery."

"Yeah, discovering the *weed*," Ava said with a snort.

"Ava!" my parents admonished at the same time. Ava shrugged in response.

I was still shocked by their reaction. "Wow, okay," I said. "I thought you wanted me to be a banker or something. And I didn't know how to tell you guys that I didn't want to do that. That I didn't know what I wanted to do for so long. But now I know."

My mom nodded. "That's all we want, Jack. For you to work hard at what you want."

Nothing could have made me happier than to hear those words. "Thank you. I promise, I will."

"But you still have to finish your internship until you start college," my dad said.

I nodded. College. The disdain I had for it had melted away with each second that passed since my fight with Lucky. "Okay, well, I still haven't researched schools yet . . ."

Ava pulled out her phone. "I've already started a spreadsheet."

My dad laughed and sprang up from the sofa. "Who wants breakfast?"

We gathered around the kitchen table—and I felt lighter than I had in weeks. Months. Years.

Once the task of talking to my parents was over, I was able to think about Lucky again. I spent the afternoon moping around my apartment since I had the day off from the bank anyway.

I kept wondering if her bodyguard actually gave the photo to her. Wondering if she had even opened it or lit it on fire. Wondering if she saw the photo.

If she saw the note.

I stared up at my cracked ceiling, sprawled across my sofa. Being brokenhearted was a *drag*. Was this what other people went through? It was freaking horrible!

The air in the apartment was stale and smelled pretty gross. Like boys and old food.

I finally dragged myself to a window and cracked it open. The soft yellow sunshine streamed into the room, highlighting every single mote of dust. It was also loud. The sound of shopkeepers yelling mixed with car horns drifted in through the window.

Something about the relentlessness of this city depressed me further. How did everyone keep living when I felt like this?

Oh my God. I wished I could slap myself.

My phone buzzed on the coffee table, interrupting my morose staring-out-window melancholy.

I dragged myself over to look at the text. From Charlie.

Hey, isn't Lucky on the Later Tonight Show like . . . now?

I glanced at the time on my phone. It was past three o'clock. I did the math—we were fifteen hours ahead. Lucky would be on in a few minutes.

If I were a more stoic man, I would have coldly turned off my phone and stepped into the shower. Washed away the memories. Started brand-new, fresh and ready to seize the day.

Who was I kidding? I flipped open my laptop on the coffee table and found the streaming site for the network.

I crouched down by the table, hunched over and balanced on the balls of my feet. Like five hundred commercials later, the show started streaming live.

Some superhero actor dude was talking to the host, James Perriweather. "Come on!" I yelled at the screen, like these two smiley-faced goofs could hear me. But they wrapped up soon after and I clutched the edges of my laptop, my face so close to the screen that I could feel its buzzy energy brush over my skin.

It cut to a commercial.

I fell backward, my head hitting the sofa, my butt sliding on the tiled floor. The ceiling had so many cracks in it. Paint peeled off of it in small chunks. My thoughts raced, matching the rate of my heart. It was going to burst out of my chest and run laps around the room, it was thumping so hard.

Was I ready to see her? And not only see her, but see her as Lucky? Lucky who existed on a different planet from the girl I spent the entire day with?

The show's theme music sucked me back into reality and I rolled onto my feet again, arms cradling the laptop.

I happened to be positioned in the one shady spot between the beams of dusty sunshine. Everything seemed to still—the fluttering of the curtains, the orbit of dust motes around my head.

James stood onstage, his hands clasped in front of him. "She has over ten million followers on Twitter. Her single 'Heartbeat' is the most downloaded song in *history* in Asia." The screaming and chanting from the audience almost drowned out his words. He made a shocked face and grinned. "Enough said! Here to make her American debut, K-pop sensation *Lucky!*" James swept his arms up in the air and the camera panned to his left. The roar of the crowd distorted the sound on my laptop.

God, I could barely breathe. I actually clutched my chest, taking a handful of sweatshirt into my fist.

The stage was dark, and then suddenly, there she was.

Standing under a single spotlight. Wearing those silver boots that stretched up her long legs. Tiny shorts. Some sort of sparkly jacket that hung over her frame. Her head was tilted down, a curtain of pink hair artfully messy and covering her face. The hand holding her microphone was weighed down with shiny, chunky rings.

She already felt so far away.

The music started up for "Heartbeat," but she didn't move. Okay, maybe this was part of the act. But it kept going and there was a palpable sense of unease in the air. I chewed my lip nervously. What was happening?

With the music still going, she slipped off her jacket and it fell to the floor. The audience cheered.

Something was weird about this.

Then she pulled off the rings, one by one, and they fell with punctuated thuds on the floor. The music kept playing, in a loop, confusion lacing everything.

Her face still covered by her hair, she placed the mic on the floor, stayed bent over, and unzipped her left boot.

Took it off and tossed it aside. Unzipped the other one.

Only when she was barefoot and holding the mic again did she look up and toss the pink wig off. The audience gasped.

She looked directly into the camera with her hair pulled back in a low bun. Her eyes were sparkling, her smile huge.

My breath caught in my throat.

"Stop the music," she said into the mic. Her voice was commanding but calm. Confused cheering and exclamations came from the audience. She held up her index finger to her mouth with a wink. Shushing them. Only wearing a pair of black shorts and a plain white tank top.

She started singing. Without accompaniment. Only that shimmering voice of hers, as clear and beautiful as a bell. Equal parts fragile and delicate, and then a sudden powerhouse when she really let it out. When she sang so hard that her voice cracked with emotion, her body swayed in subtle but beautiful movements. An arm lifted here, a leg sweeping around her there. It was like a ballet performance and torch ballad wrapped up into something so unique and special that you wanted to weep with the privilege of witnessing it.

It took a few transfixed seconds for me to realize what she was singing. "Heartbeat." But so totally deconstructed and slowed down that it was an entirely new song. Her eyes fluttered closed at one particularly low, throaty moment. Then she whispered, "Music."

The background music kicked in, thumping and loud, and her eyes snapped open. She stared directly into the camera, clear-eyed and sure.

Into me, into my eyes.

Much too suddenly, she winked and whipped her head around, pulling her hair out of the bun and shaking it out. Then she launched into her signature dance for "Heartbeat." Familiarity settled into her moves, but even in this, she was different. Looser limbed, more playful. Her iciness and cyborg-perfection were gone—in their place was a kind of joy and warmth that made me want to throw myself into the screen.

To witness it firsthand. To share her air, again.

She made silly faces at the camera, smoldered, acknowledged crowd chants and cheers with nods and winks. She enjoyed every second of it.

Then it was over. The applause and chanting was so thunderous that she started laughing, covering her mouth with her hands, bending at the waist.

I was so proud of her. Prouder than I'd ever been for anyone. There she was, continuing to live her dreams even when it was hard. Even when she wanted to give up. Taking risks to make it work for her. Because she had changed.

What would happen after this bold move of hers? Was it sanctioned by her label? I couldn't imagine it was. The statement was so obvious, so clear: I am doing this on my own terms.

I thought it was over, that I would have to see the screen cut to another offensive commercial. But James waved Lucky over to the couch.

She hopped over nimbly, completely at ease. When they both settled into their seats, the crowd was still cheering. Lucky was resplendent in the glow of it. She couldn't stop smiling, her teeth so white, her eyes so sparkling. I wanted to reach out and feel it all.

"Wow. Lucky, wow! What was *that*?" James exclaimed. "Welcome to K-pop, America!"

The crowd cheered and Lucky laughed, pushing her hair back from her face. A gesture that was so familiar to me now, I ached to see it. "K-pop's been here, James," she said. Another roar from the crowd.

He had the grace to look chagrined. "True, true. But you also brought out something else—I mean, wow. Everyone's going to know you by tomorrow."

She flushed but dropped her eyes modestly. "Thank you. It felt good," she said.

"You *looked* good, girl!" he said with cartoonish movements of his body. Everyone cheered again. "So, what's your deal? You come on the heels of your Asia tour, correct?"

She nodded, bringing her hands together in her lap. I could see her wringing them slightly. I could see everything. The world was a blur, but she was crystallized into something sharp and shining. "Yeah, finished a couple days ago."

"What was that like? Crazy, I bet?"

Lucky smiled. "That's an understatement. I visited fifteen cities in two months." The crowd made a "wowwww" kind of noise, impressed and reverent.

James raised his eyebrows. "Wow is right. What was your last stop?"

"Hong Kong," she answered, quick and precise.

"Speaking of Hong Kong," James said while glancing at the audience. A wink and nod in his expression. "There were some rumors online that you had an adventure there."

I made a choking sound. No way. Were they allowed to bring this up? K-pop stars were so fiercely protected. Even *mentioning* scandal was complete sacrilege.

But everything she'd done on the show had been sacrilegious.

Lucky's features stilled. She went blank in this way that I'd seen on her social media—that familiar placid expression that insinuated a secret buried deep inside of her. Unreachable. I'd never felt so far away from her.

A few uncomfortable seconds passed, and you could see James glance at someone off camera, to see if he should shift directions. Then it was like a switch turned on in Lucky. A spark lit in her eyes as she twisted her lips into a grimace. "What have you heard?" Her voice was so conspiratorial, so full of mischief, that everyone burst out laughing.

His face turning red, James stammered, "Well, only that, well . . . you might have had a romantic kind of day."

God, really, James Perriweather? I kept my eyes on Lucky, every nerve attuned to what she was going to say in response.

She leaned back on the sofa, pulled her leg up onto the couch. Like an ajumma about to trim some bean sprouts on her deck. It was so graceful and so Korean and so comfortable. "I had a good day," she said with a big smile.

People whooped for a second, and then there was silence. You could almost feel everyone in the audience, everyone watching the show, lean forward. Including me. To await whatever she was going to offer next.

Not that my entire life was hanging on this one moment or anything.

With her arm draped around her knee, Lucky looked directly into the camera. "I took a day off after a long tour. And it was . . ." Her voice trailed off, her gaze shifting down toward the floor. "It was *transcendent*."

The word shot from the screen directly into my body, filling me with an intense heat—like the sun breaking from the clouds.

Her eyes moved back up to the camera, and she sat up, running a hand through her hair. I could almost feel the strands between my own fingers. After a beat that felt like a hundred thousand years . . .

She smiled, a soft one full of secrets. "I spent the day with a photographer. He's going to release a very, very exclusive photo story on me. Look for it. By Jack Lim."

I fell back into the sofa. She hadn't given up on me, either.

ONE YEAR LATER

CHAPTER FIFTY-NINE
CATHERINE

"FERN! MY GOD!"

The Pomeranian stared at me, her chin held up defiantly as she hopped around on her tiny, stupid feet.

She had peed on my silver Birkenstocks. For the third time that month.

"I'm going to have you stuffed and perched jauntily on a *fedora*!" I screeched.

"Catherine!" my mom yelled from my bedroom doorway. "Don't talk to your little sister that way."

I sputtered, holding up the defiled sandal. "Sister?! She's not my sister, you weirdo!"

Fern hopped into my mom's arms and my mom crooned into her fur. "Don't worry, you're a better daughter than her." I had to laugh and my mom looked up at me with twinkling eyes. "Clean your room.

There are no hotel maids here." She padded down the hallway with the dog smugly nestled in her arms. There was only one princess in this house and it wasn't me.

It had only taken a few days for my family to get used to having me back home. No coddling, no fussing. I had to do chores, follow curfew, and have dinner with my family every night. My *actual* human sister, Vivian, immediately borrowed my clothes.

I loved it.

The October day was warm, not that unusual for the Valley. I cracked open a window and stared out into the cul-de-sac. Neighbors were unloading their groceries from their compact SUVs. A few kids were riding bikes. The day was coming to an end and the sky was a pale blue edged with pink.

It was familiar and foreign, and I relished every second I was home.

When the infamous *Later Tonight Show* episode was recorded that afternoon a year ago, Joseph had almost burst a forehead vein from the shock. I had braced myself for the screaming and yelling, but was met with confusion instead.

"Was that what your rebellious day was about? You want to change your image?" Joseph had asked.

Ji-Yeon was frazzled, sitting cross-legged on the floor of the green-room. "We could have planned it so much better."

I stared at them in shock. "What? You mean, I'm not fired?"

They both looked at each other before Joseph answered. "I don't know. The management label isn't going to like this. You might lose everything."

I took a deep breath. "What did you guys think of the performance, though?"

A few seconds passed and my heart stopped beating.

"I loved it," Ji-Yeon said with a smile.

Hope flared through my chest. "You did?"

Joseph cleared his throat. "We have to see how the public reacts. But it was good. Very good, Lucky."

Those words unleashed a flood of tears. It was relief, it was exhaustion—it was everything that I had been holding back.

And soon after, the reactions from fans and media had been equally affirming.

Everyone wanted my sponsorship.

Everyone wanted to book me on their shows.

Everyone wanted a tour of the "New Lucky."

Despite the success of that performance and Joseph's initial support, I had eventually left my label a few months after the show. There was simply no way to make my new vision of Lucky mesh with their original. My label refused to budge.

From down the hall, I could hear my mom scolding my dad for putting the tomatoes in the refrigerator again. "It's not right to leave them out!" he protested.

"Don't you ever watch the Cooking Channel?" my mom snapped. "None of *those* people refrigerate them. You think *you* know better?" They continued to argue, and I smiled as I closed my bedroom door to the noise.

Despite their hapless-married-couple routine, my parents had proven themselves to be extremely sharp. I had only been able to break my contract because, very early on, my parents had a lawyer comb through it and make adjustments based on American labor laws and other legalities.

I plopped down on my bed and pulled out my phone. I had a bunch of emails from Ji-Yeon. I clicked on the first one, with the subject line: **This week's recording schedule.**

Cat,

As requested, here's the schedule for this week. You're in the studio Tuesday and Thursday with therapy on Wednesday as usual. I've made sure that lunches are delivered and that they are NOT salads. (But they're not hamburgers, either!)

Also, find attached costume ideas for the next music video. The costume designer loved your idea of a jumpsuit, although of course I wish it could be shorts. (Those legs!)

See you in a couple months!

JY

I smiled. It pained Ji-Yeon to allow me to eat so many carbs and wear less-skimpy costumes. In a shocking move, she had left the label with me to become my new manager. "Who else is going to make sure you do your ten-step skin-care routine?" she had said with a sniff.

We were now with a smaller company based in LA. They repped a few K-pop bands but mostly independent artists. Like me. It was scary, but after a few months back in LA, I was finally falling into a routine and working on a new album again. It was still K-pop, but I was working closely with the songwriters, and I would be releasing it as Cat. Short for my full name, Catherine Nam.

The best part? My home base was LA with occasional long trips to Korea. And my schedule was so blessedly manageable—recording a few days a week, dinners with my family. And therapy. Regularly. Moving back home had eased a lot of my anxiety, but I still needed help, and my parents insisted on regular appointments with a therapist. So far, I liked her, though it was hard to shake off the feeling of shame at first. Cultural stigmas die hard.

I closed out of my email and glanced at the time on my home-screen. It was almost six. Time to roll.

A half-hour later, my sister dropped me off in front of a bar in Hollywood. I still couldn't believe the state allowed her to get behind the wheel of a dangerous killing machine.

"Take the freeway back home, don't get creative and go on Mulholland or something," I said to her firmly as I unbuckled my seat belt.

Vivian made a fart noise. "Not that I need your permission, but I'm *fine* with driving on Mulholland."

"If you want to *die* driving off a cliff!" I said with my body twisted around reaching for my guitar case in the back seat.

"*Why* would I randomly *drive off* a cliff?!" she screeched.

The guitar almost hit her in the head. "Oops, sorry. I don't know, even good drivers can—"

"Oh my God, I'm so excited for this Lilith Fair phase of your life to be over!" Vivian unlocked the doors with an aggressive jab on the button.

"Maybe I'll do this *forever* to torture you," I said, pulling on my black, wide-brimmed hat.

"Go play your stupid music!"

The car left with a roar, leaving me in the wake of its exhaust. Nice. It actually made me happy to be treated like garbage by my sister again.

Hollywood was already in full swing on this warm Friday evening. Bros in dress shirts with a sheen, girls in short skirts and high heels, tourists gawking at everyone, parking dudes peddling their thirty-dollar lots, homeless people navigating around all of it deftly, a

Korean-Brazilian food truck with customers lined up along the curb, hipsters walking briskly like they had somewhere to go . . .

It was both gross and great—the dichotomy of Hollywood. City of dreams.

I entered the bar through the back door and someone was already onstage, playing with a four-piece band. Something jazzy. The place wasn't too full yet; it was still early for the weekend.

After grabbing a soda water from the bar, I found a seat in the very back, a dark corner lit by a single candle.

"Excuse me."

I glanced over at a young woman who was standing in front of me, clutching a purse to her chest. "Yes?"

"Are you . . . Lucky?" She whispered the last part.

"Yes," I whispered back. "But can we keep that between us? I don't want everyone to know I'm here yet."

She nodded vigorously. "Oh my gosh, of course!"

I was playing in small venues across LA as an experiment. It wasn't as Lucky or even Cat. It was only me, Catherine Nam, a guitar, and my own songs.

I had tried to keep my identity a secret at first, but my cover was blown almost immediately. Even without the pink hair, people recognized me in America now. It had frustrated me at first, but I had turned it into yet another way to connect with fans. I decided to make the appearances an exclusive show for Lucky fans—only giving out twenty tickets per "secret show." It was a lottery and people were informed of the location day-of. They even had to leave their phones and cameras at the door.

The first time I had gone onstage here, last month, I was terrified.

It seemed cliché, the K-pop star who performed in front of sixty thousand–seat stadiums being nervous about being solo on a small stage.

Playing my own music required a level of vulnerability that was brand-new to me. I had felt naked.

But I also felt the same energy from my old shows as Lucky. Like I did that last night in Hong Kong. The adoration and love had poured through. I felt it in the air as keenly as I did one year ago.

It had been exhilarating. This was only my third time performing and I wasn't anywhere near getting sick of it yet.

"Thank you," I said to the woman. "And thanks for coming to see me."

She bit her lip. "I am trying *really* hard to keep my cool right now."

I laughed, relaxing considerably. "You're being very cool."

"Can I do one uncool thing?" She fished for something in her bag. "Could I get your autograph?"

It was an issue of *Remixed* magazine. The issue from a few months back that had a special photo spread.

AS LUCKY WOULD HAVE IT

The headline still made me smile. The article opened with the photo of me at Victoria Peak. The one Jack had printed out for me.

The Reigning Queen of K-pop Spends a Day in Hong Kong Before She Takes Over the World

When this issue came out, the photos had blown up and so, I assume, had Jack's prospects.

I had to assume, because, aside from a few emails and texts, we didn't talk much anymore. Overhauling my career was no joke, and then moving to the US further distanced us.

It was sad, at first. But life moved on. Months passed like days. And my days were so hectic, so packed, that I blinked, and it was a year later.

The photos were special because they gave an exclusive look into my life, not through a paparazzi or fashion editorial lens, but something more intimate and thoughtful. With very few words to accompany the photos, the images captured me in very real, unstaged moments—on the brink of conquering America. It somehow told a story about me via one day spent in Hong Kong. He saw me.

It was the work of a gifted photographer. I had almost laughed when I saw the spread—photography was so obviously Jack's passion. And he was so *good* at it. He only needed to recognize it.

I was pretty sure I had something to do with that, and it made me incredibly proud.

I signed the magazine and handed it back to the girl.

She gave me a thumbs-up sign. "Good luck!" She giggled nervously after saying it. "No pun intended."

I laughed. "Thanks."

"Oh, and also!" She stood there a beat longer, shy suddenly. "I'm a huge, huge fan. All your fans—we're so proud of you. We'll follow you anywhere. We want you to be happy."

I could only nod through the lump in my throat. My fans had proven to be amazing after everything went down. I had worried about losing my base, the virtual army around the globe that supported me without fail. Instead, they had rallied behind me.

And while I was doing all this for myself, I was also doing it for them. What I had been doing before started to lack balance. It had only been for my management label and for them. To keep them happy and excited. Or so I had thought. But what had been made clear after

The Later Tonight Show performance was that my fans wanted me to be happy. It was a symbiotic relationship.

Jack was right—a bit of selfishness went a long way. But for me, I knew that being purely selfish wouldn't be fulfilling. To sit in a dark café alone playing music for myself? That wasn't me, either. This new era of my career was finally including both. It was deeply satisfying that I *could* do both.

The jazz band ended their set and the crowd applauded politely. I finished the last of my water and headed to the stage.

What was noticeable and astonishing the first time I did this with my fans was the silence. They didn't scream my name or attempt to rush me. Like the time I performed at the karaoke bar, I had an unspoken agreement with everyone there. They wanted to help me practice in this safe space.

After spending a few minutes tuning my guitar, I tapped the mic. The sound echoed pleasantly through the bar.

"Hi, I'm Catherine Nam." I tilted my head down and played the first few notes on my guitar. It vibrated through me.

Then it was me on that stage with my cautious guitar plucking, my words and notes ringing out into the air.

Every feeling from that day was in this song. Encapsulated neatly, or not-so-neatly, into three minutes and forty-eight seconds. Each time I sang it, I felt it. I lived it. Time had passed quickly but when I performed this song, it hadn't passed at all.

When it was over, I took a deep breath that echoed out into the speakers. I looked up to see people clapping and cheering loudly.

The noises of the bar rushed in around me and I felt cocooned in the warmth of it. Tinkling glasses, laughter, the buzz of voices deep in conversation. The scent of alcohol and bodies and a fragrant candle burning somewhere. I took a moment before I started my next song, soaking in the feeling of this show.

Then something felt different.

The air was charged in a particular way, like when someone turns on a TV in a quiet house—you can *feel* it before you hear or see it. I peered out from under the brim of my hat. What was it? It was tugging at me, insistent.

My eyes skimmed the room, but it was hard to see with the dim lighting.

I stopped on a dark figure in the arched entryway. The familiarity of that silhouette zapped me. That buzz in the air amplified by a billion.

I dropped my guitar onto the floor, the thud reverberating through the room. "Sorry, guys. I'll be back in a few minutes," I said into the microphone. Then I stood up and walked across the room, shouldering past people, moving too slow. He was so close.

When I reached him, he hadn't moved an inch. His hands shoved into his pockets, his shoulder leaning against the doorway.

It was him.

CHAPTER SIXTY

JACK

AS I WATCHED HER WALK TOWARD ME, I COULDN'T move. I'd come here to see her but couldn't quite believe it was actually happening.

She stood in front of me, her eyes bright and disbelieving.

"Jack?" She said my name with a question mark, even though she *knew*.

Time had passed, and it hadn't.

"Hi." It was the only thing I could say. It was so good to see her.

She nodded—quick and awkward. "Hi!"

We stared at each other. The so-muchness of it was overwhelming. I had no idea how to talk to her anymore. My eyes traced over her, memorizing every new thing. Her shorter hair and the way it grazed her collarbones. The bronzed glow of her tan skin, the loose cropped tank top she wore with blue jeans. It was Lucky and it was Catherine.

"Cool, glad we got those pleasantries out of the way," I finally managed to say.

Catherine laughed, quick and pure, and it was a gift to be able to hear it again. Then she threw her arms around me.

The hug was brief but incredibly strong, her arms tight around my back before she pulled away. I took a deep breath. I had forgotten what her proximity did to me.

She grinned. "How did you know I was here? Wait, no, what are you doing here?"

A man pushed by her then, jostling her to the right, and I reached out to steady her without thinking. That one familiar move brought us back to Hong Kong instantly. Heat scorched between us. We moved away from the doorway, into a dark corner of the bar where we were hidden by gauzy curtains. I thought of all the spaces in Hong Kong where we had stood so closely, surrounded by people but always alone, somehow.

There was so much to say but I gave her a quick answer. "I won the lottery today."

She looked incredulous. "You *entered*?"

"How could I not?" I said with a teasing smile. "I, uh. I live in LA now."

"*What!*" I couldn't tell if the startled expression was happily surprised or . . .

I nodded. "There's a lot to catch up on, I guess."

Her expression softened. "Yeah."

Our text messages had dropped off considerably the past few months, and while it had felt natural at the time, it felt totally insubstantial now that we were standing here face-to-face.

She gave me an inscrutable look. "I can't talk for long right now, so I want to say something quickly."

I braced myself.

"Thank you."

The words zapped me in the chest. Even though she had said as much in text, it was an entirely different thing to hear it. Especially since the last words we exchanged in person were so hurtful.

"Thank you for the photos you published," she continued. "They were beautiful. You're . . . what did you say to me that day? You're incredibly accomplished, Jack."

The zap was now sending warmth through my entire chest cavity. "The subject made it easy," I said, swallowing hard. There was so much to tell her. How seeing her be so brave on that stage—putting everything on the line, taking control of her career—how that had changed the entire trajectory of my life.

How she taught me that pursuing your dreams was worth it. That your dreams could change and that change might be hard. But you should still try. Because anything short of that wasn't a quality life.

She brushed her hair back from her face, and my eyes followed her every movement. I was so greedy for all of it.

"I'm so proud of you," she said with a smile. "You did it."

Wow, I wanted to kiss her then. I crossed my arms to stop myself. "*You* did it. You gave me that challenge. You gave me the story. You gave me—" and I couldn't keep going anymore. My voice cracked with the overwhelming emotion of it. *Everything*.

But she knew what I was trying to say. She had always been able to see the heart of me, even when I wasn't able to. She reached out and touched my arm. "Jack. The feeling's mutual. You were right. I was scared. I needed someone to tell me that. To help me *see* that."

Even though I actually knew this, had seen it confirmed on live television, I was shocked by the intense pleasure I felt at having it confirmed. The way she was looking at me . . . could it be possible that she still had some feelings for me? After everything?

I smiled. "You sound awesome up there. You're doing some cool stuff."

She threw her head back and laughed. "Ooh, am I Jack-approved now?"

"You've always been," I said without thinking.

Even in the dim lighting, I could tell she was blushing. That small sign bolstered me and I reached for her hand—my fingers gently lacing with hers. "I'm proud of *you*."

She looked down at our hands and gave mine a tight squeeze. I held my breath. "That's nice. But I'm starving and we should go eat after this," she said.

I laughed. "Of course we will."

"CATHERINE!" A man's voice boomed through the bar and we pulled apart.

Catherine rolled her eyes. "I have to go." The familiarity of the words, the shortness of our time together, came back like a spectral presence lingering between us. "Wait for me?" she asked.

I nodded. "I'll be here."

Her eyes flashed and before I could react, she reached up and kissed me. Hard. It was the kiss of an outlaw, of a soldier back from war. I gladly submitted, letting her wrap her arms around me, feeling her body lift up as she stood on her toes to reach me.

"Um, I hope you don't have a girlfriend," she said breathlessly when we broke apart.

I shook my head with a laugh. "No. Not yet."

We looked at each other for a long time.

"New city, new start," she finally said. Her brow furrowed in thought for a second. "Let's pretend that kiss didn't happen."

I bit back laughter and she lifted the curtain to step outside. But she stopped mid-step. She turned and looked at me with an odd expression. Her gaze moved from my face to my chest. My T-shirt.

"UCLA?" she asked, eyes lifting back up to mine.

Right. "There's a lot to catch up on."

It was like a light came on within her—she started to glow and radiate with a warmth that filled me with the most unfamiliar feeling. Pride. In myself.

We held that moment for one absolutely perfect second before she ducked out.

It came back then—every single feeling from that day one year ago. I had moved on, figured my stuff out. Pretty sure Catherine did the same. Even if it had been the most intense day of my life, it was still one day.

The *I love you* I had scrawled on the back of that photo sometimes woke me up in the middle of the night. I had wished the earth would open up and swallow me and my bed whole.

Otherwise, though, that day managed to fade into a pleasant memory. A memory as I applied to colleges the following winter. As I sent the photos of Catherine, of Lucky, out to various magazines. As I negotiated with my parents about college—they would let me double-major in photography with another more practical subject. So I had decided on UCLA, to pair photography with journalism. At the time, I convinced myself I didn't pick UCLA because of Catherine. I almost believed it.

After living in LA for a month, I came across Catherine's first

Instagram post about her secret shows. It seemed impossible to get in, so I had ignored it at the time. Moving back to the US had been so nuts that I actually didn't have much time to think about the fact that we were in the same city.

The third time she posted, though, I entered. With zero expectations. I thought we'd exchange a hug and I'd be able to apologize and let that day go.

Now that we were back in the same room, though? It was so clear that our feelings had been simmering right under the surface. Catherine wasn't someone I could forget.

I watched her step up lightly back onstage, that happy glow still radiating from her as she sat down on her stool and picked up her guitar.

This feeling right now? The tingles and light-headedness?

It was the anticipation of something extraordinary.

Something special with another human being who was going to leave an indelible mark on your life and change you forever. Drawn together by an otherworldly force. I recognized it for the first time in my life.

We would start again, and do it with eyes wide open.

"Hi, sorry for the interruption," she said into the mic. She glanced up at me. "But I'm yours for the rest of the night."

ACKNOWLEDGMENTS

BTS has their ARMY, and I have mine.

Thank you to Judith Hansen, who has believed in me since day one. I am so grateful for everything.

I feel incredibly lucky to work with Janine O'Malley and Melissa Warten. Thank you for your editorial expertise, chill reactions to my nonchill, and enthusiasm for my books. So much gratitude to the entire Macmillan team for getting these words out to the world. Special thanks to Elizabeth Clark, Brittany Pearlman, Madison Furr, Allegra Green, Lauren Festa, Lucy del Priore, Katie Halata, Kerianne Steinberg, Janine Barlow, and Jessica White.

Thank you to Faye Bender. So excited for everything to come.

A couple years ago, I needed an education in K-pop, and woo, boy, did I get one. Thank you to K-pop Twitter for coming through. To Amerie, Nahri Lee, Lisa Espinosa, and Asela Lee. Special thanks to

Tamar Herman for her expertise and guidance through this fascinating world. Thanks to Sunmi and Neon Bunny for the music.

I fell in love with Hong Kong while writing this book. Thank you to Kita Huynh, Morgan Chevassus, and Diana Jou for navigating me through this magical city. Thank you to Gustav Lindquist and Yujin Choo for the extra help.

As always, thank you to all the booksellers, librarians, teachers, bloggers, and readers who have supported my books over the years. I am incredibly grateful for all of you.

Thank you to superstar Mel Jolly. I was able to finish writing this book because of your valuable support.

My writer friendships are what have sustained me since this book was just a spark of an idea. Thank you to my LA YA essentials: Elissa Sussman, Zan Romanoff, Brandy Colbert, Robin Benway, Aminah Mae Safi (the cross-out epigraph!), Diya Mishra, Kirsten Hubbard, and Anna Carey. Shout-out especially to the masters of puns (puns . . . ters?) and my own personal creative brain trust, Sarah Enni and Morgan Matson. Thank you to the hags for the wisdom and support. Special thanks to Veronica Roth, Courtney Summers, and Somaiya Daud—I am a better writer and person because of you all.

Thank you to my entire family whose support is the reason I can do any of this. To the Appelhans, Appelwats, and Peterhans, thank you for always caring. And reading. So fast. In front of me. In one sitting.

To my sister, Christine, who took good care of my home and Maeby while I worked on this book in another country. To my parents, for a lifetime of support and love.

To my husband, Chris, whose work and art inspire me every day. Thank you for enduring the distance and time so that I could create my art, too.